A. Whitney

Real Folks

Anatiposi

A. Whitney

Real Folks

Reprint of the original, first published in 1872.

1st Edition 2023 | ISBN: 978-3-38213-345-0

Anatiposi Verlag is an imprint of Outlook Verlagsgesellschaft mbH.

Verlag (Publisher): Outlook Verlag GmbH, Zeilweg 44, 60439 Frankfurt, Deutschland
Vertretungsberechtigt (Authorized to represent): E. Roepke, Zeilweg 44, 60439 Frankfurt, Deutschland
Druck (Print): Books on Demand GmbH, In de Tarpen 42, 22848 Norderstedt, Deutschland

REAL FOLKS.

BY

MRS. A. D. T. WHITNEY,

AUTHOR OF "WE GIRLS," "A SUMMER IN LESLIE GOLDTHWAITE'S LIFE," "FAITH GARTNEY'S GIRLHOOD," ETC.

WITH ILLUSTRATIONS.

BOSTON:

JAMES R. OSGOOD AND COMPANY,

LATE TICKNOR & FIELDS, AND FIELDS, OSGOOD, & CO.

1872.

RIVERSIDE, CAMBRIDGE:
STEREOTYPED AND PRINTED BY
H. O. HOUGHTON AND COMPANY.

CONTENTS.

REAL FOLKS.

I.

THIS WAY, AND THAT.

THE parlor blinds were shut, and all the windows of the third-story rooms were shaded; but the pantry window, looking out on a long low shed, such as city houses have to keep their wood in and to dry their clothes upon, was open; and out at this window had come two little girls, with quiet steps and hushed voices, and carried their books and crickets to the very further end, establishing themselves there, where the shade of a tall, round fir tree, planted at the foot of the yard below, fell across the building of a morning.

"It was prettier down on the bricks," Luclarion had told them. But they thought otherwise.

"Luclarion doesn't know," said Frank. "People *don't* know things, I think. I wonder why, when they've got old, and ought to? It's like the sea-shore here, I guess; only the stones are all stuck down, and you mustn't pick up the loose ones either."

Frank touched lightly, as she spoke, the white and black and gray bits of gravel that covered the flat roof.

"And it smells — like the pine forests!"

The sun was hot and bright upon the fir branches and along the tar-cemented roof.

"How do you know about sea-shores and pine forests?" asked Laura, with crushing common sense.

"I don't know; but I do," said Frank.

"You don't know anything but stories and pictures; and one tree, and a little gravel, all stuck down tight."

"I'm glad I've got one tree. And the rest of it,—why listen! It's in the *word*, Laura. *Forest.* Doesn't that sound like thousands of them, all fresh and rustling? And Ellen went to the sea-shore, in that book; and picked up pebbles; and the sea came up to her feet, just as the air comes up here, and you can't get any farther,"—said Frank, walking to the very edge and putting one foot out over, while the wind blew in her face up the long opening between rows of brick houses of which theirs was in the midst upon one side.

"A great sea!" exclaimed Laura, contemptuously. "With all those other wood-sheds right out in it, all the way down!"

"Well, there's another side to the sea; and capes, and islands," answered Frank, turning back. "Besides, I don't pretend it *is;* I only think it seems a little bit like it. I'm often put in mind of things. I don't know why."

"I'll tell you what it is like," said Laura. "It's like the gallery at church, where the singers stand up in a row, and look down, and all the people look up at them. I like high places. I like Cecilia, in the 'Bracelets,' sitting at the top, behind, when her name was called out for the prize; and 'they all made way, and she was on the floor in an instant.' I should like to have been Cecilia!"

"Leonora was a great deal the best."

"I know it; but she don't *stand out.*"

"Laura! You're just like the Pharisees! You're always wishing for long clothes and high seats!"

"There ain't any Pharisees, nowadays," said Laura, securely. After which, of course, there was nothing more to be insisted.

Mrs. Lake, the housekeeper, came to the middle upper window, and moved the blind a little. Frank and Laura were behind the fir. They saw her through the branches. She, through the farther thickness of the tree, did not notice them.

"That was good," said Laura. "She would have beckoned us in. I hate that forefinger of hers; it's always hushing or beckoning. It's only two inches long. What makes us have to mind it so?"

"She puts it all into those two inches," answered Frank. "All the *must* there is in the house. And then you've got to."

"I wouldn't — if father wasn't sick."

"Laura," said Frank, gravely, "I don't believe father is going to get well. What do you suppose they're letting us stay at home from school for?"

"O, that," said Laura, "was because Mrs. Lake didn't have time to sew the sleeves into your brown dress."

"I could have worn my gingham, Laura. What if he should die pretty soon? I heard her tell Luclarion that there must be a change before long. They talk in little bits, Laura, and they say it solemn."

The children were silent for a few minutes. Frank sat looking through the fir-tree at the far-off flecks of blue.

Mr. Shiere had been ill a long time. They could hardly think, now, what it would seem again not to have a sick father; and they had had no mother for several years, — many out of their short remembrance of life. Mrs. Lake had kept the house, and mended their clothes, and held up her forefinger at them. Even when Mr. Shiere was well, he had been a reserved man, much absorbed in business; since his wife's death, he had been a very sad man. He loved his children, but he was very little with them. Frank and Laura could not feel the shock and loss that children feel when death comes and robs them suddenly of a close companionship.

"What do you suppose would happen then?" asked Laura, after awhile. "We shouldn't be anybody's children."

"Yes, we should," said Frank; "we should be God's."

"Everybody else is that, — *besides*," said Laura.

"We shall have black silk pantalets again, I suppose," — she began, afresh, looking down at her white ones with double crimped ruffles, — "and Mrs. Gibbs will come in and help, and we shall have to pipe and overcast."

"O, Laura, how nice it was ever so long ago!" cried Frank, suddenly, never heeding the pantalets, "when mother sent us out to ask company to tea, — that pleasant Saturday, you know, — and made lace pelerines for our dolls while we were gone! It's horrid, when other girls have mothers, only to have a *housekeeper!* And pretty soon we sha'n't have anything, only a little corner, away back, that we can't hardly recollect."

"They'll do something with us; they always do," said Laura, composedly.

The children of this world, even *as* children, are wisest in their generation. Frank believed they would be God's children; she could not see exactly what was to come of that, though, practically. Laura knew that people always did something; something would be sure to be done with them. She was not frightened; she was even a little curious.

A head came up at the corner of the shed behind them;

a pair of shoulders, — high, square, turned forward; a pair of arms, long thence to the elbows, as they say women's are who might be good nurses of children; the hands held on to the sides of the steep steps that led up from the bricked yard. The young woman's face was thin and strong; two great, clear, hazel eyes looked straight out, like arrow shots; it was a clear, undeviating glance; it never wandered, or searched, or wavered, any more than a sunbeam; it struck full upon whatever was there; it struck *through* many things that were transparent to their quality. She had square, white, strong teeth, that set together like the faces of a die; they showed easily when she spoke, but the lips closed over them absolutely and firmly. Yet they were pleasant lips, and had a smile in them that never went quite out; it lay in all the muscles of the mouth and chin; it lay behind, in the living spirit that had moulded to itself the muscles.

This was Luclarion.

"Your Aunt Oldways and Mrs. Oferr have come. Hurry in!"

Now Mrs. Oldways was only an uncle's wife; Mrs. Oferr was their father's sister. But Mrs. Oferr was a rich woman who lived in New York, and who came on grand and potent, with a scarf or a pair of shoe-bows for each of the children in her big trunk, and a hundred and one suggestions for their ordering and behavior at her tongue's end, once a year. Mrs. Oldways lived up in the country, and was "aunt" to half the neighborhood at home, and turned into an aunt instantly, wherever she went and found children. If there were no children, perhaps older folks did not call her by the name, but they felt the special human kinship that is of no blood or law, but is next to motherhood in the spirit.

Mrs. Oferr found the open pantry window, before the children had got in.

"Out there!" she exclaimed, "in the eyes of all the neighbors in the circumstances of the family! Who does, or *don't* look after you?"

"Hearts'-sake!" came up the pleasant tones of Mrs. Oldways from behind, "how can they help it? There isn't any other out-doors. If they were down at Homesworth now, there'd be the lilac garden and the old chestnuts, and the seat under the wall. Poor little souls!" she added, pitifully, as she lifted them in, and kissed them. "It's well they can take any comfort. Let 'em have all there is."

Mrs. Oferr drew the blinds, and closed the window.

Frank and Laura remembered the strangeness of that day all their lives. How they sat, shy and silent, while Luclarion brought in cake and wine; how Mrs. Oferr sat in the large morocco easy-chair and took some; and Mrs. Oldways lifted Laura, great girl as she was, into her lap first, and broke a slice for her; how Mrs. Oldways went up-stairs to Mrs. Lake, and then down into the kitchen to do something that was needed; and Mrs. Oferr, after she had visited her brother, lay down in the spare chamber for a nap, tired with her long journey from New York, though it had been by boat and cars, while there was a long staging from Homesworth down to Nashua, on Mrs. Oldways' route. Mrs. Oldways, however, was "used," she said, "to stepping round." It was the sitting that had tired her.

How they were told not to go out any more, or to run up and down-stairs; and how they sat in the front windows, looking out through the green slats at so much of the street world as they could see in strips; how they obtained surreptitious bits of bread from dinner, and opened a bit of the sash, and shoved out crumbs under the blinds for the pigeons that flew down upon the sidewalk; how they wondered what kind of a day it was in other houses, where there were not circumstances in the family, where children played, and fathers were not ill, but came and went to and from their stores; and where two aunts had not come, both at once, from great ways off, to wait for something strange and awful that was likely to befall.

When they were taken in, at bedtime, to kiss their father and say good-night, there was something portentous in the stillness there; in the look of the sick man, raised high against the pillows, and turning his eyes wistfully toward them, with no slightest movement of the head; in the waiting aspect of all things, — the appearance as of everybody being to sit up all night except themselves.

Edward Shiere brought his children close to him with the magnetism of that look; they bent down to receive his kiss and his good-night, so long and solemn. He had not been in the way of talking to them about religion in his life. He had only insisted on their truth and obedience; that was the beginning of all religion. Now it was given him in the hour of his death what he should speak; and because he had never said many such words to them before, they fell like the very touch of the Holy Ghost upon their young spirits now, —

"Love God, and keep His commandments. Good-by."

In the morning, when they woke, Mrs. Lake was in their room, talking in a low voice with Mrs. Oferr, who stood by an open bureau. They heard Luclarion dusting down the stairs.

Who was taking care of their father?

They did not ask. In the night, he had been taken care of. It was morning with him, now, also.

Mrs. Lake and Mrs. Oferr were calculating, — about black pantalets, and other things.

This story is not with the details of their early orphan life. When Edward Shiere was buried came family consultations. The two aunts were the nearest friends. Nobody thought of Mr. Titus Oldways. He never was counted. He was Mrs. Shiere's uncle, — Aunt Oldways' uncle-in-law, therefore, and grand-uncle to these children. But Titus Oldways never took up any family responsibilities; he had been shy of them all his single, solitary life. He seemed to think he could not drop them as he could other things, if he did not find them satisfactory. Besides, what would he know about two young girls?

He saw the death in the paper, and came to the funeral; then he went away again to his house in Greenley Street at the far West End, and to his stiff old housekeeper, Mrs. Froke, who knew his stiff old ways. And, turning his back on everybody, everybody forgot all about him. Except as now and then, at intervals of years, there broke out here or there, at some distant point in some family crisis, a sudden recollection from which would spring a half suggestion, "Why, there's Uncle Titus! If he was only," — or, "if he would only," — and there it ended. Much as it might be with a housewife, who says of some stored-away possession forty times, perhaps, before it ever turns out available, "Why, there's that old gray taffety! If it were only green, now!" or, "If there were three or four yards more of it!"

Uncle Titus was just Uncle Titus, neither more nor less; so Mrs. Oferr and Aunt Oldways consulted about their own measures and materials; and never reckoned the old taffety at all. There was money enough to clothe and educate; little more.

"I will take home *one*," said Mrs. Oferr, distinctly.

So, they were to be separated?

They did not realize what this was, however. They were told of letters and visits; of sweet country-living, of city sights and pleasures; of kittens and birds' nests, and the great barns; of music and dancing lessons, and little parties, — "by-and-by, when it was proper."

"Let me go to Homesworth," whispered Frank to Aunt Oldways.

Laura gravitated as surely to the streets and shops, and the great school of young ladies.

"One taken and the other left," quoted Luclarion, over the packing of the two small trunks.

"We're both going," says Laura, surprised. "*One* taken? Where?"

"Where the carcass is," answered Luclarion.

"There's one thing you'll have to see to for yourselves. I can't pack it. It won't go into the trunks."

"What, Luclarion?"

"What your father said to you that night."

They were silent. Presently Frank answered, softly, — "I hope I shan't forget that."

Laura, the pause once broken, remarked, rather glibly, that she "was afraid there wouldn't be much chance to recollect things at Aunt Oferr's."

"She isn't exactly what I call a heavenly-minded woman," said Luclarion, quietly.

"She is very much *occupied*," replied Laura, grandly taking up the Oferr style. "She visits a great deal, and she goes out in the carriage. You have to change your dress every day for dinner, and I'm to take French lessons."

The absurd little sinner was actually proud of her magnificent temptations. She was only a child. Men and women never are, of course.

"I'm afraid it will be pretty hard to remember," repeated Laura, with condescension.

"*That's* your stump!"

Luclarion fixed the steadfast arrow of her look straight upon her, and drew the bow with this twang.

II.

LUCLARION.

HOW Mrs. Grapp ever came to, was the wonder. Her having the baby was nothing. Her having the name for it was the astonishment.

Her own name was Lucy; her husband's Luther; that, perhaps, accounted for the first syllable; afterwards, whether her mind lapsed off into combinations of such outshining appellatives as "Clara" and "Marion," or whether Mr. Grapp having played the clarionet, and wooed her sweetly with it in her youth, had anything to do with it, cannot be told; but in those prescriptive days of quiet which followed the domestic advent, the name did somehow grow together in the fancy of Mrs. Luther; and in due time the life-atom which had been born indistinguishable into the natural world, was baptized into the Christian Church as "Luclariŏn" Grapp. Thenceforth, and no wonder, it took to itself a very especial individuality, and became what this story will partly tell.

Marcus Grapp, who had the start of Luclarion in this "meander," — as their father called the vale of tears, — by just two years' time, and was y-*clipped*, by everybody but his mother "Mark," — in his turn, as they grew old together, cut his sister down to "Luke." Then Luther Grapp called them both "The Apostles." And not far wrong; since if ever the kingdom of heaven does send forth its Apostles — nay, its little Christs — into the work on earth, in these days, it is as little children into loving homes.

The Apostles got up early one autumn morning, when Mark was about six years old, and Luke four. They crept out of their small trundle-bed in their mother's room adjoining the great kitchen, and made their way out softly to the warm wide hearth.

There were new shoes, a pair apiece, brought home from the Mills the night before, set under the little crickets in the corners. These had got into their dreams, somehow, and into the red rooster's first halloo from the end room roof, and into the streak of pale daylight that just stirred and lifted the darkness, and showed doors and windows, but not yet the blue meeting-houses on the yellow wall-paper, by which they always knew when it was really morning; and while Mrs. Grapp was taking that last beguiling nap in which one is conscious that one means to get up presently, and rests so sweetly on one's good intentions, letting the hazy mirage of the day's work that is to be done play along the horizon of dim thoughts with its unrisen activities, — two little flannel night-gowns were cuddled in small heaps by the chimney-side, little bare feet were trying themselves into the new shoes, and lifting themselves up, crippled with two inches of stout string between the heels.

Then the shoes were turned into spans of horses, and chirruped and trotted softly into their cricket-stables; and then — what else was there to do, until the strings were cut, and the flannel night-gowns taken off?

It was so still out here, in the big, busy, day-time room; it was like getting back where the world had not begun; surely one must do something wonderful with the materials all lying round, and such an opportunity as that.

It was old-time then, when kitchens had fire-places; or rather the house was chiefly fire-place, in front of and about which was more or less of kitchen-space. In the deep fire-place lay a huge mound of gray ashes, a Vesuvius, under which red bowels of fire lay hidden. In one corner of the chimney leaned an iron bar, used sometimes in some forgotten, old fashioned way, across dogs or pothooks, — who knows now? At any rate, there it always was.

Mark, ambitious, put all his little strength to it this morning, and drew it down, carefully, without much clatter, on the hearth. Then he thought how it would turn red under those ashes, where the big coals were, and how it would shine and sparkle when he pulled it out again, like the red-hot, hissing iron Jack-the-Giant-Killer struck into the one-eyed monster's eye. So he shoved it in; and forgot it there, while he told Luke — very much twisted and dislocated, and misjoined — the leading incidents of the giant story; and then lapsed off, by some queer association, into the Scripture narrative of Joseph and his brethren, who "pulled his red coat off, and put him in a *fit*, and left him there."

"And then what?" says Luke.

"Then, — O, my iron 's done! See here, Luke!" — and taking it prudently with the tongs, he pulled back the rod, till the glowing end, a foot or more of live, palpitating, flamy red, lay out upon the broad open bricks.

"There, Luke! You daresn't put your foot on *that!*"

Dear little Luke, who wouldn't, at even four years old, be dared!

And dear little white, tender, pink-and-lily foot!

The next instant, a shriek of pain shot through Mrs. Grapp's ears, and sent her out of her dreams and out of her bed, and with one single impulse into the kitchen, with her own bare feet, and in her night-gown.

The little foot had only touched; a dainty, timid, yet

most resolute touch; but the sweet flesh shriveled, and the fierce anguish ran up every fibre of the baby body, to the very heart and brain.

"O! O, O!" came the long, pitiful, shivering cries, as the mother gathered her in her arms.

"What is it? What did you do? How came you to?" And all the while she moved quickly here and there, to cupboard and press-drawer, holding the child fast, and picking up as she could with one hand, cotton wool, and sweet-oil flask, and old linen bits; and so she bound it up, saying still, every now and again, as all she could say, — "What *did* you do? How came you to?"

Till, in a little lull of the fearful smart, as the air was shut away, and the oil felt momentarily cool upon the ache, Luke answered her, —

"He hed I dare-hn't, and ho I did!"

"You little fool!"

The rough word was half reaction of relief, that the child could speak at all, half horrible spasm of all her own motherly nerves that thrilled through and through with every pang that touched the little frame, hers also. Mothers never do part bonds with babies they have borne. Until the day they die, each quiver of their life goes back straight to the heart beside which it began.

"You Marcus! What did you mean?"

"I meant she darsn't; and she no business to 'a dars't," said Mark, pale with remorse and fright, but standing up stiff and manful, with bare common sense, when brought to bay. And then he marched away into his mother's bedroom, plunged his head down into the clothes, and cried, — harder than Luclarion.

Nobody wore any new shoes that day; Mark for a punishment, — though he flouted at the penalty as such, with an, "I guess you'd see me!" And there were many days before poor little Luclarion could wear any shoes at all.

The foot got well, however, without hindrance. But Luke was the same little fool as ever; that was not burnt out. She would never be "dared" to anything.

They called it "stumps" as they grew older. They played "stumps" all through the barns and woods and meadows; over walls and rocks, and rafters and house-roofs. But the burnt foot saved Luke's neck scores of times, doubtless. Mark remembered it; he never "stumped" her to any certain hurt, or where he could not lead the way himself.

The mischief they got into and out of is no part of my story; but one day something happened — things do happen as far back in lives as that — which gave Luclarion her clew to the world.

They had got into the best parlor, — that sacred place of the New England farm-house, that is only entered by the high-priests themselves on solemn festivals, weddings and burials, Thanksgivings and quiltings; or devoutly, now and then to set the shrine in order, shut the blinds again, and so depart, leaving it to gather the gloom and grandeur that things and places and people do when they are good for nothing else.

The children had been left alone; for their mother had gone to a sewing society, and Grashy, the girl, was upstairs in her kitchen-chamber-bedroom, with a nail over the door-latch to keep them out while she "fixed over" her best gown.

"Le's play Lake Ontario," says Marcus.

Now Lake Ontario, however they had pitched upon it, stood with them for all the waters that are upon the face of the earth, and all the confusion and peril of them. To play it, they turned the room into one vast shipwreck, of upset and piled up chairs, stools, boxes, buckets, and what else they could lay hands on; and among and over them they navigated their difficult and hilarious way. By no means were they to touch the floor; that was the Lake,—that were to drown.

It was Columbus sometimes; sometimes it was Captain Cook; to-day, it was no less than Jason sailing after the golden fleece.

Out of odd volumes in the garret, and out of "best books" taken down from the secretary in the "settin'-room," and put into their hands, with charges, of a Sunday, to keep them still, they had got these things, jumbled into strange far-off and near fantasies in their childish minds. "Lake Ontario" included and connected all.

"I'll tell you what it is," said Marcus, tumbling up against the parlor door and an idea at once. "In here!"

"What?" asked Luke, breathless, without looking up, and paddling with the shovel, from an inverted rocking-chair.

"The golden thing! Hush!"

At this moment Grashy came into the kitchen, took a little tin kettle from a nail over the dresser, and her sun-bonnet from another behind the door, and made her way through the apartment as well as she could for bristling chair-legs, with exemplary placidity. She was used to "Lake Ontario."

"Don't get into any mischief, you Apostles," was her injunction. "I'm goin' down to Miss Ruddock's for some 'east."

"Good," says Mark, the instant the door was shut. "Now this is Colchis, and I'm going in."

He pronounced it much like "cold-cheese," and it never occurred to him that he was naming any unusual or ancient locality. There was a "Jason" in the Mills Village. He kept a grocer's shop. Colchis might be close by for all he knew; out beyond the wall, perhaps, among the old barrels. Children *place* all they read or hear about, or even all they imagine, within a very limited horizon. They cannot go beyond their world. Why should they? Neither could those very venerable ancients.

"'Tain't," says Luclarion, with unbeguiled practicality. "It's just ma's best parlor, and you mustn't."

It was the "mustn't" that was the whole of it. If Mark had asserted that the back kitchen, or the cellar-way closet was Colchis, she would have indorsed it with enthusiasm, and followed on like a loyal Argonaut, as she was. But her imagination here was prepossessed. Nothing in old fable could be more environed with awe and mystery than this best parlor.

"And, besides," said Luclarion, "I dont care for the golden fleece; I'm tired of it. Let's play something else."

"I'll tell you what there is in here," persisted Mark. "There's two enchanted children. I've seen 'em!"

"Just as though," said Luke contemptuously. "Ma ain't a witch."

"Tain't ma. She don't know. They aint visible to her. *She* thinks it's nothing but the best parlor. But it opens out, right into the witch country, — not for her. 'Twill if we go. See if it dont."

He had got hold of her now; Luclarion could not resist that. Anything might be true of that wonderful best room, after all. It was the farthest Euxine, the witch-land, everything, to them.

So Mark turned the latch, and they crept in.

"We must open a shutter," Mark said, groping his way.

"Grashy will be back," suggested Luke, fearfully.

"Guess so!" said Mark. "She ain't got coaxed to take her sun-bonnet off yet, an' it 'll take her ninety-'leven hours to get it on again.

He had let in the light now from the south window.

The red carpet on the floor; the high sofa of figured hair-cloth, with brass-headed nails, and brass rosettes in the ends of the hard, cylinder pillows; the tall, carved cupboard press, its doors and drawers glittering with hanging brass handles; right opposite the door by which they had come in, the large, leaning mirror, gilt — garnished with grooved and beaded rim and an eagle and ball-chains over the top, — all this, opening right in from the familiar every-day kitchen and their Lake Ontario, — it certainly meant something that such a place should be. It meant a great deal more than sixteen feet square could hold, and what it really was did not stop short at the gray-and-crimson stenciled walls.

The two were all alone in it; perhaps they had never been all alone in it before. I think, notwithstanding their mischief and enterprise, they never had.

And deep in the mirror, face to face with them, coming down, it seemed, the red slant of an inner and more brilliant floor, they saw two other little figures. Their own they knew, really, but elsewhere they never saw their own figures entire. There was not another looking-glass in the house that was more than two feet long, and they were all hung up so high!

"There!" whispered Mark. "There they are, and they can't get out."

"Of course they can't," said sensible Luclarion.

"If we only knew the right thing to say, or do, they might," said Mark. "It's that they're waiting for, you see. They always do. It's like the sleeping beauty Grashy told us."

"Then they've got to wait a hundred years," said Luke.

"Who knows when they began?"

"They do everything that we do," said Luclarion, her imagination kindling, but as under protest. "If we could jump in perhaps they would jump out."

"We might jump *at* 'em," said Marcus. "Jest get 'em going, and may-be they'd jump over. Le's try."

So they set up two chairs from Lake Ontario in the kitchen doorway, to jump from; but they could only jump to the middle round of the carpet, and who could expect that the shadow children should be beguiled by that into a leap over bounds? They only came to the middle round of *their* carpet.

"We must go nearer; we must set the chairs in the middle, and jump close. Jest *shave*, you know," said Marcus.

"O, I'm afraid," said Luclarion.

"I'll tell you what! Le's *run* and jump! Clear from the other side of the kitchen, you know. Then they'll have to run too, and may-be they can't stop."

So they picked up chairs and made a path, and ran from across the broad kitchen into the parlor doorway, quite on to the middle round of the carpet, and then with great leaps came down bodily upon the floor close in front of the large glass that leaned over them, with two little fallen figures in it, rolling aside quickly also, over the slanting red carpet.

But, O dear, what did it?

Had the time come, anyhow, for the old string to part its last fibre, that held the mirror tilting from the wall, — or was it the crash of a completed spell?

There came a snap, — a strain, — as some nails or screws that held it otherwise gave way before the forward pressing weight, and down, flat-face upon the floor, between the children, covering them with fragments of splintered glass and gilded wood, — eagle, ball-chains, and all, — that whole magnificence and mystery lay prostrate.

Behind, where it had been, was a blank, brown-stained cobwebbed wall, thrown up harsh and sudden against them, making the room small, and all the enchanted chamber, with its red slanting carpet, and its far reflected corners, gone.

The house hushed up again after that terrible noise, and stood just the same as ever. When a thing like that happens, it tells its own story, just once, and then it is over. *People* are different. They keep talking.

There was Grashy to come home. She had not got there in time to hear the house tell it. She must learn it from the children. Why?

"Because they knew," Luclarion said. "Because, then, they could not wait and let it be found out."

"We never touched it," said Mark.

"We jumped," said Luke.

"We couldn't help it, if *that* did it. S'posin' we'd jumped in the kitchen, or — the — flat-irons had tumbled down, — or anything? That old string was all wore out."

"Well, we was here, and we jumped; and we know."

"We was here, of course; and of course we couldn't help knowing, with all that slam-bang. Why, it almost upset Lake Ontario! We can tell how it slammed, and how we thought the house was coming down. I did."

"And how we were in the best parlor, and how we jumped," reiterated Luclarion, slowly. "Marcus, it's a stump!"

They were out in the middle of Lake Ontario now, sitting right down underneath the wrecks, upon the floor; that is, under water, without ever thinking of it. The parlor door was shut, with all that disaster and dismay behind it.

"Go ahead, then!" said Marcus, and he laid himself back desperately on the floor. "There's Grashy!"

"Sakes and patience!" ejaculated Grashy, merrily, coming in. "They're drownded, — dead, both of 'em; down to the bottom of Lake Ontariah!"

"No we ain't," said Luclarion, quietly. "It isn't Lake Ontario now. It's nothing but a clutter. But there's an awful thing in the best parlor, and we don't know whether we did it or not. We were in there, and we jumped."

Grashy went straight to the parlor door, and opened it. She looked in, turned pale, and said "'Lection!"

That is a word the women have, up in the country, for solemn surprise, or exceeding emergency, or dire confusion. I do not know whether it is derived from religion or politics. It denotes a vital crisis, either way, and your hands full. Perhaps it had the theological association in Grashy's mind, for the next thing she said was, "My soul!"

"Do you know what that's a sign of, you children?"

"Sign the old thing was rotten," said Marcus, rather sullenly.

"Wish that was all," said Grashy, her lips white yet. "Hope there mayn't nothin' dreadful happen in this house before the year's out. It's wuss'n thirteen at the table."

"Do you s'pose we did it?" asked Luke, anxiously.

"Where was you when it tumbled?"

"Right in front of it. But we were rolling away. *We* tumbled."

"'Twould er come down the fust jar, anyway, if a door had slammed. The string's cut right through," said Grashy, looking at the two ends sticking up stiff and straight from the top fragment of the frame. "But the mercy is you war'n't smashed yourselves to bits and flinders. Think o' that!"

"Do you s'pose ma 'll think of that?" asked Luclarion.

"Well — yes; but it may make her kinder madder, — just at first, you know. Between you and me and the lookin'-glass, you see, — well, yer ma is a pretty strong-feelin' woman," said Grashy, reflectively. "'Fi was you I wouldn't say nothin' about it. What's the use? *I* shan't."

"It's a stump," repeated Luclarion, sadly, but in very resolute earnest.

Grashy stared.

"Well, if you ain't the curiousest young one, Luke Grapp!" said she, only half comprehending.

When Mrs. Grapp came home, Luclarion went into her bedroom after her, and told her the whole story. Mrs. Grapp went into the parlor, viewed the scene of calamity, took in the sense of loss and narrowly escaped danger, laid the whole weight of them upon the disobedience to be dealt with, and just as she had said, "You little fool!" out of the very shock of her own distress when Luke had burned her baby foot, she turned back now, took the two children up-stairs in silence, gave them each a good old orthodox whipping, and tucked them into their beds.

They slept one on each side of the great kitchen-chamber.

"Mark," whispered Luke, tenderly, after Mrs. Grapp's step had died away down the stairs. "How do you feel?"

"Hot!" said Mark. "How do you?"

"You ain't mad with me, be you?"

"No."

"Then I feel real cleared up and comfortable. But it *was* a stump, wasn't it?"

From that time forward, Luclarion Grapp had got her light to go by. She understood life. It was "stumps" all through. The Lord set them, and let them; she found that out afterward, when she was older, and "experienced religion." I think she was mistaken in the dates, though; it was *recognition*, this later thing; the experience was away back, — at Lake Ontario.

It was a stump when her father died, and her mother had to manage the farm, and she to help her. The mortgage they had to work off was a stump; but faith and Luclarion's dairy did it. It was a stump when Marcus wanted to go to college, and they undertook that, after the mortgage. It was a stump when Adam Burge wanted her to marry him, and go and live in the long red cottage at Side Hill, and she could not go till they had got through with helping Marcus. It was a terrible stump when Adam Burge married Persis Cone instead, and she had to live on and bear it. It was a stump when her mother died, and the farm was sold.

Marcus married; he never knew; he had a belles-lettres professorship in a new college up in D——. He would not take a cent of the farm money; he had had his share long ago; the four thousand dollars were invested for Luke. He did the best he could, and all he knew; but human creatures can never pay each other back. Only God can do that, either way.

Luclarion did not stay in ——. There were too few there now, and too many. She came down to Boston. Her two hundred and eighty dollars a year was very good, as far as it went, but it would not keep her idle; neither did she wish to live idle. She learned dress-making; she had taste and knack; she was doing well; she enjoyed going about from house to house for her days' work, and then coming back to her snug room at night, and her cup of tea and her book.

Then it turned out that so much sewing was not good for her; her health was threatened; she had been used to farm work and "all out-doors." It was a "stump" again. That was all she called it; she did not talk piously about a "cross." What difference did it make? There is another word, also, for "cross" in Hebrew.

Luclarion came at last to live with Mrs. Edward Shiere. And in that household, at eight and twenty, we have just found her.

III.

BY STORY-RAIL: TWENTY-SIX YEARS AN HOUR.

LAURA SHIERE did not think much about the "stump," when, in her dark gray merino travelling-dress, and her black ribbons, nicely appointed, as Mrs. Oferr's niece should be, down to her black kid gloves and broad-hemmed pocket-handkerchief, and little black straw travelling-basket (for morocco bags were not yet in those days), she stepped into the train with her aunt at the Providence Station, on her way to Stonington and New York.

The world seemed easily laid out before her. She was like a cousin in a story-book, going to arrive presently at a new home, and begin a new life, in which she would be very interesting to herself and to those about her. She felt rather important, too, with her money independence; there being really "property" of hers to be spoken of as she had heard it of late. She had her mother's diamond ring on her third finger, and was comfortably conscious of it when she drew off her left-hand glove. Laura Shiere's nature had only been stirred, as yet, a very little below the surface, and the surface rippled pleasantly in the sunlight that was breaking forth from the brief clouds.

Among the disreputable and vociferous crowd of New York hack drivers, that swarmed upon the pier as the *Massachusetts* glided into her dock, it was good to see that subduedly respectable and consciously private and superior man in the drab overcoat and the nice gloves and boots, who came forward and touched his hat to Mrs. Oferr, took her shawl and basket, and led the way, among the aggravated public menials, to a handsome private carriage waiting on the street.

"All well at home, David?" asked Mrs. Oferr.

"All well, ma'am, thank you," replied David.

And another man sat upon the box, in another drab coat, and touched *his* hat; and when they reached Waverley Place and alighted, Mrs. Oferr had something to say to him of certain directions, and addressed him as "Moses."

It was very grand and wonderful to order "David" and "Moses" about. Laura felt as if her aunt were something only a little less than "Michael with the sword." Laura had a susceptibility for dignities; she appreciated, as we have seen out upon the wood-shed, "high places, and all the people looking up."

David and Moses were brothers, she found out; she supposed that was the reason they dressed alike, in drab coats; as she and Frank used to wear their red merinos, and their blue ginghams. A little spasm did come up in her throat for a minute, as she thought of the old frocks and the old times already dropped so far behind; but Alice and Geraldine Oferr met her the next instant on the broad staircase at the back of the marble-paved hall, looking slight and delicate, and princess-like, in the grand space built about them for their lives to move in; and in the distance and magnificence of it all, the faint little momentary image of Frank faded away.

She went up with them out of the great square hall, over the stately staircase, past the open doors of drawing-rooms and library, stretching back in a long suite, with the conservatory gleaming green from the far end over the garden, up the second stairway to the floor where their rooms were; bedrooms and nursery, — this last called so still, though the great, airy front-room was the place used now for their books and amusements as growing young ladies, — all leading one into another around the sky-lighted upper hall, into which the sunshine came streaked with amber and violet from the richly colored glass. She had a little side apartment given to her for her own, with a recessed window, in which were blossoming plants just set there from the conservatory; opposite stood a white, low bed in a curtained alcove, and beyond was a dressing-closet. Laura thought she should not be able to sleep there at all for a night or two, for the beauty of it and the good time she should be having.

At that same moment Frank and her Aunt Oldways were getting down from the stage that had brought them over from Ipsley, where they slept after their day's journey from Boston, — at the doorstone of the low, broad-roofed, wide-built, roomy old farm-house in Homesworth.

Right in the edge of the town it stood, its fields stretching over the south slope of green hills in sunny uplands, and down in meadowy richness to the wild, hidden, sequestered river-side, where the brown water ran through a narrow, rocky valley, — Swift River they called it. There are a great many Swift Rivers in New England. It was only a vehement little tributary of a larger stream, beside which lay larger towns; it was doing no work for the world, apparently, at present; there were no mills, except a little grist-mill to which the farmers brought their corn, cuddled among the rocks and wild birches and alders, at a turn where the road came down, and half a dozen planks made a bit of a bridge.

"O, what beautiful places!" cried Frank, as they crossed the little bridge, and glanced either way into a green, gray, silvery vista of shrubs and rocks, and rushing water, with the white spires of meadow-sweet and the pink hardhack, and the first bright plumes of the golden rod nodding and shining against the shade, — as they passed the head of a narrow, grassy lane, trod by cows' feet, and smelling of their milky breaths, and the sweetness of hay-barns, — as they came up, at length, over the long slope of turf that carpeted the way, as for a bride's feet, from the roadside to the very threshold. She looked along the low, treble-piled garden wall, too, and out to the open sheds, deep with pine chips; and upon the broad brown house-roof, with its long, gradual decline, till its eaves were within reach of a child's fingers from the ground; and her quick eye took in facilities.

"O, if Laura could see this! After the old shed-top in Brier Street, and the one tree!"

But Laura had got what the shed-top stood for with her; it was Frank who had hearkened to whole forests in the stir of the one brick-rooted fir. To that which each child had, it was already given.

In a week or two Frank wrote Laura a letter. It was an old-fashioned letter, you know; a big sheet, written close, four pages, all but the middle of the last page, which was left for the "superscription." Then it was folded, the first leaf turned down twice, lengthwise; then the two ends laid over, toward each other; then the last doubling, or rather trebling, across; and the open edge slipped over the folds. A wafer sealed it, and a thimble pressed it, — and there were twenty-five cents postage to pay. That was a letter in the old times, when Laura and Frank Shiere were little girls. And this was that letter: —

DEAR LAURA, — We got here safe, Aunt Oldways and I, a week ago last Saturday, and it is *beautiful*. There is a green lane, — almost everybody has a green lane, — and the cows go up and down, and the swallows build in the barn-eaves. They fly out at sundown, and fill all the sky up. It is like the specks we used to watch in the sunshine when it came in across the kitchen, and they danced up and down and through and away, and seemed to be live things; only we couldn't tell, you know, what they were, or if they really did know how good it was. But these are big and real, and you can see their wings, and you know what they mean by it. I guess it is all the same thing, only some things are little and some are big. You can see the stars here, too, — such a sky full. And that is all the same again.

There are beautiful roofs and walls here. I guess you would think you were high up! Harett and I go up from under the cheese-room windows right over the whole house, and we sit on the peak by the chimney. Harett is Mrs. Dillon's girl. Not the girl that lives with her, — her daughter. But the girls that live with people are daughters here. Somebody's else, I mean. They are all alike. I suppose her name is Harriet, but they all call her Harett. I don't like to ask her for fear she should think I thought they didn't know how to pronounce.

I go to school with Harett; up to the West District. We carry brown bread and butter, and doughnuts, and cheese, and apple-pie in tin pails, for luncheon. Don't you remember the brown cupboard in Aunt Oldways' kitchen, how sagey, and doughnutty, and good it always smelt? It smells just so now, and everything tastes just the same.

There is a great rock under an oak tree half way up to

school, by the side of the road. We always stop there to rest, coming home. Three of the girls come the same way as far as that, and we always save some of our dinner to eat up there, and we tell stories. I tell them about dancing-school, and the time we went to the theatre to see "Cinderella," and going shopping with mother, and our little tea-parties, and the Dutch dolls we made up in the long front chamber. O, *don't* you remember, Laura? What different pieces we have got into our remembrances already! I feel as if I was making patchwork. Sometime, may-be, I shall tell somebody about living *here*. Well, they will be beautiful stories! Homesworth is an elegant place to live in. You will see when you come next summer.

There is an apple tree down in the south orchard that bends just like a horse's back. Then the branches come up over your head and shade you. We ride there, and we sit and eat summer apples there. Little rosy apples with dark streaks in them all warm with the sun. You can't think what a smell they have, just like pinks and spice boxes. Why don't they keep a little way off from each other in cities, and so have room for apple trees? I don't see why they need to crowd so. I hate to think of you all shut up tight when I am let right out into green grass, and blue sky, and apple orchards. That puts me in mind of something! Zebiah Jane, Aunt Oldways' girl, always washes her face in the morning at the pump-basin out in the back dooryard, just like the ducks. She says she can't spatter round in a room; she wants all creation for a slop-bowl. I feel as if we had all creation for everything up here. But I can't put all creation in a letter if I try. *That* would spatter dreadfully.

I expect a long letter from you every day now. But I

don't see what you will make it out of. I think I have got all the *things* and you won't have anything left but the *words*. I am sure you don't sit out on the wood-shed at Aunt Oferr's, and I dont believe you pound stones and bricks, and make colors. Do you know when we rubbed our new shoes with pounded stone and made them gray?

I never told you about Luclarion. She came up as soon as the things were all sent off, and she lives at the minister's. Where she used to live is only two miles from here, but other people live there now, and it is built on to and painted straw color, with a green door.

Your affectionate sister,

FRANCES SHIERE.

When Laura's letter came this was it:—

DEAR FRANK,—I received your kind letter a week ago, but we have been very busy having a dressmaker and doing all our fall shopping, and I have not had time to answer it before. We shall begin to go to school next week, for the vacations are over, and then I shall have ever so much studying to do. I am to take lessons on the piano, too, and shall have to practice two hours a day. In the winter we shall have dancing-school and practicing parties. Aunt has had a new bonnet made for me. She did not like the plain black silk one. This is of *gros d'Afrique*, with little bands and cordings round the crown and front; and I have a dress of *gros d'Afrique*, too, trimmed with double folds piped on. For every-day I have a new black *mousseline* with white clover leaves on it, and an all-black French chally to wear to dinner. I don't wear my black and white calico at all. Next summer aunt means to have me wear white almost all the time, with lavender and violet ribbons. I shall have a white muslin with three skirts and a black sash to wear to parties and to Public Saturdays, next winter. They have Public Saturdays at dancing-school every three weeks. But only the parents and relations can come. Alice and Geraldine dance the shawl-dance with Helena Pomeroy, with crimson and white Canton crape scarfs. They have showed me some of it at home. Aunt Oferr says I shall learn the *gavotte.*

Aunt Oferr's house is splendid. The drawing-room is full of sofas, and divans, and ottomans, and a *causeuse,* a little S-shaped seat for two people. Everything is covered with blue velvet, and there are blue silk curtains to the windows, and great looking-glasses between, that you can see all down into through rooms and rooms, as if there were a hundred of them. Do you remember the story Luclarion used to tell us of when she and her brother Mark were little children and used to play that the looking-glass-things were real, and that two children lived in them, in the other room, and how we used to make believe too in the slanting chimney glass? You could make believe it here with *forty* children. But I don't make believe much now. There is such a lot that is real, and it is all so grown up. It would seem so silly to have such plays, you know. I can't help thinking the things that come into my head though, and it seems sometimes just like a piece of a story, when I walk into the drawing-room all alone, just before company comes, with my *gros d'Afrique* on, and my puffed lace collar, and my hair tied back with long new black ribbons. It all goes through my head just how I look coming in, and how grand it is, and what the words would be in a book about it, and I seem to act a little bit, just to myself as if I were a girl in a story, and it seems to say, "And Laura walked up the long drawing-room and took a book bound in crimson morocco from the white marble pier table and sat down upon the velvet ottoman in the balcony window." But what happened then it never tells. I suppose it will by and by. I am getting used to it all, though; it isn't so *awfully* splendid as it was at first.

I forgot to tell you that my new bonnet flares a great deal, and that I have white lace quilling round the face with little black dotty things in it on stems. They don't wear those close cottage bonnets now. And aunt has had my dresses made longer and my pantalettes shorter, so that they hardly show at all. She says I shall soon wear long dresses, I am getting so tall. Alice wears them now, and her feet look so pretty, and she has such pretty slippers: little French purple ones, and sometimes dark green, and sometimes beautiful light gray, to go with different dresses. I don't care for anything but the slippers, but I *should* like such ones as hers. Aunt says I can't, of course, as long as I wear black, but I can have purple ones next summer to wear with my white dresses. That will be when I come to see you.

I am afraid you will think this is a very *wearing* kind of a letter, there are so many 'wears' in it. I have been reading it over so far, but I can't put in any other word.

Your affectionate sister,

LAURA SHIERE.

P. S. Aunt Oferr says Laura Shiere is such a good sounding name. It doesn't seem at all common. I am glad of it. I should hate to be common.

I do not think I shall give you any more of it just here

than these two letters tell. We are not going through all Frank and Laura's story. That with which we have especially to do lies on beyond. But it takes its roots in this, as all stories take their roots far back and underneath.

Two years after, Laura was in Homesworth for her second summer visit at the farm. It was convenient, while the Oferrs were at Saratoga. Mrs. Oferr was very much occupied now, of course, with introducing her own daughters. A year or two later, she meant to give Laura a season at the Springs. "All in turn, my dear, and good time," she said.

The winter before, Frank had been a few weeks in New York. But it tired her dreadfully, she said. She liked the theatres and the concerts, and walking out and seeing the shops. But there was "no place to get out of it into." It didn't seem as if she ever really got home and took off her things. She told Laura it was like that first old letter of hers; it was just "wearing," all the time.

Laura laughed. "But how can you live *without* wearing?" said she.

Frank stood by, wondering, while Laura unpacked her trunks that morning after her second arrival at Aunt Oldways'. She had done now even with the simplicity of white and violet, and her wardrobe blossomed out like the flush of a summer garden.

She unfolded a rose-colored muslin, with little raised embroidered spots, and threw it over the bed.

"Where *will* you wear that, up here?" asked Frank, in pure bewilderment.

"Why, I wear it to church, with my white Swiss mantle," answered Laura. "Or taking tea, or anything. I've a black silk *visite* for cool days. That looks nice with it. And see here, — I've a pink sunshade. They don't have them much yet, even in New York. Mr. Pemberton Oferr brought these home from Paris, for Gerry, and Alice, and me. Gerry's is blue. See! it tips back." And Laura set the dashy little thing with its head on one side, and held it up coquettishly.

"They used them in carriages in Paris, he said, and in St. Petersburg, driving out on the Nevskoi Prospekt."

"But where are your common things?"

"Down at the bottom; I haven't come to them. They were put in first, because they would bear squeezing. I've two French calicoes, with pattern trimmings; and a lilac jaconet, with ruffles, open down the front."

Laura wore long dresses now; and open wrappers were the height of the style.

Laura astonished Homesworth the first Sunday of this visit, with her rose-colored toilet. Bonnet of shirred pink silk with moss rosebuds and a little pink lace veil; the pink muslin, full-skirted over two starched petticoats; even her pink belt had gay little borders of tiny buds and leaves, and her fan had a pink tassel.

"They're the things I wear; why shouldn't I?" she said to Frank's remonstrance.

"But up here!" said Frank. "It would seem nicer to wear something — stiller."

So it would; a few years afterward Laura herself would have seen that it was more elegant; though Laura Shiere was always rather given to doing the utmost — in apparel — that the occasion tolerated. Fashions grew stiller in years after. But this June Sunday, somewhere in the last thirties or the first forties, she went into the village church like an Aurora, and the village long remembered the resplendence. Frank had on a white cambric dress, with a real rose in the bosom, cool and fresh, with large green leaves; and her "cottage straw" was trimmed with white lutestring, crossed over the crown.

"Do you feel any better?" asked Aunt Oldways of Laura, when they came home to the country tea-dinner.

"Better — how?" asked Laura, in surprise.

"After all that 'wear' and *stare*," said Aunt Oldways, quietly.

Aunt Oldways might have been astonished, but she was by no means awestruck, evidently; and Aunt Oldways generally spoke her mind.

Somehow, with Laura Shiere, pink was pinker, and ribbons were more rustling than with most people. Upon some quiet unconscious folks, silk makes no spread, and color little show; with Laura every gleam told, every fibre asserted itself. It was the live Aurora, bristling and tingling to its farthest electric point. She did not toss or flaunt, either; she had learned better of Signor Pirotti how to carry herself; but she was in conscious *rapport* with every thing and stitch she had about her. Some persons only put clothes on to their bodies; others really seem to contrive to put them on to their souls.

Laura Shiere came up to Homesworth three years later, with something more wonderful than a pink embossed muslin: — she had a lover.

Mrs. Oferr and her daughters were on their way to the mountains; Laura was to be left with the Oldways. Grant Ledwith accompanied them all thus far on their way; then he had to go back to Boston.

"I can't think of anything but that pink sunshade she used to carry round canted all to one side over her shoulder," said Aunt Oldways, looking after them down the dusty road the morning that he went away. Laura, in her white dress and her straw hat and her silly little bronze-and-blue-silk slippers printing the roadside gravel, leaning on Grant Ledwith's arm, seemed only to have gained a fresh, graceful adjunct to set off her own pretty goings and comings with, and to heighten the outside interest of that little point of eternity that she called her life. Mr. Ledwith was not so much a man who had won a woman, as Laura was a girl who had "got a beau."

She had sixteen tucked and trimmed white skirts, too, she told Frank; she should have eight more before she was married; people wore ever so many skirts now, at a time. She had been to a party a little while ago where she wore *seven*.

There were deep French embroidery bands around some of these white skirts; those were beautiful for morning dresses. Geraldine Oferr was married last winter; Laura had been her bridesmaid; Gerry had a white brocade from Paris, and a point-lace veil. She had three dozen of everything, right through. They had gone to housekeeping up town, in West Sixteenth Street. Frank would have to come to New York next winter, or in the spring, to be *her* bridesmaid; then she would see; then — who knew!

Frank was only sixteen, and she lived away up here in Homesworth among the hills; she had not "seen," but she had her own little secret, for all that; something she neither told nor thought, yet which was there; and it came across her with a queer little thrill from the hidden, unlooked-at place below thought, that "Who" *didn't* know.

Laura waited a year for Grant Ledwith's salary to be raised to marrying point; he was in a wholesale woolen house in Boston; he was a handsome fellow, with gentlemanly and taking address, — capital, this, for a young salesman; and they put his pay up to two thousand dollars within that twelvemonth. Upon this, in the spring, they married; took a house in Filbert Street, down by the river, and set up their little gods. These were: a sprinkle of black walnut and brocatelle in the drawing-room, a Sheffield-plate tea-service, and a crimson-and-gilt-edged dinner set that Mrs. Oferr gave them; twilled turkey-red curtains, that looked like thibet, in the best chamber; and the twenty-four white skirts and the silk dresses, and whatever corresponded to them on the bridegroom's part, in their wardrobes. All that was left of Laura's money, and all that was given them by Grant Ledwith's father, and Mr. Titus Oldways' astounding present of three hundred dollars, without note or comment, — the first reminder they had had of him since Edward Shiere's funeral, "and goodness knew how he heard anything now," Aunt Oferr said, — had gone to this outfit. But they were well set up and started in the world; so everybody said, and so they, taking the world into their young, confident hands for a plaything, not knowing it for the perilous loaded shell it is, thought, merrily, themselves.

Up in Homesworth people did not have to wait for two thousand dollar salaries. They would not get them if they did.

Oliver Ripwinkley, the minister's son, finished his medical studies and city hospital practice that year, and came back, as he had always said he should do, to settle down for a country doctor. Old Doctor Parrish, the parson's friend of fifty years, with no child of his own, kept the place for Oliver, and hung up his old-fashioned saddle-bags in the garret the very day the young man came home.

He was there to be "called in," however, and with this backing, and the perforce of there being nobody else, young Doctor Ripwinkley had ten patients within the first week; thereby opportunity for shewing himself in the eyes of ten families as a young man who "appeared to know pretty well what he was about."

So that when he gave further proof of the same, by asking, within the week that followed, the prettiest girl in Homesworth, Frances Shiere, to come and begin the world with him at Mile Hill village, nobody, not even Frank herself, was astonished.

She bought three new gowns, a shawl, a black silk mantle, and a straw bonnet. She made six each of every pretty white garment that a woman wears; and one bright mellow evening in September, they took their first tea in the brown-carpeted, white-shaded little corner room in the old "Rankin house;" a bigger place than they really wanted yet, and not all to be used at first; but rented "reasonable," central, sunshiny, and convenient; a place that they hoped they should buy sometime; facing on the broad sidegreen of the village street, and running back, with its field and meadow belongings, away to the foot of great, gray, sheltering Mile Hill.

And the vast, solemn globe, heedless of what lit here or there upon its breadth, or took up this or that life in its little freckling cities, or between the imperceptible foldings of its hills, — only carrying way-passengers for the centuries, — went plunging on its track, around and around, and swept them all, a score of times, through its summer and its winter solstices.

IV.

AFTERWARDS IS A LONG TIME.

OLD Mr. Marmaduke Wharne had come down from Outledge, in the mountains, on his way home to New York. He had stopped in Boston to attend to some affairs of his own, — if one can call them so, since Marmaduke Wharne never had any "own" affairs that did not chiefly concern, to their advantage, somebody else, — in which his friend Mr. Titus Oldways was interested, not personally, but Wharne fashion. Now, reader, you know something about Mr. Titus Oldways, which up to this moment, only God, and Marmaduke Wharne, and Rachel Froke, who kept Mr. Oldways' house, and wore a Friend's drab dress and white cap, and said "Titus," and "Marmaduke" to the two old gentlemen, and "thee" and "thou" to everybody, — have ever known. In a general way and relation, I mean; separate persons knew particular things; but each separate person thought the particular thing he knew to be a whimsical exception.

Mr. Oldways did not belong to any church: but he had an English Prayer-book under his Bible on his study table, and Baxter and Fenelon and à Kempis and "Wesley's Hymns," and Swedenborg's "Heaven and Hell" and "Arcana Celestia," and Lowell's "Sir Launfal," and Dickens's "Christmas Carol," all on the same set of shelves, — that held, he told Marmaduke, his religion; or as much of it as he could get together. And he had this woman, who was a Friend, and who walked by the Inner Light, and in outer charity, if ever a woman did, to keep his house. "For," said he, "the blessed truth is, that the Word of God is in the world. Alive in it. When you know that, and wherever you can get hold of his souls, then and there you've got your religion, — a piece at a time. To prove and sort your pieces, and to straighten the tangle you might otherwise get into, there's *this*," and he laid his hand down on the Four Gospels, bound in white morocco, with a silver cross upon the cover, — a volume that no earthly creature, again, knew of, save Titus and Marmaduke and Rachel Froke, who laid it into a drawer when she swept and dusted, and placed it between the crimson folds of its quilted silken wrapper when she had finished, burnishing the silver cross gently with a scrap of chamois leather cut from a clean piece every time. There was nothing else delicate and exquisite in all the plain and grim establishment; and the crimson wrapper was comfortably worn, and nobody would notice it, lying on the table there, with an almanac, a directory, the big, open Worcester's Dictionary, and the scattered pamphlets and newspapers of the day.

Out in the world, Titus Oldways went about with visor down.

He gave to no fairs nor public charities; "let them get all they could that way, it wasn't his way," he said to Rachel Froke. The world thought he gave nothing, either of purse or life.

There was a plan they had together, — he and Marmaduke Wharne, — this girls' story-book will not hold the details nor the idea of it, — about a farm they owned, and people working it that could go nowhere else to work anything; and a mill-privilege that might be utilized and expanded, to make — not money so much as safe and honest human life by way of making money; and they sat and talked this plan over, and settled its arrangements, in the days that Marmaduke Wharne was staying on in Boston, waiting for his other friend, Miss Craydocke, who had taken the River Road down from Outledge, and so come round by Z——, where she was staying a few days with the Goldthwaites and the Inglesides. Miss Craydocke had a share or two in the farm and in the mill.

And now, Titus Oldways wanted to know of Marmaduke Wharne what he was to do for Afterwards.

It was a question that had puzzled and troubled him. Afterwards.

"While I live," he said, "I will do what I can, and *as* I can. I will hand over my doing, and the wherewith, to no society or corporation. I'll pay no salaries nor circumlocutions. Neither will I — afterwards. And how is my money going to work on?"

"*Your* money?"

"Well, — God's money."

"How did it work when it came to you?"

Mr. Oldways was silent.

"He chose to send it to you. He made it in the order of things that it should come to you. You began, yourself, to work for money. You did not understand, then, that the money would be from God and was for Him."

"He made me understand."

"Yes. He looked out for that part of it too. He can look out for it again. His word shall not return unto him void."

"He has given me this, though, to pass on; and I will not put it into a machine. I want to give some living soul a body for its living. Dead charities are dead. It's of no use to will it to you, Marmaduke; I'm as likely to stay on, perhaps, as you are."

"And the youngest life might drop, the day after your own. You can't take it out of God's hand."

"I must either let it go by law, or will it — here and there. I know enough whom it would help; but I want to invest, not spend it; to invest it in a life — or lives — that will carry it on from where I leave it. How shall I know?"

"He giveth it a body as it pleaseth Him," quoted Marmaduke Wharne, thoughtfully. "I am English, you know, Oldways; I can't help reverencing the claims of next of kin. Unless one is plainly shown otherwise, it seems the appointment. How can we set aside his ways until He clearly points us out his own exception?"

"My 'next' are two women whom I don't know; my niece's children. She died thirty years ago."

"Perhaps you ought to know them."

"I know *about* them; I've kept the run; but I've held clear of family. They didn't need me, and I had no right to put it into their heads they did, unless I fully meant" —

He broke off.

"They're like everybody else, Wharne; neither better nor worse, I dare say; but the world is full of just such women. How do I know this money would be well in their hands — even for themselves?"

"Find out."

"One of 'em was brought up by an Oferr woman!"

The tone in which he *commonized* the name to a satiric general term, is not to be written down, and needed not to be interpreted.

"The other is well enough," he went on, "and contented enough. A doctor's widow, with a little property, a farm and two children, — her older ones died very young, — up in New Hampshire. I might spoil *her;* and the other, — well, you see as I said, I *don't know.*"

"Find out," said Marmaduke Wharne, again.

"People are not found out till they are tried."

"Try 'em!"

Mr. Oldways had been sitting with his head bent, thoughtfully, his eyes looking down, his hands on the two stiff, old-fashioned arms of his chair. At this last spondaic response from Marmaduke, he lifted his eyes and eyebrows, — not his head, — and raised himself slightly with his two hands pressing on the chair arms; the keen glance and the half-movement were impulsively toward his friend.

"Eh?" said he.

"Try 'em," repeated Marmaduke Wharne. "Give God's way a chance."

Mr. Oldways, seated back in his chair again, looked at him intently; made a little vibration, as it were, with his body, that moved his head up and down almost imperceptibly, with a kind of gradual assenting apprehension, and kept utterly silent.

So, their talk being palpably over for this time, Marmaduke Wharne got up presently to go. They nodded at each other, friendlily, as he looked back from the door.

Left alone, Mr. Titus Oldways turned in his swivel-chair, around to his desk beside which he was sitting.

"Next of kin?" he repeated to himself. "God's way? — Well! Afterwards is a long time. A man must give it up somewhere. Everything escheats to the king at last."

And he took a pen in his hand and wrote a letter.

"AFTERWARDS IS A LONG TIME." See p. 44.

V.

HOW THE NEWS CAME TO HOMESWORTH.

"I WISH I lived in the city, and had a best friend," said Hazel Ripwinkley to Diana, as they sat together on the long, red, sloping kitchen roof under the arches of the willow-tree, hemming towels for their afternoon "stent." They did this because their mother sat on the shed roof under the fir, when she was a child, and had told them of it. Imagination is so much greater than fact, that these children, who had now all that little Frank Shiere had dreamed of with the tar smell and the gravel stones and the one tree, — who might run free in the wide woods and up the breezy hillsides, — liked best of all to get out on the kitchen roof and play "old times," and go back into their mother's dream.

"I wish I lived in a block of houses, and could see across the corner into my best friend's room when she got up in the morning!"

"And could have that party!" said Diana.

"Think of the clean, smooth streets, with red sidewalks, and people living all along, door after door! I like things set in rows, and people having places, like the desks at school. Why, you've got to go way round Sand Hill to get to Elizabeth Ann Dorridon's. I should like to go up steps, and ring bells!"

"I don't know," said Diana, slowly. "I think birds that build little nests about anywhere in the cunning, separate places, in the woods, or among the bushes, have the best time."

"Birds, Dine! It ain't birds, it's people! What has that to do with it?"

"I mean I think nests are better than martin-boxes."

"Let's go in and get her to tell us that story. She's in the round room."

The round room was a half ellipse, running in against the curve of the staircase. It was a bit of a place, with the window at one end, and the bow at the other. It had been Doctor Ripwinkley's office, and Mrs. Ripwinkley sat there with her work on summer afternoons. The door opened out, close at the front, upon a great flat stone in an angle, where was also entrance into the hall by the house-door, at the right hand. The door of the office stood open, and across the stone one could look down, between a range of lilac bushes and the parlor windows, through a green door-yard into the street.

"Now, Mother Frank, tell us about the party!"

They called her "Mother Frank" when they wished to be particularly coaxing. They had taken up their father's name for her, with their own prefix, when they were very little ones, before he went away and left nobody to call her Frank, every day, any more.

"That same little old story? Won't you ever be tired of it, — you great girls?" asked the mother; for she had told it to them ever since they were six and eight years old.

"Yes! No, never!" said the children.

For how *should* they outgrow it? It was a sunny little bit out of their mother's own child-life. We shall go back to smaller things, one day, maybe, and find them yet more beautiful. It is the *going* back, together.

"The same old way?"

"Yes; the very same old way."

"We had little open-work straw hats and muslin pelisses, — your Aunt Laura and I," — began Mrs. Ripwinkley, as she had begun all those scores of times before. "Mother put them on for us, — she dressed us just alike, always, — and told us to take each other's hands, and go up Brier and down Hickory streets, and stop at all the houses that she named, and that we knew; and we were to give her love and compliments, and ask the mothers in each house, — Mrs. Dayton, and Mrs. Holridge (she lived up the long steps), and Mrs. Waldow, and the rest of them, to let Caroline and Grace and Fanny and Susan, and the rest of *them*, come at four o'clock, to spend the afternoon and take tea, if it was convenient."

"O, mother!" said Hazel, "you didn't say that when you *asked* people, you know."

"O, no!" said Mrs. Ripwinkley. "That was when we went to stop a little while ourselves, without being asked. Well, it was to please to let them come. And all the ladies were at home, because it was only ten o'clock; and they all sent their love and compliments, and they were much obliged, and the little girls would be very happy.

"It was a warm June day; up Brier Street was a steep walk; down Hickory we were glad to keep on the shady side, and thought it was nice that Mrs. Bemys and Mrs. Waldow lived there. The strings of our hats were very moist and clinging when we got home, and Laura had a blue mark under her chin from the green ribbon.

"Mother was in her room, in her white dimity morning gown, with little bows up the front, the ends trimmed with cambric edging. She took off our hats and our pelisses, — the tight little sleeves came off wrong side out, — sponged our faces with cool water, and brushed out Laura's curls. That was the only difference between us. I hadn't any curls, and my hair had to be kept cropped. Then she went to her upper bureau drawer and took out two little paper boxes.

"'Something has come for Blanche and Clorinda, since you have been gone,' she said, smiling. 'I suppose you have been shopping?' We took the paper boxes, laughing back at her with a happy understanding. We were used to these little plays of mother's, and she couldn't really surprise us with her kindnesses. We went and sat down in the window-seat, and opened them as deliberately and in as grown-up a way as we could. Inside them were two little lace pelerines lined with rose-colored silk. The boxes had a faint smell of musk. The things were so much better for coming in boxes! Mother knew that.

"Well, we dressed our dolls, and it was a great long sunshiny forenoon. Mother and Luclarion had done something in the kitchen, and there was a smell of sweet baking in the house. Every now and then we sniffed, and looked at each other, and at mother, and laughed. After dinner we had on our white French calicoes with blue sprigs, and mother said she should take a little nap, and we might go into the parlor and be ready for our company. She always let us receive our own company ourselves at first. And exactly at four o'clock the door-bell rang, and they began to come.

"Caroline and Fanny Dayton had on white cambric dresses, and green kid slippers. That was being very much dressed, indeed. Lucy Waldow wore a pink lawn, and Grace Holridge a buff French print. Susan Bemys said her little sister couldn't come because they couldn't find her best shoes. Her mother thought she had thrown them out of the window.

"When they all got there we began to play 'Lady Fair;' and we had just got all the 'lady fairs,' one after another, into our ring, and were dancing and singing up and down and round and round, when the door opened and mother walked in.

"We always thought our mother was the prettiest of any of the girls' mothers. She had such bright shining hair, and she put it up with shell combs into such little curly puffs. And she never seemed fussy or old, but she came in among us with such a beautiful, smiling way, as if she knew beforehand that it was all right, and there was no danger of any mischief, or that we shouldn't behave well, but she only wanted to see the good time. That day she had on a white muslin dress with little purple flowers on it, and a bow of purple ribbon right in the side of her hair. She had a little piece of fine work in her hand, and after she had spoken to all the little girls and asked them how their mothers were, she went and sat down in one of the front windows, and made little scollops and eyelets. I remember her long ivory stiletto, with a loop of green ribbon through the head of it, and the sharp, tiny, big-bowed scissors that lay in her lap, and the bright, tapering silver thimble on her finger.

"Pretty soon the door opened again, softly; a tray appeared, with Hannah behind it. On the tray were little glass saucers with confectionery in them; old-fashioned confectionery, — gibraltars, and colored caraways, and cockles with mottoes. We were in the middle of "So says the Grand Mufti,' and Grace Holridge was the Grand Mufti. Hannah went up to her first, as she stood there alone, and Grace took a saucer and held it up before the row of us, and said, '*Thus* says the Grand Mufti!' and then she bit a red gibraltar, and everybody laughed. She did it so quickly and so prettily, putting it right into the play. It was good of her not to say, '*So* says the Grand Mufti.' At least we thought so then, though Susan Bemys said it would have been funnier.

"We had a great many plays in those days, and it took a long afternoon to get through with them. We had not begun to wonder what we should do next, when tea time came, and we went down into the basement room. It wasn't tea, though; it was milk in little clear, pink mugs, some that mother only had out for our parties, and cold water in crimped-edge glasses, and little biscuits, and sponge-cakes, and small round pound-cakes frosted. These were what had smelt so good in the morning.

"We stood round the table; there was not room for all of us to sit, and mother helped us, and Hannah passed things round. Susan Bemys took cake three times, and Lucy Waldow opened her eyes wide, and Fanny Dayton touched me softly under the table.

"After tea mother played and sung some little songs to us; and then she played the 'Fisher's Hornpipe' and 'Money Musk,' and we danced a little contra-dance. The girls did not all know cotillons, and some of them had not begun to go to dancing-school. Father came home and had his tea after we had done ours, and then he came up into the parlor and watched us dancing. Mr. Dayton came in, too. At about half past eight some of the other fathers called, and some of the mothers sent their girls, and everybody was fetched away. It was nine o'clock when Laura and I went to bed, and we couldn't go to sleep until after the clock struck ten, for thinking and saying what a beautiful time we had had, and anticipating how the girls would talk it all over next day at school. That," said Mrs. Ripwinkley, when she had finished, "was the kind of a party we used to have in Boston when I was a little girl. I don't know what the little girls have now."

"Boston!" said Luclarion, catching the last words as she came in, with her pink cape bonnet on, from the Homesworth variety and finding store, and post-office. "You'll talk them children off to Boston, finally, Mrs. Ripwinkley! Nothing ever tugs so at one end, but there 's something tugging at the other; and there 's never a hint nor a hearing to anybody, that something more doesn't turn up concerning it. Here 's a letter, Mrs. Ripwinkley!"

Mrs. Ripwinkley took it with some surprise. It was not her sister's handwriting nor Mr. Ledwith's, on the cover; and she rarely had a letter from them that was posted in Boston, now. They had been living at a place out of town for several years. Mrs. Ledwith knew better than to give her letters to her husband for posting. They got lost in his big wallet, and stayed there till they grew old.

Who should write to Mrs. Ripwinkley, after all these years, from Boston?

She looked up at Luclarion, and smiled. "It didn't take a Solomon," said she, pointing to the postmark.

"No, nor yet a black smooch, with only four letters plain, on an invelup. 'Taint that, it's the drift of things. Those girls have got Boston in their minds as hard and fast as they've got heaven; and I mistrust mightily they'll get there first somehow!"

The girls were out of hearing, as she said this; they had got their story, and gone back to their red roof and their willow tree.

"Why, Luclarion!" exclaimed Mrs. Ripwinkley, as she drew out and unfolded the letter sheet. "It's from Uncle Titus Oldways."

"Then he ain't dead," remarked Luclarion, and went away into the kitchen.

"MY DEAR FRANCES, — I am seventy-eight years old. It is time I got acquainted with some of my relations. I've had other work to do in the world heretofore (at least I thought I had), and so, I believe, have they. But I have a wish now to get you and your sister to come and live nearer to me, that we may find out whether we really are anything to each other or not. It seems natural, I suppose, that we might be; but kinship doesn't all run in the veins.

"I do not ask you to do this with reference to any possible intentions of mine that might concern you after my death; my wish is to do what is right by you, in return for your consenting to my pleasure in the matter, while I am alive. It will cost you more to live in Boston than where you do now, and I have no business to expect you to break up and come to a new home unless I can make it an object to you in some way. You can do some things for your children here that you could not do in Homesworth. I will give you two thousand dollars a year to live on, and secure the same to you if I die. I have a house here in Aspen Street, not far from where I live myself, which I will give to either of you that it may suit. That you can settle between you when you come. It is rather a large house, and Mrs. Ledwith's family is larger, I think, than yours. The estate is worth ten thousand dollars, and I will give the same sum to the one who prefers, to put into a house elsewhere. I wish you to reckon this as all you are ever to expect from me, except the regard I am willing to believe I may come to have for you. I shall look to hear from you by the end of the week.

"I remain, yours truly,

"TITUS OLDWAYS."

"Luclarion!" cried Mrs. Ripwinkley, with excitement, "come here and help me think!"

"Only four days to make my mind up in," she said again, when Luclarion had read the letter through.

Luclarion folded it and gave it back.

"It won't take God four days to think," she answered quietly; "and you can ask *Him* in four minutes. You and I can talk afterwards." And Luclarion got up and went away a second time into the kitchen.

That night, after Diana and Hazel were gone to bed, their mother and Luclarion Grapp had some last words about it, sitting by the white-scoured kitchen table, where Luclarion had just done mixing bread and covered it away for rising. Mrs. Ripwinkley was apt to come out and talk things over at this time of the kneading. She could get more from Luclarion then than at any other opportunity. Perhaps that was because Miss Grapp could not walk off from the bread-trough; or it might be that there was some sympathy between the mixing of her flour and yeast into a sweet and lively perfection, and the bringing of her mental leaven wholesomely to bear.

"It looks as if it were meant, Luclarion," said Mrs. Ripwinkley, at last. "And just think what it will be for the children."

"I guess it's meant fast enough," replied Luclarion.

"But as for what it will be for the children, — why, that's according to what you all make of it. And that's the stump."

Luclarion Grapp was fifty-four years old; but her views of life were precisely the same that they had been at twenty-eight.

VI.

AND.

THERE is a piece of Z——, just over the river, that they call "And."

It began among the school-girls; Barbara Holabird had christened it, with the shrewdness and mischief of fourteen years old. She said the "and-so-forths" lived there.

It was a little supplementary neighborhood; an after-growth, coming up with the railroad improvements, when they got a freight station established on that side for the East Z—— mills. "After Z——, what should it be but 'And?'" Barbara Holabird wanted to know. The people who lived there called it East Square; but what difference did that make?

It was two miles Boston-ward from Z—— centre, where the down trains stopped first; that was five minutes gained in the time between it and the city. Land was cheap at first, and sure to come up in value; so there were some streets laid out at right angles, and a lot of houses put up after a pattern, as if they had all been turned out of blanc-mange moulds, and there was "East Square." Then people began by-and-by to build for themselves, and a little variety and a good deal of ambition came in. They had got to French roofs now; this was just before the day of the multitudinous little paper collar-boxes with beveled covers, that are set down everywhere now, and look as if they could be lifted up by the chimneys, any time, and be carried off with a thumb and finger. Two and a half story houses, Mansarded, looked grand; and the East Square people thought nothing slight of themselves, though the "old places" and the real Z—— families were all over on West Hill.

Mrs. Megilp boarded in And for the summer.

"Since Oswald had been in business she couldn't go far from the cars, you know; and Oswald had a boat on the river, and he and Glossy enjoyed that so much. Besides, she had friends in Z——, which made it pleasant; and she was tired, for her part, of crowds and fashion. All she wanted was a quiet country place. She knew the Goldthwaites and the Haddens; she had met them one year at Jefferson."

Mrs. Megilp had found out that she could get larger rooms in And than she could have at the mountains or the sea-shore, and at half the price; but this she did not mention. Yet there was nothing shabby in it, except her carefully *not* mentioning it.

Mrs. Megilp was Mrs. Grant Ledwith's chief intimate and counselor. She was a good deal the elder; that was why it was mutually advantageous. Grant Ledwith was one of the out-in-the-world, up-to-the-times men of the day; the day in which everything is going, and everybody that is in active life has, somehow or other, all that is going. Grant Ledwith got a good salary, an inflated currency salary; and he spent it all. His daughters were growing up, and they were stylish and pretty; Mrs. Megilp took a great interest in Agatha and Florence Ledwith, and was always urging their mother to "do them justice." "Agatha and Florence were girls who had a right to every advantage." Mrs. Megilp was almost old enough to be Laura Ledwith's mother; she had great experience, and knowledge of the world; and she sat behind Laura's conscience and drove it tandem with her inclination.

Per contra, it was nice for Mrs. Megilp, who was a widow, and whose income did not stretch with the elasticity of the times, to have friends who lived like the Ledwiths, and who always made her welcome; it was a good thing for Glossy to be so fond of Agatha and Florence, and to have them so fond of her. "She needed young society," her mother said. One reason that Glossy Megilp needed young society might be in the fact that she herself was twenty-six.

Mrs. Megilp had advised the Ledwiths to buy a house in Z——. "It was just far enough not to be suburban, but to have a society of its own; and there *was* excellent society in Z——, everybody knew. Boston was hard work, nowadays; the distances were getting to be so great." Up to the West and South Ends, — the material distances, — she meant to be understood to say; but there was an inner sense to Mrs. Megilp's utterances, also.

"One might as well be quite out of town; and then it was always something, even in such city connection as one might care to keep up, to hail from a well-recognized social independency; to belong to Z—— was a standing, always. It wasn't like going to Forest Dell, or Lakegrove, or Bellair; cheap little got-up places with fancy names, that were strung out on the railroads like French gilt beads on a chain."

But for all that, Mrs. Ledwith had only got into "And;" and Mrs. Megilp knew it.

Laura did not realize it much; she had bowing and speaking acquaintance with the Haddens and the Hendees, and even with the Marchbankses, over on West Hill; and the Goldthwaites and the Holabirds, down in the town, she knew very well. She did not care to come much nearer; she did not want to be bound by any very stringent and exclusive social limits; it was a bother to keep up to all the demands of such a small, old-established set. Mrs. Hendee would not notice, far less be impressed by the advent of her new-style Brussels carpet with a border, or her full, fresh, Nottingham lace curtains, or the new covering of her drawing-room set with cuir-colored terry. Mrs. Tom Friske and Mrs. Philgry, down here at East Square, would run in, and appreciate, and admire, and talk it all over, and go away perhaps breaking the tenth commandment amiably in their hearts.

Mrs. Ledwith's nerves had extended since we saw her as a girl; they did not then go beyond the floating ends of her blue or rose-colored ribbons, or, at furthest, the tip of her jaunty laced sunshade; now they ramified, — for life still grows in some direction, — to her chairs, and her china, and her curtains, and her ruffled pillow-shams. Also, savingly, to her children's "suits," and party dresses, and pic-nic hats, and double button gloves. Savingly; for there is a leaven of grace in mother-care, even though it be expended upon these. Her friend, Mrs. Inchdeepe, in Helvellyn Park, with whom she dined when she went shopping in Boston, had *nothing* but her modern improvements and her furniture. "My house is my life," she used to say, going round with a Canton crape duster, touching tenderly carvings and inlayings and gildings.

Mrs. Megilp was spending the day with Laura Ledwith; Glossy was gone to town, and thence down to the sea-shore, with some friends.

Mrs. Megilp spent a good many days with Laura. She had large, bright rooms at her boarding-house, but then she had very gristly veal pies and thin tapioca puddings for dinner; and Mrs. Megilp's constitution required something more generous. She was apt to happen in at this season, when Laura had potted pigeons. A little bird told her; a dozen little birds, I mean, with their legs tied together in a bunch; for she could see the market wagon from her window, when it turned up Mr. Ledwith's avenue.

Laura had always the claret pitcher on her dinner table, too; and claret and water, well-sugared, went deliciously with the savory stew.

They were up-stairs now, in Laura's chamber; the bed and sofa were covered with silk and millinery; Laura was looking over the girls' "fall things;" there was a smell of sweet marjoram and thyme and cloves, and general richness coming up from the kitchen; there was a bland sense of the goodness of Providence in Mrs. Megilp's — no, not heart, for her heart was not very hungry; but in her eyes and nostrils.

She was advising Mrs. Ledwith to take Desire and Helena's two green silks and make them over into one for Helena.

"You can get two whole back breadths then, by piecing it up under the sash; and you *can't* have all those gores again; they are quite done with. Everybody puts in whole breadths now. There's just as much difference in the *way* of goring a skirt, as there is between gores and straight selvages."

"They do hang well, though; they have such a nice slope."

"Yes, — but the stripes and the seams! Those tell the story six rods off; and then there *must* be sashes, or postillions, or something; they don't make anything without them; there isn't any finish to a round waist unless you have something behind."

"They wore belts last year, and I bought those expensive gilt buckles. I'm sure they used to look sweetly. But there! a fashion doesn't last nowadays while you're putting a thing on and walking out of the house!"

"And don't put in more than three plaits," pursued Mrs. Megilp, intent on the fate of the green silks. "Everything is gathered; you see that is what requires the sashes; round waists and gathers have a queer look without."

"If you once begin to alter, you've got to make all over," said Mrs. Ledwith, a little fractiously, putting the scissors in with unwilling fingers. She knew there was a good four days' work before her, and she was quick with her needle, too.

"Never mind; the making over doesn't cost anything; you turn off work so easily; and then you've got a really stylish thing."

"But with all the ripping and remodelling, I don't get time to turn round, myself, and *live!* It is all fall work, and spring work, and summer work and winter work. One drive rushes pell-mell right over another. There isn't time enough to make things and have them; the good of them, I mean."

"The girls get it; we have to live in our children," said Mrs. Megilp, self-renouncingly. "I can never rest until Glossy is provided with everything; and you know, Laura, I *am* obliged to contrive."

Mrs. Megilp and her daughter Glaucia spent about a thousand dollars a year, between them, on their dress. In these days, this is a limited allowance — for the Megilps. But Mrs. Megilp was a woman of strict pecuniary principle; the other fifteen hundred must pay all the rest; she submitted cheerfully to the Divine allotment, and punctually made the two ends meet. She will have this to show, when the Lord of these servants cometh and reckoneth with them, and that man who has been also in narrow circumstances, brings his nicely kept talent out of his napkin.

Desire Ledwith, a girl of sixteen, spoke suddenly from a corner where she sat with a book, —

"I do wonder who '*they*' are, mamma!"

"Who?" said Mrs. Ledwith, half rising from her chair, and letting some breadths of silk slide down upon the floor from her lap, as she glanced anxiously from the window down the avenue. She did not want any company this morning.

"Not that, mamma; I don't mean anybody coming. The 'theys' that wear, and don't wear, things; the theys you have to be just like, and keep ripping and piecing for."

"You absurd child!" exclaimed Mrs. Ledwith, pettishly. "To make me spill a whole lapful of work for that! They? Why, everybody, of course."

"Everybody complains of them, though. Jean Friske says her mother is all discouraged and worn out. There isn't a thing they had last year that won't have to be made over this, because they put in a breadth more behind, and they only gore side seams. And they don't wear black capes or cloth sacks any more with all kinds of dresses; you must have suits, clear through. It seems to me 'they' is a nuisance. And if it's everybody, we must be part of it. Why doesn't somebody stop?"

"Desire, I wish you'd put away your book, and help, instead of asking silly questions. You can't make the world over, with 'why don'ts?'"

"I'll *rip*," said Desire, with a slight emphasis; putting her book down, and coming over for a skirt and a pair of scissors. "But you know I'm no good at putting together again. And about making the world over, I don't know but that might be as easy as making over all its clothes. I'd as lief try, of the two."

Desire was never cross or disagreeable; she was only "impracticable," her mother said. "And besides that, she didn't know what she really did want. She was born hungry and asking, with those sharp little eyes, and her mouth always open while she was a baby. 'It was a sign,' the nurse said, when she was three weeks old. And then the other sign, — that she should have to be called 'Desire!'"

Mrs. Megilp — for Mrs. Megilp had been in office as long ago as that — had suggested ways of getting over or around the difficulty, when Aunt Desire had stipulated to have the baby named for her, and had made certain persuasive conditions.

"There's the pretty French turn you might give it, — 'Desirée.' Only one more 'e,' and an accent. That is so sweet, and graceful, and distinguished!"

"But Aunt Desire won't have the name twisted. It is to be real, plain Desire, or not at all."

Mrs. Megilp had shrugged her shoulders.

"Well; of course it can be that, to christen by, and marry by, and be buried by. But between whiles, — people pick up names, — you'll see!"

Mrs. Megilp began to call her "Daisy" when she was two years old. Nobody could help what Mrs. Megilp took a fancy to call her by way of endearment, of course; and Daisy she was growing to be in the family, when one day, at seven years old, she heard Mrs. Megilp say to her mother, —

"I don't see but that you've all got your *Desire*, after all. The old lady is satisfied; and away up there in Hanover, what can it signify to her? The child is "Daisy," practically, now, as long as she lives."

The sharp, eager little gray eyes, so close together in the high, delicate head, glanced up quickly at speaker and hearer.

"What old lady, mamma, away up in Hanover?"

"Your Aunt Desire, Daisy, whom you were named for. She lives in Hanover. You are to go and see her there, this summer."

"Will she call me Daisy?"

The little difficulty suggested in this question had singularly never occurred to Mrs. Ledwith before. Miss Desire Ledwith never came down to Boston; there was no danger at home.

"No. She is old-fashioned, and doesn't like pet names. She will call you Desire. That is your name, you know."

"Would it signify if she thought you called me Daisy?" asked the child frowning half absently over her doll, whose arm she was struggling to force into rather a tight sleeve of her own manufacture.

"Well, perhaps she might not exactly understand. People always went by their names when she was a child, and now hardly anybody does. She was very particular about having you called for her, and you *are*, you know. I always write 'Desire Ledwith' in all your books, and — well, I always *shall* write it so, and so will you. But you can be Daisy when we make much of you here at home, just as Florence is Flossie."

"No, I can't," said the little girl, very decidedly, getting up and dropping her doll. "Aunt Desire, away up in Hanover, is thinking all the time that there is a little Desire Ledwith growing up down here. I don't mean to have her cheated. I'm going to went by my name, as she did. Don't call me Daisy any more, all of you; for I shan't come!"

The gray eyes sparkled; the whole little face scintillated, as it were. Desire Ledwith had a keen, charged little face; and when something quick and strong shone through it, it was as if somewhere behind it there had been struck fire.

She was true to that through all the years after; going to school with Mabels and Ethels and Graces and Ediths, — not a girl she knew but had a pretty modern name, — and they all wondering at that stiff little "Desire" of hers that she would go by. When she was twelve years old, the old lady up in Hanover had died, and left her a gold watch, large and old-fashioned, which she could only keep on a stand in her room, — a good solid silver tea-set, and all her spoons, and twenty-five shares in the Hanover Bank.

Mrs. Megilp called her Daisy, with gentle inadvertence, one day after that. Desire lifted her eyes slowly at her, with no other reply in her face, or else.

"You might please your mother now, I think," said Mrs. Megilp. "There is no old lady to be troubled by it."

"A promise isn't ever dead, Mrs. Megilp," said Desire, briefly. "I shall keep our words."

"After all," Mrs. Megilp said privately to the mother, "there is something quietly aristocratic in an old, plain, family name. I don't know that it isn't good taste in the child. Everybody understands that it was a condition, and an inheritance."

Mrs. Megilp had taken care of that. She was watchful for the small impressions she could make in behalf of her particular friends. She carried about with her a little social circumference in which all was preëminently as it should be.

But, — as I would say if you could not see it for yourself, — this is a digression. We will go back again.

"If it were any use!" said Desire, shaking out the deep plaits as she unfastened them from the band. "But you're only a piece of everybody after all. You haven't anything really new or particular to yourself, when you've done. And it takes up so much time. Last year, this was so pretty! *Isn't* anything actually pretty in itself, or can't they settle what it is? I should think they had been at it long enough."

"Fashions never were so graceful as they are this minute," said Mrs. Megilp. "Of course it is art, like everything else, and progress. The world is getting educated to a higher refinement in it, every day. Why, it's duty, child!" she continued, exaltedly. "Think what the world would be if nobody cared. We ought to make life beautiful. It's meant to be. There's not only no virtue in ugliness, but almost no virtue *with* it, I think. People are more polite and good-natured when they are well dressed and comfortable."

"*That's* dress, too, though," said Desire, sententiously. "You've got to stay at home four days, and rip, and be tired, and cross, and tried-on-to, and have no chance to do anything else, before you can put it all on and go out and be good-natured and bland, and help put the beautiful face on the world, *one* day. I don't believe it's political economy."

"Everybody doesn't have to do it for themselves. Really, when I hear people blamed for dress and elegance, — why, the very ones who have the most of it are those who sacrifice the least time to it. They just go and order what they want, and there's the end of it. When it comes home, they put it on, and it might as well be a flounced silk as a plain calico."

"But we *do* have to think, Mrs. Megilp. And work and worry. And then we *can't* turn right round in the things we know every stitch of and have bothered over from beginning to end, and just be lilies of the field!"

"A great many people do have to wash their own dishes, and sweep, and scour; but that is no reason it ought not to be done. I always thought it was rather a pity that was said, *just so*," Mrs. Megilp proceeded, with a mild deprecation of the Scripture. "There *is* toiling and spinning; and will be to the end of time, for some of us."

"There's cauliflower brought for dinner, Mrs. Ledwith," said Christina, the parlor girl, coming in. "And Hannah says it won't go with the pigeons. Will she put it on the ice for to-morrow?"

"I suppose so," said Mrs. Ledwith, absently, considering a breadth that had a little hitch in it. "Though what we shall have to-morrow I'm sure I don't know," she added, rousing up "I wish Mr. Ledwith wouldn't send home the first thing he sees, without any reference."

"And here's the milkman's bill, and a letter," continued Christina, laying them down on a chair beside her mistress, and then departing.

Great things come into life so easily, when they do come, right alongside of milk-bills and cabbages! And yet one may wait so long sometimes for anything to happen *but* cabbages!

The letter was in a very broad, thick envelope, and sealed with wax.

Mrs. Ledwith looked at it curiously before she opened it. She did not receive many letters. She had very little time for correspondence. It was addressed to "Mrs. Laura Ledwith." That was odd and unusual, too.

Mrs. Megilp glanced at her over the tortoise-shell rims of her eye-glasses, but sat very quiet, lest she should delay the opening. She would like to know what could be in that very business-like looking despatch, and Laura would be sure to tell her. It must be something pretty positive, one way or another; it was no common-place negative communication. Laura might have had property left her. Mrs. Megilp always thought of possibilities like that.

When Laura Ledwith had unfolded the large commercial sheet, and glanced down the open lines of square, upright characters, whose purport could be taken in at sight, like print, she turned very red with a sudden excitement. Then all the color dropped away, and there was nothing in her face but blank, pale, intense surprise.

"It is a most *won*derful thing!" said she, at last, slowly; and her breath came like a gasp with her words. "My great-uncle, Mr. Oldways."

She spoke those four words as if from them Mrs. Megilp could understand everything.

Mrs. Megilp thought she did.

"Ah! Gone?" she asked, pathetically.

"Gone! No, indeed!" said Mrs. Ledwith. "He wrote the letter. He wants me to *come;* me, and all of us, — to Boston, to live; and to get acquainted with him."

"My dear," said Mrs. Megilp, with the promptness and benignity of a Christian apostle, "it's your duty to go."

"And he offers me a house, and two thousand dollars a year."

"My dear," said Mrs. Megilp, "it is *emphatically* your duty to go."

All at once something strange came over Laura Ledwith. She crumpled the letter tight in her hands with a clutch of quick excitement, and began to choke with a little sob, and to laugh at the same time.

"Don't give way!" cried Mrs. Megilp, coming to her and giving her a little shake and a slap. "If you do once you will again, and you're *not* hystericky!"

"He 's sent for Frank, too. Frank and I will be together again in dear old Boston! But—we can't be children and sit on the shed any more; and—it *isn't* dear old Boston, either!"

And then Laura gave right up, and had a good cry for five minutes. After that she felt better, and asked Mrs. Megilp how she thought a house in Spiller Street would do.

But she couldn't rip any more of those breadths that morning.

Agatha and Florence came in from some calls at the Goldthwaites and the Haddens, and the news was told, and they had their bonnets to take off, and the dinner-bell rang, and the smell of the spicy pigeon-stew came up the stairs, all together. And they went down, talking fast; and one said "house," and another "carpets," and another "music and German;" and Desire, trailing a breadth of green silk in her hand that she had never let go since the letter was read, cried out, "oratorios!" And nobody quite knew what they were going down stairs for, or had presence of mind to realize the pigeons, or help each other or themselves properly, when they got there! Except Mrs. Megilp, who was polite and hospitable to them all, and picked two birds in the most composed and elegant manner.

When the dessert was put upon the table, and Christina, confusedly enlightened as to the family excitement, and excessively curious, had gone away into the kitchen, Mrs. Ledwith said to Mrs. Megilp, —

"I'm not sure I should fancy Spiller Street, after all; it's a sort of a corner. Westmoreland Street or Helvellyn Park might be nice. I know people down that way, — Mrs. Inchdeepe."

"Mrs. Inchdeepe isn't exactly 'people,'" said Mrs. Megilp, in a quiet way that implied more than grammar. "Don't get into 'And' in Boston, Laura! — With such an addition to your income, and what your uncle gives you toward a house, I don't see why you might not think of Republic Avenue."

"We shall have plenty of thinking to do about everything," said Laura.

"Mamma," said Agatha, insinuatingly, "I'm thinking, already; about that rose-pink paper for my room. I'm glad now I didn't have it here."

Agatha had been restless for white lace, and rose-pink, and a Brussels carpet ever since her friend Zarah Thoole had come home from Europe and furnished a morning-room.

All this time Mr. Grant Ledwith, quite unconscious of the impending changes with which his family were so far advanced in imagination, was busy among bales and samples in Devonshire Street. It got to be an old story by the time the seven o'clock train was in, and he reached home. It was almost as if it had all happened a year ago, and they had been waiting for him to come home from Australia.

There was so much to explain to him that it was really hard to make him understand, and to bring him up to the point from which they could go on together.

VII.

WAKING UP.

THE Ledwiths took apartments in Boston for a month. They packed away the furniture they wanted to keep for upper rooms, in the attics of their house at Z——. They had an auction of all the furniture of their drawing-room, dining-room, library, and first floor of sleeping-rooms. Then they were to let their house. Meanwhile, one was to be fixed upon and fitted up in Boston. In all this Mrs. Megilp advised, invaluably.

"It's of no use to move things," she said. "Three removes are as bad as a fire; and nothing ever fits in to new places. Old wine and new bottles, you know! Clear all off with a country auction. Everybody comes, and they all fight for everything. Things bring more than their original cost. Then you've nothing to do but order according to your taste."

Mr. Oldways had invited both his nieces to his own house on their arrival. But here again Mrs. Megilp advised, — so judiciously.

"There are too many of you; it would be a positive infliction. And then you'll have all your running about and planning and calculating to do, and the good old gentleman would think he had pulled half Boston down about his ears. Your sister can go there; it would be only generous and thoughtful to give way to her. There are only three of them, and they are strange, you know, to everything, and wouldn't know which way to turn. I can put you in the way of rooms at the Bellevue, exactly the thing, for a hundred and fifty a month. No servants, you see; meals at the restaurant, and very good, too. The Wedringtons are to give them up unexpectedly; going to Europe; poor Mrs. Wedrington is so out of health. And about the house; don't decide in a hurry; see what your uncle says, and your sister. It's very likely she'll prefer the Aspen Street house; and it *would* be out of the way for you. Still it is not to be *refused*, you know; of course it is very desirable in many respects; roomy, old-fashioned, and a garden. I think your sister will like those things; they're what she has been used to. If she does, why it's all comfortably settled, and nobody refuses. It is so ungracious to appear to object; a gift horse, you know."

"Not to be refused; only by no means to be taken; masterly inactivity till somebody else is hooked; and then somebody else is to be grateful for the preference. I wish Mrs. Megilp wouldn't shine things up so; and that mother wouldn't go to her to black all her boots!"

Desire said this in secret, indignant discomfort, to Helena, the fourth in the family, her chum-sister. Helena did very well to talk to; she heard anything; then she pranced round the room and chaffed the canary.

"Chee! chee! chee! chiddle, iddle, iddle, iddle, e-e-ee! Where do you keep all your noise and your breath? You're great, aren't you? You do that to spite people that have to work up one note at a time. You don't take it in away down under your belt, do you? You're not particular about that. You don't know much, after all. You don't know *how* you do it. You aren't learning of Madame Caroletti. And you haven't learned two quarters, any way. You were only just born last spring. Set up! Tr-r-r-e-e-ee! I can do that myself. I don't believe you've got an octave in you. Poh!"

Mrs. Ripwinkley came down from the country with a bonnet on that had a crown, and with not a particle of a chignon. When she was married, twenty-five years before, she wore a French twist,—her hair turned up in waves from her neck as prettily as it did away from her forehead,—and two thick coiled loops were knotted and fastened gracefully at the top. She had kept on twisting her hair so, all these years; and the rippling folds turned naturally under her fingers into their places. The color was bright still, and it had not thinned. Over her brows it parted richly, with no fuzz or crimp; but a sweet natural wreathing look that made her face young. Mrs. Ledwith had done hers over slate-pencils till she had burned it off; and now tied on a friz, that came low down, for fashion's sake, and left visible only a little bunch of puckers between her eyebrows and the crowsfeet at the corners. The back of her head was weighted down by an immense excrescence in a bag. Behind her ears were bare places. Mrs. Ledwith began to look old-young. And a woman cannot get into a worse stage of looks than that. Still, she was a showy woman—a good exponent of the reigning style; and she was handsome—she and her millinery—of an evening, or in the street.

When I began that last paragraph I meant to tell you what else Mrs. Ripwinkley brought with her, down out of the country and the old times; but hair takes up a deal of room. She brought down all her dear old furniture. That is, it came after her in boxes, when she had made up her mind to take the Aspen Street house.

"Why, that's the sofa Oliver used to lie down on when he came home tired from his patients; and that's the rocking-chair I nursed my babies in; and this is the old oak table we've sat round three times a day, the family of us, growing and thinning, as the time went on, all through these years. It's like a communion table, now, Laura. Of course such things had to come."

This was what she answered, when Laura ejaculated her amazement at her having brought "old Homesworth truck" to Boston.

"You see it isn't the walls that make the home; we can go away from them and not break our hearts, so long as our own goes with us. The little things that we have used, and that have grown around us with our living,— they are all of living that we can handle and hold on to; and if I went to Spitzbergen, I should take as many of them as I could."

The Aspen Street house just suited Mrs. Ripwinkley, and Diana, and Hazel.

In the first place, it was wooden; built side to the street, so that you went up a little paved walk, in a shade of trees, to get to the door; and then the yard, on the right hand side as you came in, was laid out in narrow walks between borders of blossoming plants. There were vines against the brick end of the next building,— creepers and morning-glories, and white and scarlet runners; and a little martin-box was set upon a pole in the still, farther corner.

The rooms of the house were low, but large; and some of the windows had twelve-paned sashes,— twenty-four to a window. Mrs. Ripwinkley was charmed with these also. They were like the windows at Mile Hill.

Mrs. Ledwith, although greatly relieved by her sister's prompt decision for the house which she did *not* want, felt it in her conscience to remonstrate a little.

"You have just come down from the mountains, Frank, after your twenty-five years' sleep; you've seen nothing;

by and by you will think differently. This house is fearfully old-fashioned, *fearfully ;* and it's away down here on the wrong side of the hill. You can never get up over Summit Street from here."

"We are used to hills, and walking."

"But I mean — that isn't all. There are other things you won't be able to get over. You'll never shake off Aspen Street dust, — you nor the children."

"I don't think it is dusty. It is quiet, and sheltered, and clean. I like it ever so much," said Mrs. Ripwinkley.

"O, dear, you don't understand in the least! It's wicked to let you go on so! You poor, dear, simple little old soul!"

"Never mind," said Mrs. Megilp. "It's all well enough for the present. It pleases the old gentleman, you know; and after all he's done, he ought to be pleased. One of you should certainly be in his neighborhood. *He* has been here from time immemorial; and any place grows respectable by staying in it long enough — from *choice.* Nobody will wonder at Mrs. Ripwinkley's coming here at his request. And when she *does* move, you see, she will know exactly what she is about."

"I almost doubt if she ever *will* know what she is about," said Laura.

"In that case, — well," — said Mrs. Megilp, and stopped, because it really was not in the least needful to say more.

Mrs. Megilp felt it judicious, for many reasons, that Mrs. Ripwinkley should be hidden away for awhile, to get that mountain sleep out of her eyes, if it should prove possible; just as we rub old metal with oil and put it by till the rust comes off.

The Ledwiths decided upon a house in Shubarton Place; that would not seem quite like taking old Uncle Titus's money and rushing away with it as far as city limits would allow; and Laura really did wish to have the comfort of her sister's society, in a cozy way, of mornings, up in her room; that was her chief idea about it. There were a good many times and things in which she scarcely expected much companionship from Frank. She would not have said even to herself, that Frank was rusty; and she would do her faithful and good-natured best to rub her up; but there was an instinct with her of the congruous and the incongruous; and she would not do her Bath-brick polishing out on the public promenade.

They began by going together to the carpet stores and the paper warehouses; but they ended in detailing themselves for separate work; their ideas clashed ridiculously, and perpetually confused each other. Frank remembered loyally her old brown sofa and chairs; she would not have gay colors to put them out of countenance; for even if she re-covered them, she said they should have the same old homey complexion. So she chose a fair, soft buff, with a pattern of brown leaves, for her parlor paper; Mrs. Ledwith, meanwhile, plunging headlong into glories of crimson and garnet and gold. Agatha had her blush pink, in panels, with heart-of-rose borders, set on with delicate gilt beadings; you would have thought she was going to put herself up, in a fancy-box, like a French *mouchoir* or a *bonbon*.

"Why *don't* you put your old brown things all together in an up-stairs room, and call it Mile Hill? You could keep it for old times' sake, and sit there mornings; the house is big enough; and then have furniture like other people's in the parlor?"

"You see it wouldn't be *me*," said Mrs. Ripwinkley, simply.

"They keep saying it 'looks,' and 'it looks,' said Diana to her mother, at home. "Why must everything *look* somehow?"

"And every*body*, too," said Hazel. "Why, when we meet any one in the street that Agatha and Florence know, the minute they have gone by they say, 'She didn't look well to-day,' or, 'How pretty she did look in that new hat!' And after the great party they went to at that Miss Hitchler's, they never told a word about it except how girls 'looked.' I wonder what they *did*, or where the good time was. Seems to me people ain't living, — they are only just looking; or *is* this the same old Boston that you told about, and where are the real folks, mother?"

"We shall find them," said Mrs. Ripwinkley, cheerily; "and the real of these, too, when the outsides are settled. In the meantime, we'll make our house say, and not look. Say something true, of course. Things won't say anything else, you see; if you try to make them, they don't speak out; they only stand in a dumb show and make faces."

"That's looking!" said Hazel. "Now I know."

"How those children do grow!" said Mrs. Ripwinkley, as they went off together. "Two months ago they were sitting out on the kitchen roof, and coming to me to hear the old stories!"

"Transplantin'," said Luclarion. "That's done it."

At twelve and fourteen, Hazel and Diana could be simple as birds, — simpler yet, as human children waiting for all things, — in their country life and their little dreams of the world. Two months' contact with people and things in a great city had started the life that was in them, so that it showed what manner of growth it was to be of.

And little Hazel Ripwinkley had got hold already of the small end of a very large problem.

But she could not make it out that this was the same old Boston that her mother had told about, or where the nice neighbors were that would be likely to have little tea-parties for their children.

VIII.

EAVESDROPPING IN ASPEN STREET.

SOME of the old builders, — not the *very* old ones, for they built nothing but rope-walks down behind the hill, — but some of those who began to go northwest from the State House to live, made a pleasant group of streets down there on the level stretching away to the river, and called them by fresh, fragrant, country — suggesting names. Names of trees and fields and gardens, fruits and blossoms; and they built houses with gardens around them. In between the blocks were deep, shady places; and the smell of flowers was tossed back and forth by summer winds between the walls. Some nice old people stayed on there, and a few of their descendants stay on there still, though they are built in closely now, for the most part, and coarse, common things have much intruded, and Summit Street overshadows them with its palaces.

Here and there a wooden house, set back a little, like this of the Ripwinkleys in Aspen Street, gives you a feeling of Boston in the far back times, as you go by; and here and there, if you could get into the life of the neighborhood, you might perhaps find a household keeping itself almost untouched with change, though there has been such a rush and surge for years up and over into the newer and prouder places.

At any rate, Titus Oldways lived here in Greenley Street; and he owned the Aspen Street house, and another over in Meadow Place, and another in Field Court. He meant to stretch his control over them as long as he could, and keep them for families; therefore he valued them at such rates as they would bring for dwellings; he would not sell or lease them for any kind of "improvements;" he would not have their little door-yards choked up, or their larger garden spaces destroyed, while he could help it.

Round in Orchard Street lived Miss Craydocke. She was away again, now, staying a little while with the Josselyns in New York. Uncle Titus told Mrs. Ripwinkley that when Miss Craydocke came back it would be a neighborhood, and they could go round; now it was only back and forth between them and him and Rachel Froke. There were other people, too, but they would be longer finding them out. "You'll know Miss Craydocke as soon as you see her; she is one of those you always seem to have seen before."

Now Uncle Titus would not have said this to everybody; not even if everybody had been his niece, and had come to live beside him.

Orchard Street is wide and sunny and pleasant; the river air comes over it and makes it sweet; and Miss Craydocke's is a big, generous house, of which she only uses a very little part herself, because she lets the rest to nice people who want pleasant rooms and can't afford to pay much rent; an old gentleman who has had a hard time in the world, but has kept himself a gentleman through it all, and his little cheery old lady-wife who puts her round glasses on and stitches away at fine women's under-garments and flannel embroideries, to keep things even, have the two very best rooms; and a clergyman's widow, who copies for lawyers, and writes little stories for children, has another; and two orphan sisters who keep school have another; and Miss Craydocke calls her house the Beehive, and buzzes up and down in it, and out and in, on little "seeing-to" errands of care and kindness all day long, as never any queen-bee did in any beehive before, but in a way that makes her more truly queen than any sitting in the middle cell of state to be fed on royal jelly. Behind the Beehive, is a garden, as there should be; great patches of lily-of-the valley grow there that Miss Craydocke ties up bunches from in the spring and gives away to little children, and carries into all the sick rooms she knows of, and the poor places. I always think of those lilies of the valley when I think of Miss Craydocke. It seems somehow as if they were blooming about her all the year through; and so they are, perhaps, invisibly. The other flowers come in their season; the crocuses have been done with first of all; the gay tulips and the snowballs have made the children glad when they stopped at the gate and got them, going to school. Miss Craydocke is always out in her garden at school-time. By and by there are the tall white lilies, standing cool and serene in the July heats; then Miss Craydocke is away at the mountains, pressing ferns and drying grasses for winter parlors; but there is somebody on duty at the garden dispensary always, and there are flower-pensioners who know they may come in and take the gracious toll.

Late in the autumn, the nasturtiums and verbenas and marigolds are bright; and the asters quill themselves into the biggest globes they can, of white and purple and rose, as if it were to make the last glory the best, and to do the very utmost of the year. Then the chrysanthemums go into the house and bloom there for Christmas-time.

There is nothing else like Miss Craydocke's house and garden, I do believe, in all the city of the Three Hills. It is none too big for her, left alone with it, the last of her family; the world is none too big for her; she is glad to know it is all there. She has a use for everything as fast as it comes, and a work to do for everybody, as fast as she finds them out. And everybody, — almost, — catches it as she goes along, and around her there is always springing up a busy and a spreading crystallizing of shining and blessed elements. The world is none too big for her, or for any such, of course, because, — it has been told why better than I can tell it, — because "ten times one is always ten."

It was a gray, gusty morning. It had not set in to rain continuously; but the wind wrung handfuls of drops suddenly from the clouds, and flung them against the panes and into the wayfarers' faces.

Over in the house opposite the Ripwinkley's, at the second story windows, sat two busy young persons. Hazel, sitting at her window, in "mother's room," where each had a corner, could see across; and had got into the way of innocent watching. Up in Homesworth, she had used to watch the robins in the elm-trees; here, there was human life, in little human nests, all about her.

"It's the same thing, mother," she would say, "isn't it, now? Don't you remember in that book of the "New England Housekeeper," that you used to have, what the woman said about the human nature of the beans? It's in beans, and birds, and bird's nests; and folks, and folks' nests. It don't make much difference. It's just snugness, and getting along. And it's so nice to see!"

Hazel put her elbows up on the window-sill, and looked straight over into that opposite room, undisguisedly.

The young man, in one window, said to his sister in the other, at the same moment, —

"Our company's come! There's that bright little girl again!"

And the sister said, "Well, it's pretty much all the company we can take in! She brings her own seat and her own window; and she doesn't interrupt. It's just the kind for us, Kentie!"

"She's writing, — copying something, — music, it looks like; see it there, set up against the shutter. She always goes out with a music roll in her hand. I wonder whether she gives or takes?" said Diana, stopping on her way to her own seat to look out over Hazel's shoulder.

"Both, I guess," said Mrs. Ripwinkley. "Most people do. Why don't you put your flowers in the window, Hazel?"

"Why, so I will!"

They were a great bunch of snowy white and deep crimson asters, with green ivy leaves, in a tall gray glass vase. Rachel Froke had just brought them in from Miss Craydocke's garden.

"They're looking, mother! Only I do think it's half too bad! That girl seems as if she would almost reach across after them. Perhaps they came from the country, and haven't had any flowers."

"Thee might take them over some," said Mrs. Froke, simply.

"O, I shouldn't dare! There are other people in the house, and I don't know their names, or anything. I wish I could, though."

"I can," said Rachel Froke. "Thee'll grow tall enough to step over pebbles one of these days. Never mind; I'll fetch thee more to-morrow; and thee'll let the vase go for a while? Likely they've nothing better than a tumbler."

Rachel Froke went down the stairs, and out along the paved walk, into the street. She stopped an instant on the curb-stone before she crossed, and looked up at those

HAZEL AT THE WINDOW. See p. 82.

second story windows. Hazel watched her. She held up the vase slightly with one hand, nodding her little gray bonnet kindly, and beckoned with the other.

The young girl started from her seat.

In another minute Hazel saw them together in the doorway.

There was a blush and a smile, and an eager brightness in the face, and a quick speaking thanks, that one could read without hearing, from the parted lips, on the one side, and the quiet, unflutterable gray bonnet calmly horizontal on the other; and then the door was shut, and Rachel Froke was crossing the damp pavement again.

"I'm so glad Aspen Street is narrow!" said Hazel. "I should hate to be way off out of sight of people. What did you say to her, Mrs. Froke?" she asked, as the Friend reëntered. Hazel could by no means take the awful liberty of "Rachel."

"I said the young girl, Hazel Ripwinkley, being from the country, knew how good flowers were to strangers in the town, and that she thought they might be strange, and might like some."

Hazel flushed all up. At that same instant, a gentle nod and smile came across from window to window, and she flushed more, till the tears sprung with the shy, glad excitement, as she returned it and then shrunk away.

"And she said, 'Thank her, with Dorris Kincaid's love,'" proceeded Rachel Froke.

"O, *mother!* exclaimed Hazel. "And you did it all, right off so, Mrs. Froke. I don't see how grown up people dare, and know how!"

Up the stairs ran quick feet in little clattering heeled boots. Desire Ledwith, with a purple waterproof on, came in.

"I couldn't stay at home to-day," she said, "I wanted to be where it was all-togetherish. It never is at our house. Now it's set up, they don't do anything with it."

"That's because it '*looks*' — so elegant," said Hazel, catching herself up in dismay.

"It's because it's the crust, I think," said Desire. "Puff paste, like an oyster patty; and they haven't got anything cooked yet for the middle. I wonder when they will. I had a call yesterday, all to myself," she went on, with a sudden change of tone and topic. "Agatha was hopping! and I wouldn't tell her what I said, or how I behaved. That new parlor girl of ours thinks we're all or any of us 'Miss Ledwith,' mamma included, and so she let him in. He had on lavender pantaloons and a waxed moustache."

"The rain is just pouring down!" said Diana, at the garden window.

"Yes; I'm caught. That's what I meant," said Desire. "You 've got to keep me all day, now. How will you get home, Mrs. Froke? Or won't you have to stay, too?"

"Thee may call me Rachel, Desire Ledwith, if thee pleases. I like it better. I am no mistress. And for getting home, it is but just round the corner. But there is no need yet. I came for an hour, to sit here with friend Frances. And my hour is not yet up."

"I'm glad of that, for there is something I want you to tell me. I haven't quite got at it myself, yet; so as to ask, I mean. Wait a minute!" And she put her elbows up on her knees, and held her thumbs against her ears, and her fingers across her forehead; sitting squarely opposite the window to which she had drawn up her chair beside Diana, and looking intently at the driving streams that rushed and ran down against the glass.

"I was sitting in the bay-window at home, when it

began this morning; that made me think. All the world dripping wet, and I just put there dry and safe in the middle of the storm, shut up behind those great clear panes and tight sashes. How they did have to contrive, and work, before there were such places made for people! What if they had got into their first scratchy little houses, and sat behind the logs as we do behind glass windows; and thought, as I was thinking, how nice it was just to be covered up from the rain? Is it all finished now? Hasn't anybody got to contrive anything more? And who's going to do it — and everything. And what are we good for, — just *we*, — to come and expect it all, modern-improved! I don't think much of our place among things, do you, Mrs. Froke? — There, I believe that's it, as near as I can!"

"Why does thee ask me, Desire?"

"I don't know. I don't know any whys or what fors. 'Behold we know not anything,' — Tennyson and I! But you seem so — pacified — I suppose I thought you must have settled most things in your mind."

"Every builder — every little joiner — did his piece, — thought his thought out, I think likely. There's no little groove or moulding or fitting or finish, but is a bit of somebody's living; and life grows, going on. We've all got our piece to do," said Rachel.

"I asked Mrs. Mig," Desire pursued, "and she said some people's part was to buy and employ and encourage; and that spending money helps all the world; and then she put another cushion to her back, and went on tatting."

"Perhaps it does — in spite of the world," said Rachel Froke, quietly.

"But I guess nobody is to sit by and *only* encourage;

God has given out no such portion as that, I do believe. We can encourage each other, and every one do his own piece too."

"I didn't really suppose Mrs. Mig knew," said Desire, demurely. "She never began at the bottom of anything. She only finishes off. She buys pattern worsted work, and fills it in. That's what she's doing now, when she don't tat; a great bunch of white lilies, grounding it with olive. It's lovely; but I'd rather have made the lilies. She'll give it to mother, and then Glossy will come and spend the winter with us. Mrs. Mig is going to Nassau with a sick friend; she 's awfully useful—for little overseeings and general touchings up, after all the hard part is done. Mrs. Mig's sick friends always have nurses and waiting maids — Mrs. F—— Rachel! Do you know, I haven't got any piece!"

"No, I don't know; nor does thee either, yet," said Rachel Froke.

"It's all such bosh!" said Kenneth Kincaid, flinging down a handful of papers. "I've no right, I solemnly think, to help such stuff out into the world! A man can't take hold anywhere, it seems, without smutting his fingers!"

Kenneth Kincaid was correcting proof for a publisher. What he had to work on this morning was the first chapters of a flimsy novel.

"It isn't even confectionery," said he. "It's terra alba and cochineal. And when it comes to the sensation, it will be benzine for whiskey. Real things are bad enough, for the most part, in this world; but when it comes to sham fictions and adulterated poisons, Dorris, I'd rather help bake bread, if it were an honest loaf, or make strong shoes for laboring men!"

"You don't always get things like that," said Dorris. "And you know you're not responsible. Why will you torment yourself so?"

"I was so determined not to do anything but genuine work; work that the world wanted; and to have it come down to this!"

"Only for a time, while you are waiting."

"Yes; people must eat while they are waiting; that's the — devil of it! I'm not swearing, Dorris, dear; it came truly into my head, that minute, about the Temptation in the Wilderness." Kenneth's voice was reverent, saying this; and there was an earnest thought in his face.

"You'll never like anything heartily but your Sunday work."

"That's what keeps me here. My week-day work might be wanted somewhere else. And perhaps I ought to go. There's Sunday work everywhere."

"If you've found one half, hold on to it;" said Dorris. "The other can't be far off."

"I suppose there are a score or two of young architects in this city, waiting for a name or a chance to make one, as I am. If it isn't here for all of them, somebody has got to quit."

"And somebody has got to hold on," repeated Dorris. "You are morbid, Kent, about this 'work of the world.'"

"It's overdone, everywhere. Fifth wheels trying to hitch on to every coach. I'd rather be the one wheel of a barrow."

"The Lord is Wheelwright, and Builder," said Dorris, very simply. "You *are* a wheel, and He has made you; He'll find an axle for you and put you on; and you shall go about his business, so that you shall wonder to remember that you were ever leaning up against a wall. Do you know, Kentie, life seems to me like the game we used to play at home in the twilight. When we shut our eyes and let each other lead us, until we did not know where we were going, or in what place we should come out. I should not care to walk up a broad path with my eyes wide open, now. I'd rather feel the leading. To-morrow always makes a turn. It's beautiful! People don't know, who *never* shut their eyes!"

Kenneth had taken up a newspaper.

"The pretenses at doing! The dodges and go-betweens that make a sham work between every two real ones! There's hardly a true business carried on, and if there is, you don't know where or which. Look at the advertisements. Why, they cheat with their very tops and faces! See this man who puts in big capitals: 'Lost! $5,000! $1,000 reward!' and then tells you, in small type, that five thousand dollars are lost every year by breaking glass and china, that his cement will mend! What business has he to cry 'Wolf!' to the hindrance of the next man who may have a real wolf to catch? And what business has the printer, whom the next man will pay to advertise his loss, to help on a lie like this beforehand? I'm only twenty-six years old, Dorris, and I'm getting ashamed of the world!"

"Don't grow hard, Kenneth. 'The Son of Man came not to condemn the world, but to save it.' Let's each try to save our little piece!"

We are listening across the street, you see; between the windows in the rain; it is strange what chords one catches that do not catch each other, and were never planned to be played together, — by the *players*.

Kenneth Kincaid's father Robert had been a ship-builder. When shipping went down in the whirlpool of 1857, Robert Kincaid's building had gone; and afterward he had died leaving his children little beside their education, which he thanked God was secured, and a good repute that belonged to their name, but was easily forgotten in the crowd of young and forward ones, and in the strife and scramble of a new business growth.

Between college and technical studies Kenneth had been to the war. After that he had a chance to make a fortune in Wall Street. His father's brother, James, offered to take him in with him, to buy and sell stocks and gold, to watch the market, to touch little unseen springs, to put the difference into his own pocket every time the tide of value shifted, or could be made to seem to shift. He might have been one of James R. Kincaid and Company. He would have none of it. He told his uncle plainly that he wanted real work; that he had not come back from fighting to — well, there he stopped, for he could not fling the truth in his uncle's face; he said there were things he meant to finish learning, and would try to do; and if nobody wanted them of him he would learn something else that was needed. So with what was left to his share from his father's little remnant of property, he had two years at the Technological School, and here he was in Boston waiting. You can see what he meant by real work, and how deep his theories and distinctions lay. You can see that it might be a hard thing for one young man, here or there, to take up the world on these terms now, in this year of our Lord eighteen hundred and sixty-nine.

Over the way Desire Ledwith was beginning again, after a pause in which we have made our little chassée.

"I know a girl," she said, "who has got a studio. And she talks about art, and she knows styles, and who has done what, and she runs about to see pictures, and she copies things, and she has little plaster legs and toes and things hanging round everywhere. She thinks it is something great; but it 's only Mig, after all. Everything is. Florence Migs into music. And I won't Mig, if I never do anything. I'm come here this morning to darn stockings." And she pulled out of her big waterproof pocket a bundle of stockings and a great white ball of darning cotton and a wooden egg.

"There is always one thing that is real," said Mrs. Ripwinkley, gently, "and that shows the way surely to all the rest."

"I know what you mean," said Desire, "of course; but they've mixed that all up too, like everything else, so that you don't know where it is. Glossy Megilp has a velvet prayer-book, and she blacks her eyelashes and goes to church. We've all been baptized, and we've learned the Lord's Prayer, and we're all Christians. What is there more about it? I wish, sometimes, they had let it all alone. I think they vaccinated us with religion, Aunt Frank, for fear we should take it the natural way."

"Thee is restless," said Rachel Froke, tying on her gray cloak. "And to make us so is oftentimes the first thing the Lord does for us. It was the first thing He did for the world. Then He said, 'Let there be light!' In the meantime, thee is right; just darn thy stockings." And Rachel went.

They had a nice morning, after that, "leaving frets alone," as Diana said. Diana Ripwinkley was happy in things just as they were. If the sun shone, she rejoiced in the glory; if the rain fell, it shut her in sweetly to the heart of home, and the outside world grew fragrant for her breathing. There was never anything in her day that she could spare out of it, and there were no holes in the hours either. "Whether she was most bird or bee, it was hard to tell," her mother said of her; from the time she used to sweep and dust her garret baby-house along the big beams in the old house at Homesworth, and make little cheeses, and set them to press in wooden pill-boxes from which she had punched the bottoms out, till now, that she began to take upon herself the daily freshening of the new parlors in Aspen Street, and had long lessons of geometry to learn, whose dry demonstrations she set to odd little improvised recitatives of music, and chanted over while she ran up and down putting away clean linen for her mother, that Luclarion brought up from the wash.

As for Hazel, she was only another variation upon the same sweet nature. There was more of outgo and enterprise with her. Diana made the thing or the place pleasant that she was in or doing. Hazel sought out new and blessed inventions. "There was always something coming to the child that wouldn't ever have come to no one else," Luclarion said. "And besides that, she was a real 'Witch Hazel;' she could tell where the springs were, and what's more, where they warn't."

Luclarion Grapp would never have pleaded guilty to "dropping into poetry" in any light whatsoever; but what she meant by this was not exactly according to the letter, as one may easily see.

IX.

HAZEL'S INSPIRATION.

WHAT was the use of "looking," unless things were looked at? Mrs. Ledwith found at the end of the winter that she ought to give a party. Not a general one; Mrs. Ledwith always said "not a general one," as if it were an exception, whereas she knew better than ever to undertake a general party; her list would be *too* general, and heterogeneous. It would simply be a physical, as well as a social, impossibility. She knew quantities of people separately and very cordially, in her easy have-a-good-time-when-you-can style, that she could by no means mix, or even gather together. She picked up acquaintances on summer journeys, she accepted civilities wherever she might be, she asked everybody to her house who took a fancy to her, or would admire her establishment, and if she had had a spring cleaning or a new carpeting, or a furbishing up in any way, the next thing was always to light up and play it off, — to try it on to somebody. What were houses for? And there was always somebody who ought to be paid attention to; somebody staying with a friend, or a couple just engaged, or if nothing else, it was her turn to have the sewing-society; and so her rooms got aired. Of course she had to air them now! The drawing-room, with its apricot and coffee-brown furnishings, was lovely in the evening, and the crimson and garnet in the dining-room was rich and cozy, and set off brilliantly her show of silver and cut-glass; and then, there was the new, real, sea-green China.

So the party was had. There were some people in town from New York; she invited them and about a hundred more. The house lit up beautifully; the only pity was that Mrs. Ledwith could not wear her favorite and most becoming colors, buff and chestnut, because she had taken that family of tints for her furniture; but she found a lovely shade of violet that would hold by gas-light, and she wore black Fayal lace with it, and white roses upon her hair. Mrs. Treweek was enchanted with the brown and apricot drawing-room, and wondered where on earth they had got that particular shade, for "my dear! she had ransacked Paris for hangings in just that perfect, soft, ripe color that she had in her mind and never could hit upon." Mrs. MacMichael had pushed the grapes back upon her plate to examine the pattern of the bit of china, and had said how lovely the coloring was, with the purple and pale green of the fruit. And these things, and a few more like them, were the residuum of the whole, and Laura Ledwith was satisfied.

Afterward, "while they were in the way of it," Florence had a little *musicale;* and the first season in Shubarton Place was over.

It turned out, however, as it did in the old rhyme, — they shod the horse, and shod the mare, and let the little colt go bare. Helena was disgusted because she could not have a "German."

"We shall have to be careful, now that we have fairly settled down," said Laura to her sister; "for every bit of Grant's salary will have been taken up with this winter's expenses. But one wants to begin right, and after that one can go on moderately. I'm good at contriving, Frank; only give me something to contrive with!"

"Isn't it a responsibility," Frank ventured, "to think what we shall contrive *for?*"

"Of course," returned Mrs. Ledwith, glibly. "And my first duty is to my children. I don't mean to encourage them to reckless extravagance; as Mrs. Megilp says, there's always a limit; but it's one's duty to make life beautiful, and one can't do too much for home. I want my children to be satisfied with theirs, and I want to cultivate their tastes and accustom them to society. I can't do *everything* for them; they will dress on three hundred a year apiece, Agatha and Florence; and I can assure you it needs management to accomplish that, in these days!"

Mrs. Ripwinkley laughed, gently.

"It would require management with us to get rid of that, upon ourselves."

"O, my dear, don't I tell you continually, you haven't waked up yet? Just rub your eyes a while longer, — or let the girls do it for you, — and you'll see! Why, I know of girls, — girls whose mothers have limited incomes, too, — who have been kept plain, actually *plain*, all their school days, but who must have now six and eight hundred a year to go into society with. And really I wouldn't undertake it for less, myself, if I expected to keep up with everything. But I must treat mine all alike, and we must be contented with what we have. There's Helena, now, crazy for a young party; but I couldn't think of it. Young parties are ten times worse than old ones; there's really no *end* to the expense, with the German, and everything. Helena will have to wait; and yet, — of course, if I could, it is desirable, almost necessary; acquaintances begin in the school-room, — society, indeed; and a great deal would depend upon it. The truth is, you're no sooner born, now-a-days, than you have to begin to keep up; or else — you're dropped out."

"O, Laura! do you remember the dear little parties our mother used to make for us? From four till half-past eight, with games, and tea at six, and the fathers looking in?"

"And cockles, and mottoes, and printed cambric dresses, and milk and water! Where are the children, do you suppose, you dear old Frau Van Winkle, that would come to such a party now?"

"Children must be born simple, as they were then. There's nothing my girls would like better, even at their age, than to help at just such a party. It is a dream of theirs. Why shouldn't somebody do it, just to show how good it is?"

"You can lead a horse to water, you know, Frank, but you can't make him drink. And the colts are forty times worse. I believe you might get some of the mothers together for an ancient tea-drink, just in the name of old association; but the *babies* would all turn up their new-fashioned little noses."

"O, dear!" sighed Frau Van Winkle. "I wish I knew people!"

"By the time you do, you'll know the reason why, and be like all the rest."

Hazel Ripwinkley went to Mrs. Hilman's school, with her cousin Helena. That was because the school was a thoroughly good one; the best her mother could learn of; not because it was kept in parlors in Dorset Street, and there were girls there who came from palaces west of the Common, in the grand avenues and the A B C streets; nor did Hazel wear her best gray and black velvet suit for every day, though the rich colored poplins with their over-skirts and sashes, and the gay ribbons for hair and neck made the long green baize covered tables look like garden-plots with beds of bloom, and quite extinguished with their brilliancy the quiet, one skirted brown merino that she brushed and folded every night, and put on with fresh linen cuffs and collar every morning.

"It is an idiosyncrasy of Aunt Frances," Helena explained, with the grandest phrase she could pick out of her "Synonymes," to cow down those who "wondered."

Privately, Helena held long lamentations with Hazel, going to and fro, about the party that she could not have.

"I'm actually ashamed to go to school. There isn't a girl there, who can pretend to have anything, that hasn't had some kind of a company this winter. I've been to them all, and I feel real mean, — sneaky. What's 'next year?' Mamma puts me off with that. Poh? Next year they'll all begin again. You can't skip birthdays."

"I'll tell you what!" said Hazel, suddenly, inspired by much the same idea that had occurred to Mrs. Ripwinkley; "I mean to ask my mother to let *me* have a party!"

"You! Down in Aspen Street! Don't, for pity's sake, Hazel!"

"I don't believe but what it could be done over again!" said Hazel, irrelevantly, intent upon her own thought.

"It couldn't be done *once!* For gracious grandmother's sake, don't think of it!" cried the little world-woman of thirteen.

"It's gracious grandmother's sake that made me think of it," said Hazel, laughing. "The way she used to do."

"Why don't you ask them to help you hunt up old Noah, and all get back into the ark, pigeons and all?"

"Well, I guess they had pretty nice times there, any how; and if another big rain comes, perhaps they'll have to!"

Hazel did not intend her full meaning; but there is many a faint, small prophecy hid under a clover-leaf.

Hazel did not let go things; her little witch-wand, once pointed, held its divining angle with the might of magic until somebody broke ground.

"It's awful!" Helena declared to her mother and sisters, with tears of consternation. "And she wants me to go round with her and carry 'compliments!' It'll never be got over, — never! I wish I could go away to boarding-school!"

For Mrs. Ripwinkley had made up her unsophisticated mind to try this thing; to put this grain of a pure, potent salt, right into the seethe and glitter of little Boston, and find out what it would decompose or precipitate. For was not she a mother, testing the world's chalice for her children? What did she care for the hiss and the bubble, if they came?

She was wider awake than Mrs. Ledwith knew; perhaps they who come down from the mountain heights of long seclusion can measure the world's paces and changes better than they who have been hurried in the midst of them, on and on, or round and round.

Worst of all, old Uncle Titus took it up.

It was funny, — or it would have been funny, reader, if anybody but you and I and Rachel Froke knew exactly how, — to watch Uncle Titus as he kept his quiet eye on all these things, — the things that he had set going, — and read their revelations; sheltered, disguised, under a character that the world had chosen to put upon him, like Haroun Alraschid in the merchant's cloak.

They took their tea with him, — the two families, — every Sunday night. Agatha Ledwith "filled him in" a pair of slippers that very first Christmas; he sat there in the corner with his old leather ones on, when they came, and left them, for the most part, to their own mutual entertainment, until the tea was ready. It was a sort of family exchange; all the plans and topics came up, particularly on the Ledwith side, for Mrs. Ripwinkley was a good listener, and Laura a good talker; and the fun, — that you and I and Rachel Froke could guess, — yes, and a good deal of unsuspected earnest, also, — was all there behind the old gentleman's "Christian Age," as over brief mentions of sermons, or words about books, or little brevities of family inquiries and household news, broke small floods of excitement like water over pebbles, as Laura and her daughters discussed and argued volubly the matching and the flouncing of a silk, or the new flowering and higher pitching of a bonnet, — since "they are wearing everything all on the top, you know, and mine looks terribly meek;" or else desçanted diffusely on the unaccountbleness of the somebodies not having called, or the bother and forwardness of the some-other-bodies who had, and the eighty-three visits that were left on the list to be paid, and "never being able to take a day to sit down for anything."

"What is it all for?" Mrs. Ripwinkley would ask, over again, the same old burden of the world's weariness falling upon her from her sister's life, and making her feel as if it were her business to clear it away somehow.

"Why, to live!" Mrs. Ledwith would reply. "You've got it all to do, you see."

"But I don't really see, Laura, where the living comes in."

Laura opens her eyes.

"*Slang?*" says she. "Where did you get hold of that?"

"Is it slang? I'm sure I don't know. I mean it."

"Well, you *are* the funniest! You don't *catch* anything. Even a by-word must come first-hand from you, and mean something!"

"It seems to me such a hard-working, getting-ready-to-be, and then not being. There's no place left for it,—because it's all place."

"Gracious me, Frank! If you are going to sift everything so, and get back of everything! I can't live in metaphysics: I have to live in the things themselves, amongst other people."

"But isn't it scene and costume, a good deal of it, without the play? It may be that I don't understand, because I have not got into the heart of your city life; but what comes of the parties, for instance? The grand question, beforehand, is about wearing, and then there's a retrospection of what was worn, and how people looked. It seems to be all surface. I should think they might almost send in their best gowns, or perhaps a photograph,—if photographs ever were becoming,—as they do visiting cards."

"Aunt Frank," said Desire, "I don't believe the 'heart of city life' is in the parties, or the parlors. I believe there's a great lot of us knocking round amongst the dry goods and the furniture that never get any further. People must be *living*, somewhere, *behind* the fixings. But there are so many people, nowadays, that have never quite got fixed!"

"You might live all your days here," said Mrs. Ledwith to her sister, passing over Desire, "and never get into the heart of it, for that matter, unless you were born into it. I don't care so much, for my part. I know plenty of nice people, and I like to have things nice about me, and to have a pleasant time, and to let my children enjoy themselves. The 'heart,' if the truth was known, is a dreadful still place. I'm satisfied."

Uncle Titus's paper was folded across the middle; just then he reversed the lower half; that brought the printing upside down; but he went on reading all the same.

"*I'm* going to have a real party," said Hazel, "a real, gracious-grandmother party; just such as you and mother had, Aunt Laura, when you were little."

Her Aunt Laura laughed good-naturedly.

"I guess you'll have to go round and knock up the grandmothers to come to it, then," said she. "You'd better make it a fancy dress affair at once, and then it will be accounted for."

"No; I'm going round to invite; and they are to come at four, and take tea at six; and they're just to wear their afternoon dresses; and Miss Craydocke is coming at any rate; and she knows all the old plays, and lots of new ones; and she is going to show how."

"I'm coming, too," said Uncle Titus, over his newspaper, with his eyes over his glasses.

"That's good," said Hazel, simply, least surprised of any of the conclave.

"And you'll have to play the muffin man. 'O, don't you know,'"—she began to sing, and danced two little steps toward Mr. Oldways. "O, I forgot it was Sunday!" she said, suddenly stopping.

"Not much wonder," said Uncle Titus. "And not much matter. *Your* Sunday's good enough."

And then he turned his paper right side up; but, before he began really to read again, he swung half round toward them in his swivel-chair, and said,—

"Leave the sugar-plums to me, Hazel; I'll come early and bring 'em in my pocket."

"It's the first thing he's taken the slightest notice of, or interest in, that any one of us has been doing," said Agatha Ledwith, with a spice of momentary indignation, as they walked along Bridgeley Street to take the car.

For Uncle Titus had not come to the Ledwith party. "He never went visiting, and he hadn't any best coat," he told Laura, in verbal reply to the invitation that had come written on a square satin sheet, once folded, in an envelope with a big monogram.

"It's of no consequence," said Mrs. Ledwith, "any way. Only a child's play."

"But it will be, mother; you don't know," said Helena. "She 's going right in everywhere, with that ridiculous little invitation; to the Ashburnes and the Geoffreys, and all! She hasn't the least idea of any difference; and just think what the girls will say, and how they will stare, and laugh! I wish she wasn't my cousin!"

"Helena!"

Mrs. Ledwith spoke with real displeasure; for she was good-natured and affectionate in her way; and her worldly ambitions were rather wide than high, as we have seen.

"Well, I can't help it; you don't know, mother," Helena repeated. "It's horrid to go to school with all those stiffies, that don't care a snap for you, and only laugh."

"Laughing is vulgar," said Agatha. If any indirect question were ever thrown upon the family position, Agatha immediately began expounding the ethics of high breeding, as one who had attained.

"It is only half-way people who laugh," she said. "Ada Geoffrey and Lilian Ashburne never laugh — *at* anybody — I am sure."

"No, they don't; not right out. They're awfully polite. But you can feel it, underneath. They have a way of keeping so still, when you know they would laugh if they did anything."

"Well, they'll neither laugh nor keep still, about this. You need not be concerned. They'll just not go, and that will be the end of it."

Agatha Ledwith was mistaken. She had been mistaken about two things to-night. The other was when she had said that this was the first time Uncle Oldways had noticed or been interested in anything they did.

X.

COCKLES AND CRAMBO.

HAZEL RIPWINKLEY put on her nankeen sack and skirt, and her little round, brown straw hat. For May had come, and almost gone, and it was a day of early summer warmth.

Hazel's dress was not a "suit;" it had been made and worn two summers before suits were thought of; yet it suited very well, as people's things are apt to do, after all, who do not trouble themselves about minutiæ of fashion, and so get no particular antediluvian marks upon them that show when the flood subsides.

Her mother knew some things that Hazel did not. Mrs. Ripwinkley, if she had been asleep for five and twenty years, had lost none of her perceptive faculties in the trance. But she did not hamper her child with any doubts; she let her go on her simple way, under the shield of her simplicity, to test this world that she had come into, for herself.

Hazel had written down her little list of the girls' names that she would like to ask; and Mrs. Ripwinkley looked at it with a smile. There was Ada Geoffrey, the banker's daughter, and Lilian Ashburne, the professor's, — heiresses each, of double lines of birth and wealth. She could remember how, in her childhood, the old names sounded, with the respect that was in men's tones when they were spoken; and underneath were Lois James and Katie Kilburnie, children of a printer and a hatter. They had all been chosen for their purely personal qualities. A child, let alone, chooses as an angel chooses.

It remained to be seen how they would come together.

At the very head, in large, fair letters, was, —

"MISS CRAYDOCKE."

Down at the bottom, she had just added, —

"MR. KINCAID AND DORRIS."

"For, if I have *some* grown folks, mother, perhaps I ought to have *other* grown folks, — 'to keep the balance true.' Besides, Mr. Kincaid and Dorris always like the *little* nice times."

From the day when Dorris Kincaid had come over with the gray glass vase and her repeated thanks, when the flowers had done their ministry and faded, there had been little simple courtesies, each way, between the opposite houses; and once Kenneth and his sister had taken tea with the Ripwinkleys, and they had played "crambo" and "consequences" in the evening. The real little game of "consequences," of which this present friendliness was a link, was going on all the time, though they did not stop to read the lines as they folded them down, and "what the world said" was not one of the items in their scheme of it at all.

It would have been something worth while to have followed Hazel as she went her rounds, asking quietly at each house to see Mrs. This or That, "as she had a message;" and being shown, like a little representative of an almost extinct period, up into the parlor, or the dressing-room of each lady, and giving her quaint errand.

"I am Hazel Ripwinkley," she would say, "and my mother sends her compliments, and would like to have Lilian,"— or whoever else, — "come at four o'clock to-day, and spend the afternoon and take tea. I'm to have a little party such as she used to have, and nobody is to be much dressed up, and we are only to play games."

"I AM HAZEL RIPWINKLEY." See p. 105.

"Why, that is charming!" cried Mrs. Ashburne; for the feeling of her own sweet early days, and the old B—— Square house, came over her as she heard the words. "It is Lilian's music afternoon; but never mind; give my kind compliments to your mother, and she will be very happy to come."

And Mrs. Ashburne stooped down and kissed Hazel, when she went away.

She stood in the deep carved stone entrance-way to Mrs. Geoffrey's house, in the same fearless, Red Riding Hood fashion, just as she would have waited in any little country porch up in Homesworth, where she had need indeed to knock.

Not a whit dismayed was she either, when the tall man-servant opened to her, and admitted her into the square, high, marble-paved hall, out of which great doors were set wide into rooms rich and quiet with noble adorning and soft shading, — where pictures made such a magic upon the walls, and books were piled from floor to ceiling; and where her little figure was lost as she went in, and she hesitated to take a seat anywhere, lest she should be quite hidden in some great arm-chair or sofa corner, and Mrs. Geoffrey should not see her when she came down.

So, as the lady entered, there she was, upright and waiting, on her two feet, in her nankeen dress, just within the library doors, with her face turned toward the staircase.

"I am Hazel Ripwinkley," she began; as if she had said, I am Pease-blossom or Mustard-seed; "I go to school with Ada." And went on, then, with her compliments and her party. And at the end she said, very simply, —

"Miss Craydocke is coming, and she knows the games."

"Miss Craydocke, of Orchard Street? And where do you live?"

"In Aspen Street, close by, in Uncle Oldways' house. We haven't lived there very long, — only this winter; before that we always lived in Homesworth."

"And Homesworth is in the country? Don't you miss that?"

"Yes; but Aspen Street isn't very bad; we've got a garden. Besides, we like streets and neighbors."

Then she added, — for her little witch-stick felt spiritually the quality of what she spoke to, — "Wouldn't Mr. Geoffrey come for Ada in the evening?"

"I haven't the least doubt he would!" said Mrs. Geoffrey, her face all alive with exquisite and kindly amusement, and catching the spirit of the thing from the inimitable simplicity before her, such as never, she did believe, had walked into anybody's house before, in this place and generation, and was no more to be snubbed than a flower or a breeze or an angel.

It was a piece of Witch Hazel's witchery, or inspiration, that she named Miss Craydocke; for Miss Craydocke was an old, dear friend of Mrs. Geoffrey's, in that "heart of things" behind the fashions, where the kingdom is growing up. But of course Hazel could not have known that; something in the lady's face just made her think of the same thing in Miss Craydocke's, and so she spoke, forgetting to explain, nor wondering in the very least, when she was met with knowledge.

It was all divining, though, from the beginning to the end. That was what took her into these homes, rather than to a score of other places up and down the self-same streets, where, if she had got in at all, she would have met strange, lofty stares, and freezing "thank you's," and "engagements."

"I've found the real folks, mother, and they're all coming!" she cried, joyfully, running in where Mrs. Ripwinkley was setting little vases and baskets about on shelf and table, between the white, plain, muslin draperies of the long parlor windows. In vases and baskets were sweet May flowers; bunches of deep-hued, rich-scented violets, stars of blue and white periwinkle, and Miss Craydocke's lilies of the valley in their tall, cool leaves; each kind gathered by itself in clusters and handfuls. Inside the wide, open fireplace, behind the high brass fender and the shining andirons, was a "chimney flower pot," country fashion, of green lilac boughs, — not blossoms, — and woodbine sprays, and crimson and white tulips. The room was fair and fragrant, and the windows were wide open upon vines and grass.

"It looks like you, mother, just as Mrs. Geoffrey's house looks like her. Houses ought to look like people, I think."

"There's your surprise, children. We shouldn't be doing it right without a surprise, you know."

And the surprise was not dolls' pelerines, but books. "Little Women" was one, which sent Diana and Hazel off for a delicious two hours' read up in their own room until dinner.

After dinner, Miss Craydocke came, in her purple and white striped mohair and her white lace neckerchief; and at three o'clock Uncle Titus walked in, with his coat pockets so bulgy and rustling and odorous of peppermint and sassafras, that it was no use to pretend to wait and be unconscious, but a pure mercy to unload him so that he might be able to sit down.

Nobody knows to this day where he got them; he must have ordered them somewhere, one would think, long enough before to have special moulds and implements made; but there were large, beautiful cockles, — not of the old flour-paste sort, but of clear, sparkling sugar, rose-color, and amber, and white, with little slips of tinted paper tucked within, and these printed delicately with pretty rhymes and couplets, from real poets; things to be truly treasured, yet simple, for children's apprehension, and fancy, and fun. And there were "Salem gibraltars," such as we only get out of Essex County now and then, for a big charitable Fair, when Salem and everywhere else gets its spirit up to send its best and most especial; and there were toys and devices in sugar — flowers and animals, hats, bonnets, and boots, apples, and cucumbers, — such as Diana and Hazel, and even Desire and Helena had never seen before.

"It isn't quite fair," said good Miss Craydocke. "We were to go back to the old, simple fashions of things; and here you are beginning over again already with sumptuous inventions. It's the very way it came about before, till it was all spoilt."

"No," said Uncle Titus, stoutly. "It's only 'Old *and* New,' — the very selfsame good old notions brought to a little modern perfection. They're not French flummery, either; and there's not a drop of gin, or a flavor of prussic acid, or any other abominable chemical, in one of those contrivances. They're as innocent as they look; good honest mint and spice and checkerberry and lemon and rose. I know the man that made 'em!"

Helena Ledwith began to think that the first person, singular or plural, might have a good time; but that awful third! Helena's "they" was as potent and tremendous as her mother's.

"It's nice," she said to Hazel; "but they don't have such things. I never saw them at a party. And they don't play games; they always dance. And it's broad, hot daylight; and — you haven't asked a single boy!"

"Why, I don't know any! Only Jimmy Scarup; and I guess he'd rather play ball, and break windows!"

"Jimmy Scarup!" And Helena turned away, hopeless of Hazel's comprehending.

But "they" came; and "they" turned right into "we."

It was not a party; it was something altogether fresh and new; the house was a new, beautiful place; it was like the country. And Aspen Street, when you got down there, was so still and shady and sweet smelling and pleasant. They experienced the delight of finding out something.

Miss Craydocke and Hazel set them at it, — their good time; they had planned it all out, and there was no stiff, shy waiting. They began, right off, with the "Muffin Man." Hazel danced up to Desire: —

"O, *do* you know the Muffin Man,
The Muffin Man, the Muffin Man?
O, *do* you know the Muffin Man
That lives in Drury Lane?"

"O, yes, I know the Muffin Man,
The Muffin Man, the Muffin Man,
O, yes, I know the Muffin Man
That lives in Drury Lane."

And so they danced off together: —

"Two of us know the Muffin Man,
The Muffin Man, the Muffin Man,
Two of us know the Muffin Man
That lives in Drury Lane."

And then they besieged Miss Craydocke; and then the three met Ada Geoffrey, just as she had come in and spoken to Diana and Mrs. Ripwinkley; and Ada had caught the refrain, and responded instantly; and *four* of them knew the Muffin Man.

"I know they'll think it's common and queer, and they'll laugh to-morrow," whispered Helena to Diana, as Hazel drew the lengthening string to Dorris Kincaid's corner and caught her up; but the next minute they were around Helena in her turn, and they were laughing already, with pure glee; and five faces bent toward her, and five voices sang, —

"O, *don't* you know the Muffin Man?"

And Helena had to sing back that she did; and then the six made a perfect snarl around Mrs. Ripwinkley herself, and drew her in; and then they all swept off and came down across the room upon Mr. Oldways, who muttered, under the singing, "seven women! Well, the Bible says so, and I suppose it's come!" and then he held out both hands, while his hard face unbent in every wrinkle, with a smile that overflowed through all their furrowed channels, up to his very eyes; like some sparkling water that must find its level; and there were eight that knew the Muffin Man.

So nine, and ten, and up to fifteen; and then, as their line broke away into fragments, still breathless with fun, Miss Craydocke said, — her eyes brimming over with laughing tears, that always came when she was gay, —

"There, now! we all know the 'Muffin Man;' therefore it follows, mathematically, I believe, that we must all know each other. I think we'll try a sitting-down game next. I'll give you all something. Desire, you can tell them what to do with it, and Miss Ashburne shall predict the consequences."

So they had the "Presentation Game;" and the gifts, and the dispositions, and the consequences, when the whispers were over, and they were all declared aloud, were such hits and jumbles of sense and nonsense as were almost too queer to have been believed.

"Miss Craydocke gave me a butter firkin," said Mrs. Ripwinkley. "I was to put it in the parlor and plant vanilla beans in it; and the consequence would be that Birnam Wood would come to Dunsinane."

"She gave me a wax doll," said Helena. "I was to buy it a pair of high-heeled boots and a chignon; and the consequence would be that she would have to stand on her head."

"She gave me," said Mr. Oldways, "an iron spoon. I was to deal out sugar-plums with it; and the consequence would be that you would all go home."

"She gave me," said Lois James, "Woman's Rights. I should'nt know what to do with them; and the consequence would be a terrible mortification to all my friends."

"She gave me," said Hazel, "a real good time. I was to pass it round; and the consequence would be an earthquake."

Then they had "Scandal;" a whisper, repeated rapidly from ear to ear. It began with, "Luclarion is in the kitchen making tea-biscuits;" and it ended with the horrible announcement that there were "two hundred gallons of hot pitch ready, and that everybody was to be tipped into it."

"Characters," and "Twenty Questions," and "How, When, and Where," followed; and then they were ready for a run again, and they played "Boston," in which Mr. Oldways, being "Sceattle," was continually being left out, whereupon he declared at last, that he didn't believe there was any place for him, or even that he was down anywhere on the map, and it wasn't fair, and he was going to secede; and that broke up the play; for the great fun of all the games had come to be Miss Craydocke and Uncle Titus, as it always is the great fun to the young ones when the elders join in, — the older and the soberer, the better sport; there is always something in the "fathers looking on;" that is the way I think it is among them who always do behold the Face of the Father in heaven, — smiling upon their smiles, glowing upon their gladness.

In the tea-room, it was all even more delightful yet; it was further out into the garden, shaded at the back by the deep leafiness of grape-vines, and a trellis work with arches in it that ran up at the side, and would be gay by and by with scarlet runners, and morning-glories, and nasturtiums, that were shooting up strong and swift already, from the neatly weeded beds.

Inside, was the tall old semicircular sideboard, with gingerbread grooves carved all over it; and the real brass "dogs," with heads on their fore-paws, were lying in the fire-place, under the lilac boughs; and the square, plain table stood in the midst, with its glossy white cloth that touched the floor at the corners, and on it were the identical pink mugs, and a tall glass pitcher of milk, and plates of the thinnest and sweetest bread and butter, and early strawberries in a white basket lined with leaves, and the traditional round frosted cakes upon a silver plate with a network rim.

And Luclarion and Mrs. Ripwinkley waited upon them all, and it was still no party, to be compared or thought of with any salad and ice-pudding and Germania-band affair, such as they had had all winter; but something utterly fresh and new and by itself, — place, and entertainment, and people, and all.

After tea, they went out into the garden; and there, under the shady horse-chestnuts, was a swing; and there were balls with which Hazel showed them how to play "class;" tossing in turn against the high brick wall, and taking their places up and down, according to the number of their catches. It was only Miss Craydocke's "Thread the Needle" that got them in again; and after that, she showed them another simple old dancing game, the "Winding Circle," from which they were all merrily and mysteriously untwisting themselves with Miss Craydocke's bright little thin face and her fluttering cap ribbons, and her spry little trot leading them successfully off, when the door opened, and the grand Mr. Geoffrey walked in; the man who could manage State Street, and who had stood at the right hand of Governor and President, with his clear brain, and big purse, and generous hand, through the years of the long, terrible war; the man whom it was something for great people to get to their dinners, or to have walk late into an evening drawing-room and dignify an occasion for the last half hour.

Mrs. Ripwinkley was just simply glad to see him; so she was to see Kenneth Kincaid, who came a few minutes after, just as Luclarion brought the tray of sweetmeats in, which Mrs. Ripwinkley had so far innovated upon the gracious-grandmother plan as to have after tea, instead of before.

The beautiful cockles and their rhymes got their heads all together around the large table, for the eating and the reading. Mr. Geoffrey and Uncle Titus sat talking European politics together, a little aside. The sugar-plums lasted a good while, with the chatter over them; and then, before they quite knew what it was all for, they had got slips of paper and lead pencils before them, and there was to be a round of "Crambo" to wind up.

"O, I don't know how!" and "I never can!" were the first words, as they always are, when it was explained to the uninitiated; but Miss Craydocke assured them that "everybody could;" and Hazel said that "nobody expected real poetry; it needn't be more than two lines, and those might be blank verse, if they were *very* hard, but jingles were better;" and so the questions and the words were written and folded, and the papers were shuffled and opened amid outcries of, "O, this is awful!" "*What* a word to get in!" "Why, they haven't the least thing to do with each other!"

"That's the beauty of it," said Miss Craydocke, unrelentingly; "to *make* them have; and it is funny how much things do have to do with each other when they once happen to come across."

Then there were knit brows, and desperate scratchings, and such silence that Mr. Geoffrey and Uncle Titus stopped short on the Alabama question, and looked round to see what the matter was.

Kenneth Kincaid had been modestly listening to the older gentlemen, and now and then venturing to inquire or remark something, with an intelligence that attracted Mr. Geoffrey; and presently it came out that he had been south with the army; and then Mr. Geoffrey asked questions of him, and they got upon Reconstruction business, and comparing facts and exchanging conclusions, quite as if one was not a mere youth with only his eyes and his brains and his conscience to help him in his first grapple with the world in the tangle and crisis at which he found it, and the other a grave, practiced, keen-judging man, the counsellor of national leaders.

After all, they had no business to bring the great, troublesome, heavy-weighted world into a child's party. I wish men never would; though it did not happen badly, as it all turned out, that they did a little of it in this instance. If they had thought of it, "Crambo" was good for them too, for a change; and presently they did think of it; for Dorris called out in distress, real or pretended, from the table, —

"Kentie, here's something you must really take off my hands! I haven't the least idea what to do with it."

And then came a cry from Hazel, —

"No fair! We're all just as badly off, and there isn't one of us that has got a brother to turn to. Here's another for Mr. Kincaid."

"There are plenty more. Come, Mr. Oldways, Mr. Geoffrey, won't you try 'Crambo?' There's a good deal in it, as there is in most nonsense."

"We'll come and see what it is," said Mr. Geoffrey; and so the chairs were drawn up, and the gray, grave heads looked on over the young ones.

"Why, Hazel's got through!" said Lois, scratching violently at her paper, and obliterating three obstinate lines.

"O, I didn't bother, you see! I just stuck the word right in, like a pin into a pincushion, and let it go. There wasn't anything else to do with it."

"I've got to make my pincushion," said Dorris.

"I should think you had! Look at her! She's writing her paper all over! O, my gracious, she must have done it before!"

"Mother and Mr. Geoffrey are doing heaps, too! We shall have to publish a book," said Diana, biting the end of her pencil, and taking it easy. Diana hardly ever got the rhymes made in time; but then she always admired everybody's else, which was a good thing for somebody to be at leisure to do.

"Uncle Oldways and Lilian are folding up," said Hazel.

"Five minutes more," said Miss Craydocke, keeping the time with her watch before her. "Hush!"

When the five minutes were rapped out, there were seven papers to be read. People who had not finished this time might go on when the others took fresh questions.

Hazel began reading, because she had been ready first.

"'What is the difference between sponge-cake and doughnuts?' 'Hallelujah.'"

"'Airiness, lightness, and insipidity;
Twistiness, spiciness, and solidity.
Hallelujah! I've got through!
That is the best that I can do!'"

There was a shout at Hazel's pinsticking.

"Now, Uncle Titus! You finished next."

"My question is a very comprehensive one," said Uncle Titus, "with a very concise and suggestive word. 'How wags the world?' 'Slambang.'"

"'The world wags on
With lies and slang;
With show and vanity,
Pride and inanity,
Greed and insanity,
And a great slambang!'"

"That's only *one* verse," said Miss Craydocke. "There's another; but he didn't write it down."

Uncle Titus laughed, and tossed his Crambo on the table. "It's true, so far, anyway," said he.

"*So far* is hardly ever quite true," said Miss Craydocke.

Lilian Ashburne had to answer the question whether she had ever read "Young's Night Thoughts;" and her word was "Comet."

"'Pray might I be allowed a pun,
To help me through with just this one?

I've tried to read Young's Thoughts of Night,
But never yet could come it, quite.' "

"O, O, O! That's just like Lilian, with her soft little 'prays' and 'allow me's,' and her little pussy-cat ways of sliding through tight places, just touching her whiskers!"

"It's quite fair," said Lilian, smiling, "to slide through if you can."

"Now, Mr. Geoffrey."

And Mr. Geoffrey read,—

"'What is your favorite color?' 'One-hoss.'"

"'Do you mean, my friend, for a one-hoss shay,
Or the horse himself,—black, roan, or bay?
In truth, I think I can hardly say;
I believe, for a nag, "I bet on the gray."

"'For a shay, I would rather not have yellow,
Or any outright, staring color,
That makes the crowd look after a fellow,
And the little *gamins* hoot and bellow.

"'Do you mean for ribbons? or gowns? or eyes?
Or flowers? or gems? or in sunset skies?
For many questions, as many replies,
Drops of a rainbow take rainbow dyes.

"'The world is full, and the world is bright;
Each thing to its nature parts the light;
And each for its own to the Perfect sight
Wears that which is comely, and sweet, and right.'"

"O, Mr. Geoffrey! That's lovely!" cried the girl-voices, all around him. And Ada made a pair of great eyes at her father, and said,—

"What an awful humbug you have been, papa! To have kept the other side up with care all your life! Who ever suspected *that* of you?"

Diana and Hazel were not taken so much by surprise; their mother had improvised little nursery jingles for them all their baby days, and had played Crambo with them since; so they were very confident with their "Now, mother:" and looked calmly for something creditable.

"'What is your favorite name?'" read Mrs. Ripwinkley. "And the word is 'Stuff.'"

"'When I was a little child,
Looking very meek and mild,
I liked grand, heroic names, —
Of warriors, or stately dames:
Zenobia, and Cleopatra;
(No rhyme for that this side Sumatra;)
Wallace, and Helen Mar, — Clotilda,
Berengaria, and Brunhilda;
Maximilian; Alexandra;
Hector, Juno, and Cassandra;
Charlemagne and Britomarte,
Washington and Bonaparte;
Victoria and Guinevere,
And Lady Clara Vere de Vere.
— Shall I go on with all this stuff,
Or do you think it is enough?
I cannot tell you what dear name
I love the best; I play a game;
And tender earnest doth belong
To quiet speech, not silly song.'"

"That's just like mother; I should have stopped as soon as I'd got the 'stuff' in; but she always shapes off with a little morriowl," said Hazel. "Now, Desire!"

Desire frantically scribbled a long line at the end of what she had written; below, that is, a great black morass of scratches that represented significantly the "Slough of Despond" she had got into over the winding up, and then gave, —

"'Which way would you rather travel, — north or south?' 'Goosey-gander.'"

"'O, goosey-gander!
If I might wander,
It should be toward the sun;
The blessed South
Should fill my mouth
With ripeness just begun.
For bleak hills, bare,
With stunted, spare,
And scrubby, piney trees,
Her gardens rare,
And vineyards fair,
And her rose-scented breeze.
For fearful blast,
Skies overcast,
And sudden blare and scare,
Long, stormless moons,
And placid noons, —
And — all sorts of comfortablenesses, — there!'"

"That makes me think of father's horse running away with him once," said Helena, "when he had to head him right up against a brick wall, and knock everything all to smash before he could stop!"

"Anybody else?"

"Miss Kincaid, I think," said Mr. Geoffrey. He had been watching Dorris's face through the play, flashing and smiling with the excitement of her rhyming, and the slender, nervous fingers twisting tremulously the penciled slip while she had listened to the others.

"If it isn't all rubbed out," said Dorris, coloring and laughing to find how badly she had been treating her own effusion.

"You see it *was* rather an awful question, — 'What do you want most?' And the word is, 'Thirteen.'"

She caught her breath a little quickly as she began: —

"'Between yourself, dear, myself, and the post,
There are the thirteen things that I want the most.

I want to be, sometimes, a little stronger;
I want the days to be a little longer;
I'd like to have a few less things to do;
I'd better like to better do the few:
I want — and this might almost lead my wishes, —
A bigger place to keep my mops and dishes.
I want a horse; I want a little buggy,
To ride in when the days grow hot and muggy;
I want a garden; and, — perhaps it's funny, —
But now and then I want a little money.
I want an easy way to do my hair;
I want an extra dress or two to wear;
I want more patience; and when all is given,
I think I want to die and go to heaven!'"

"I never saw such bright people in all my life!" said Ada Geoffrey, when the outcry of applause for Dorris had subsided, and they began to rise to go. "But the *worst* of all is papa! I'll never get over it of you, see if I do! Such a cheat! Why, it's like playing dumb all your life, and then just speaking up suddenly in a quiet way, some day, as if it was nothing particular, and nobody cared!"

With Hazel's little divining-rod, Mrs. Ripwinkley had reached out, testing the world for her, to see what some of it might be really made of. Mrs. Geoffrey, from her side, had reached out in turn, also, into this fresh and simple opportunity, to see what might be there worth while.

"How was it, Aleck?" she asked of her husband, as they sat together in her dressing-room, while she brushed out her beautiful hair.

"Brightest people I have been among for a long time — and nicest," said the banker, concisely. "A real, fresh little home, with a mother in it. Good place for Ada to go, and good girls for her to know; like the ones I fell in love with a hundred years ago."

"That rhymed oracle, — to say nothing of the *fraction* of a compliment, — ought to settle it," said Mrs. Geoffrey, laughing.

"Rhymes have been the order of the evening. I expect to talk in verse for a week at least."

And then he told her about the "Crambo."

A week after, Mrs. Ledwith was astonished to find, lying on the mantel in her sister's room, a card that had been sent up the day before, —

"Mrs. Alexander H. Geoffrey."

XI.

MORE WITCH-WORK.

HAZEL was asked to the Geoffreys' to dinner.

Before this, she and Diana had both been asked to take tea, and spend an evening, but this was Hazel's little especial "invite," as she called it, because she and Ada were writing a dialogue together for a composition at school.

The Geoffreys dined at the good old-fashioned hour of half past two, except when they had formal dinner company; and Hazel was to come right home from school with Ada, and stay and spend the afternoon.

"What intimacy!" Florence Ledwith had exclaimed, when she heard of it.

"But it isn't at all on the grand style side; people like the Geoffreys do such things quite apart from their regular connection; it is a sort of 'behind the scenes;'" said Glossy Megilp, who was standing at Florence's dressing-glass, touching up the little heap of "friz" across her forehead.

"Where's my poker?" she asked, suddenly, breaking off from the Geoffrey subject, and rummaging in a dressing box, intent upon tutoring some little obstinate loop of hair that would be *too* frizzy.

"I should think a 'blower' might be a good thing to add to your tools, Glossy," said Desire. "You have brush, poker, and tongs, now, to say nothing of coal-hod," she added, glancing at the little open japanned box that held some kind of black powder which had to do with the

WITCH-WORK. See p. 122.

shadow of Glossy's eyelashes upon occasion, and the emphasis upon the delicate line of her brows.

"No secret," said Glossy, magnanimously. "There it is! It is no greater sin than violet powder, or false tails, for that matter; and the little gap in my left eyebrow was never deliberately designed. It was a 'lapsus naturæ;' I only follow out the hint, and complete the intention. Something *is* left to ourselves; as the child said about the Lord curling her hair for her when she was a baby and letting her do it herself after she grew big enough. What are our artistic perceptions given to us for, unless we're to make the best of ourselves in the first place?"

"But it isn't all eyebrows," said Desire, half aloud.

"Of course not," said Glossy Megilp. "Twice a day I have to do myself up somehow, and why shouldn't it be as well as I can? Other things come in their turn, and I do them."

"But, you see, the friz and the fix has to be, anyhow, whether or no. Everything isn't done, whether or no. I guess it's the 'first place,' that's the matter."

"I think you have a very theoretical mind, Des, and a slightly obscure style. You can't be satisfied till everything is all mapped out, and organized, and justified, and you get into horrible snarls trying to do it. If I were you, I would take things a little more as they come."

"I can't," said Desire. "They come hind side before and upside down."

"Well, if everybody is upside down, there's a view of it that makes it all right side up, isn't there? It seems to be an established fact that we must dress and undress, and that the first duty of the day is to get up and put on our clothes. We aren't ready for much until we do. And one person's dressing may require one thing, and another's another. Some people have a cork leg to put on, and some people have false teeth; and they wouldn't any of them come hobbling or mumbling out without them, unless there was a fire or an earthquake, I suppose."

Glossy Megilp's arguments and analogies perplexed Desire, always. They sometimes silenced her; but they did not always answer her. She went back to what they had been discussing before.

"To 'lay down the shubbel and the hoe,' — here's your poker, under the table-flounce, Glossy, — and to 'take up the fiddle and the bow,' again, — I think it's real nice and beautiful for Hazel — "

"To 'go where the good darkies go'?"

"Yes. It's the *good* of her that's got her in. And I believe you and Florence both would give your best boots to be there too, if it *is* behind. Behind the fixings and the fashions is where people *live;* 'dere's vat I za-ay!'" she ended, quoting herself and Rip Van Winkle.

"Maybe," said Florence, carelessly; "but I'd as lief be *in* the fashion, after all. And that's where Hazel Ripwinkley never will get, with all her taking little novelties."

Meanwhile, Hazel Ripwinkley was deep in the delights of a great portfolio of rare engravings; prints of glorious frescoes in old churches, and designs of splendid architecture; and Mrs. Geoffrey, seeing her real pleasure, was sitting beside her, turning over the large sheets, and explaining them; telling her, as she gazed into the wonderful faces of the Saints and the Evangelists in Correggio's frescoes of the church of San Giovanni at Parma, how the whole dome was one radiant vision of heavenly glory, with clouds and angel faces, and adoring apostles, and Christ the Lord high over all; and that these were but the filling in between the springing curves of the magnificent arches;

describing to her the Abbess's room in San Paolo, with its strange, beautiful heathen picture over the mantel, of Diana mounting her stag-drawn car, and its circular walls painted with trellis-work and medallioned with windows, where the heads of little laughing children, and graceful, gentle animals peeped in from among vines and flowers.

Mrs. Geoffrey did not wonder that Hazel lingered with delight over these or over the groups by Raphael in the Sistine Chapel,—the quiet pendentives, where the waiting of the world for its salvation was typified in the dream-like, reclining forms upon the still, desert sand; or the wonderful scenes from the "Creation,"—the majestic "Let there be Light!" and the Breathing of the breath of life into Man. She watched the surprise and awe with which the child beheld for the first time the daring of inspiration in the tremendous embodiment of the Almighty, and waited while she could hardly take her eyes away. But when, afterward, they turned to a portfolio of Architecture, and she found her eager to examine spires and arches and capitals, rich reliefs and stately façades and sculptured gates, and exclaiming with pleasure at the colored drawings of Florentine ornamentation, she wondered, and questioned her,—

"Have you ever seen such things before? Do you draw? I should hardly think you would care so much, at your age."

"I like the prettiness," said Hazel, simply, "and the grandness; but I don't suppose I should care so much if it wasn't for Dorris and Mr. Kincaid. Mr. Kincaid draws buildings; he's an architect; only he hasn't architected much yet, because the people that build things don't know him. Dorris was so glad to give him a Christmas present of 'Daguerreotypes de Paris,' with the churches and arches and bridges and things; she got it at a sale; I wonder what they would say to all these beauties!"

Then Mrs. Geoffery found what still more greatly enchanted her, a volume of engravings, of English Home Architecture; interiors of old Halls, magnificent staircases, lofty libraries and galleries dim with space; exteriors, gabled, turreted and towered; long, rambling piles of manor houses, with mixed styles of many centuries.

"They look as if they were brimfull of stories!" Hazel cried. "O, if I could only carry it home to show to the Kincaids!"

"You may," said Mrs. Geoffrey, as simply, in her turn, as if she were lending a copy of "Robinson Crusoe;" never letting the child guess by a breath of hesitation the value of what she had asked.

"And tell me more about these Kincaids. They are friends of yours?"

"Yes; we've known them all winter. They live right opposite, and sit in the windows, drawing and writing. Dorris keeps house up there in two rooms. The little one is her bedroom; and Mr. Kincaid sleeps on the big sofa. Dorris makes crackle-cakes, and asks us over. She cooks with a little gas-stove. I think it is beautiful to keep house with not very much money. She goes out with a cunning white basket and buys her things; and she does all her work up in a corner on a white table, with a piece of oil-cloth on the floor; and then she comes over into her parlor, she says, and sits by the window. It's a kind of a play all the time."

"And Mr. Kincaid?"

"Dorris says he might have been rich by this time, if he had gone into his Uncle James's office in New York. Mr. James Kincaid is a broker, and buys gold. But Kenneth says gold stands for work, and if he ever has any he'll buy it with work. He wants to do some real thing. Don't you think that's nice of him?"

"Yes, I do," said Mrs. Geoffrey. "And Dorris is that bright girl who wanted thirteen things, and rhymed them into 'Crambo?' Mr. Geoffrey told me."

"Yes, ma'am; Dorris can do almost anything."

"I should like to see Dorris, sometime. Will you bring her here, Hazel?"

Hazel's little witch-rod felt the almost impassible something in the way.

"I don't know as she would be *brought*," she said.

Mrs. Geoffrey laughed.

"You have an instinct for the fine proprieties, without a bit of respect for any conventional fences," she said. "I'll *ask* Dorris."

"Then I'm sure she'll come," said Hazel, understanding quite well and gladly the last three words, and passing over the first phrase as if it had been a Greek motto, put there to be skipped.

"Ada has stopped practicing," said Mrs. Geoffrey, who had undertaken the entertainment of her little guest during her daughter's half hour of music. "She will be waiting for you now."

Hazel instantly jumped up.

But she paused after three steps toward the door, to say gently, looking back over her shoulder with a shy glance out of her timidly clear eyes, —

"Perhaps, — I hope I haven't, — stayed too long!"

"Come back, you little hazel-sprite!" cried Mrs. Geoffrey; and when she got her within reach again, she put her hands one each side of the little blushing, gleaming face, and kissed it, saying, —

"I don't *think*, — I'm slow, usually, in making up my mind about people, big or little, — but I don't think you can stay too long, — or come too often, dear!"

"I've found another for you, Aleck," she said, that night at the hair-brushing, to her husband.

He always came to sit in her dressing-room, then; and it was at this quiet time that they gave each other, out of the day they had lived in their partly separate ways and duties, that which made it for each like a day lived twice, so that the years of their life counted up double.

"He is a young architect, who 'hasn't architected much, because he doesn't know the people who build things;' and he wouldn't be a gold broker with his uncle in New York, because he believes in doing money's worth in the world for the world's money. Isn't he one?"

"Sounds like it," said Mr. Geoffrey. "What is his name?"

"Kincaid."

"Nephew of James R. Kincaid?" said Mr. Geoffrey, with an interrogation that was also an exclamation. "And wouldn't go in with him! Why, it was just to have picked up dollars!"

"Exactly," replied his wife. "That was what he objected to."

"I should like to see the fellow."

"Don't you remember? You have seen him! The night you went for Ada to the Aspen Street party, and got into 'Crambo.' He was there; and it was his sister who wanted thirteen things. I guess they do!"

"Ask them here," said the banker.

"I mean to," Mrs. Geoffrey answered. "That is, after I've seen Hapsie Craydocke. She knows everything. I'll go there to-morrow morning."

"'Behind' is a pretty good way to get in — to some places," said Desire Ledwith, coming into the rose-pink room with news. "Especially an omnibus. And the Ripwinkleys, and the Kincaids, and old Miss Craydocke, and for all I know, Mrs. Scarup and Luclarion Grapp are going to Summit Street to tea to-night. Boston is topsy-turvey; Holmes was a prophet; and 'Brattle Street and Temple Place are interchanging cards!' Mother, we ought to get intimate with the family over the grocer's shop. Who knows what would come of it? There are fairies about in disguise, I'm sure; or else it's the millenium. Whichever it is, it's all right for Hazel, though; she's ready. Don't you feel like foolish virgins, Flo and Nag? I do."

I am afraid it was when Desire felt a little inclination to "nag" her elder sister, that she called her by that reprehensible name. Agatha only looked lofty, and vouchsafed no reply; but Florence said, —

"There's no need of any little triumphs or mortifications. Nobody crows, and nobody cries. *I'm* glad. Diana's a dear, and Hazel's a duck, besides being my cousins; why shouldn't I? Only there *is* a large hole for the cats, and a little hole for the kittens; and I'd as lief, myself, go in with the cats."

"The Marchbankses are staying there, and Professor Gregory. I don't know about cats," said Desire, demurely.

"It's a reason-why party, for all that," said Agatha, carelessly, recovering her good humor.

"Well, when any nice people ask me, I hope there *will* be a 'reason why.' It's the persons of consequence that make the 'reason why.'"

And Desire had the last word.

Hazel Ripwinkley was thinking neither of large holes

nor little ones, — cats nor kittens; she was saying to Luclarion, sitting in her shady down-stairs room behind the kitchen, that looked out into the green yard corner, "how nicely things came out, after all!"

"They seemed so hobblety at first, when I went up there and saw all those beautiful books, and pictures, and people living amongst them every day, and the poor Kincaids not getting the least bit of a stretch out of their corner, ever. I'll tell you what I thought, Luclarion;" and here she almost whispered, "I truly did. I thought God was making a mistake."

Luclarion put out her lips into a round, deprecating pucker, at that, and drew in her breath, —

"Oo — sh!"

"Well, I mean it seemed as if there was a mistake somewhere; and that I'd no business, at any rate, with what they wanted so. I couldn't get over it until I asked for those pictures; and mother said it was such a bold thing to do!"

"It was bold," said Luclarion; "but it wasn't forrud. It was gi'n you, and it hit right. That was looked out for."

"It's a stumpy world," said Luclarion Grapp to Mrs. Ripwinkley, afterward; "but some folks step right over their stumps athout scarcely knowin' when!"

XII.

CRUMBS.

DESIRE LEDWITH was, at this epoch, a perplexity and a worry, — even a positive terror sometimes, — to her mother.

It was not a case of the hen hatching ducks; it was rather as if a hen had got a hawk in her brood.

Desire's demurs and questions, — her dissatisfactions, siftings and contempts, — threatened now and then to swoop down upon the family life and comfort with destroying talons.

"She'll be an awful, strong-minded, radical, progressive, overturning woman," Laura said, in despair, to her friend Mrs. Megilp. "And Greenley Street, and Aspen Street, and that everlasting Miss Craydocke, are making her worse. And what can I do? Because there's Uncle."

Right before Desire, — not knowing the cloud of real bewilderment that was upon her young spiritual perceptions, getting their first glimpse of a tangled and conflicting and distorted world, — she drew wondering comparisons between her elder children and this odd, anxious, restless, sharp-spoken girl.

"I don't understand it," she would say. "It isn't a bit like a child of mine. I always took things easy, and got the comfort of them somehow; I think the world is a pretty pleasant place to live in, and there's lots of satisfaction to be had; and Agatha and Florence take after me; they are nice, good-natured, contented girls; managing their allowances, — that I wish were more, — trimming their own bonnets, and enjoying themselves with their friends, girl-fashion."

Which was true. Agatha and Florence were neither fretful nor dissatisfied; they were never disrespectful, perhaps because Mrs. Ledwith demanded less of deferential observance than of a kind of jolly companionship from her daughters; a go-and-come easiness in and out of what they called their home, but which was rather the trimming-up and outfitting place, — a sort of Holmes' Hole, — where they put in spring and fall, for a thorough overhaul and rig; and at other times, in intervals or emergencies, between their various and continual social trips and cruises. They were hardly ever all-togetherish, as Desire had said; if they ever were, it was over house cleaning and millinery; when the ordering was complete, — when the wardrobes were finished, — then the world was let in, or they let themselves out, and — "looked."

"Desire is different," said Mrs. Ledwith. "She's like Grant's father, and her Aunt Desire, — pudgicky and queer."

"Well, mamma," said the child, once, driven to desperate logic for defense, "I don't see how it can be helped. If you *will* marry into the Ledwith family, you can't expect to have your children all Shieres!"

Which, again, was very true. Laura laughed at the clever sharpness of it, and was more than half proud of her bold chick-of-prey, after all.

Yet Desire remembered that her Aunt Frances was a Shiere, also; and she thought there might easily be two sides to the same family; why not, since there were two sides still further back, always? There was Uncle Titus; who knew but it was the Oldways streak in her, after all?

Desire took refuge, more and more, with Miss Craydocke, and Rachel Froke, and the Ripwinkleys; she even went to Luclarion with questions, to get her quaint notions of things; and she had ventured into Uncle Titus's study, and taken down volumes of Swedenborg to pry into, while he looked at her with long keen regards over his spectacles, and she did not know that she was watched.

"That young girl, Desire, is restless, Titus," Rachel Froke said to him one day. "She is feeling after something; she wants something real to do; and it appears likely to me that she will do it, if they don't take care."

After that, Uncle Titus fixed his attention upon her yet more closely; and at this time Desire stumbled upon things in a strange way among his bookshelves, and thought that Rachel Froke was growing less precise in her fashion of putting to rights. Books were tucked in beside each other as if they had been picked up and bestowed anyhow; between "Heaven and Hell" and the "Four Leading Doctrines," she found, one day, "Macdonald's Unspoken Sermons," and there was a leaf doubled lengthwise in the chapter about the White Stone and the New Name. Another time, a little book of poems, by the same author, was slid in, open, over the volumes of Darwin and Huxley, and the pages upon whose outspread faces it lay were those that bore the rhyme of the blind Bartimeus: —

> "O Jesus Christ! I am deaf and blind;
> Nothing comes through into my mind,
> I only am not dumb:
> Although I see Thee not, nor hear,
> I cry because Thou mayst be near.
> O Son of Mary! come!"

Do you think a girl of seventeen may not be feeling out into the spiritual dark, — may not be stretching helpless hands, vaguely, toward the Hands that help? Desire Ledwith laid the book down again, with a great swelling breath coming up slowly out of her bosom, and with a warmth of tears in her earnest little eyes. And Uncle Titus Oldways sat there among his papers, and never moved, or seemed to look, but saw it all.

He never said a word to her himself; it was not Uncle Titus's way to talk, and few suspected him of having anything to say in such matters; but he went to Friend Froke and asked her, —

"Haven't you got any light that might shine a little for that child, Rachel?"

And the next Sunday, in the forenoon, Desire came in; came in, without knowing it, for her little light.

She had left home with the family on their way to church; she was dressed in her buff silk pongee suit trimmed with golden brown bands and quillings; she had on a lovely new brown hat with tea roses in it; her gloves and boots were exquisite and many buttoned; Agatha and Florence could not think what was the matter when she turned back, up Dorset Street, saying suddenly, "I won't go, after all." And then she had walked straight over the hill and down to Greenley Street, and came in upon Rachel, sitting alone in a quiet gray parlor that was her own, where there were ferns and ivies in the window, and a little canary, dressed in brown and gold like Desire herself, swung over them in a white wire cage.

When Desire saw how still it was, and how Rachel Froke sat there with her open window and her open book, all by herself, she stopped in the doorway with a sudden feeling of intrusion, which had not occurred to her as she came.

"It's just what I want to come into; but if I do, it

won't be there. I've no right to spoil it. Don't mind, Rachel. I'll go away."

She said it softly and sadly, as if she could not help it; and was turning back into the hall.

"But I do mind," said Rachel, speaking quickly. "Thee will come in, and sit down. Whatever it is thee wants, is here for thee. Is it the stillness? Then we will be still."

"That's so easy to say. But you can't do it for me. *You* will be still, and I shall be all in a stir. I want so to be just hushed up!"

"Fed, and hushed up, in somebody's arms, like a baby. I know," said Rachel Froke.

"How does she know?" thought Desire; but she only looked at her with surprised eyes, saying nothing.

"Hungry and restless; that's what we all are," said Rachel Froke, "until" —

"Well, — until?" demanded the strange girl, impetuously, as Rachel paused. "I've been hungry ever since I was born, mother says."

"Until He takes us up and feeds us."

"Why don't He? — Mrs. Froke, when does He give it out? Once a month, in church, they have the bread and the wine? Does that do it?"

"Thee knows we do not hold by ordinances, we Friends," said Rachel. "But He gives the bread of life. Not once a month, or in any place; it is his word. Does thee get no word when thee goes to church? Does nothing come to thee?"

"I don't know; it's mixed up: the church is full of bonnets; and people settle their gowns when they come in, and shake out their hitches and puffs when they go out, and there's professional music at one end, and — I suppose it's because I'm bad, but I don't know; half the time it seems to me it's only Mig at the other. Something all fixed up, and patted down, and smoothed over, and salted and buttered, like the potato hills they used to make on my plate for me at dinner, when I was little. But it's soggy after all, and has an underground taste. It isn't anything that has just grown, up in the light, like the ears of corn they rubbed in their hands. Breakfast is better than dinner. Bread, with yeast in it, risen up new. They don't feed with bread very often."

"The yeast in the bread, and the sparkle in the wine; they are the life of it; they are what make the signs."

"If they only gave it out fresh, and a little of it! But they keep it over, and it grows cold and tough and flat; and people sit round and pretend, but they don't eat. They've eaten other things, — all sorts of trash, — before they came. They've spoiled their appetites. Mine was spoiled, to-day. I felt so new and fussy, in these brown things. So I turned round, and came here."

Mr. Oldways' saying came back into Mrs. Froke's mind: —

"Haven't you got any light, Rachel, that might shine a little for that child?"

Perhaps that was what the child had come for.

What had the word of the Spirit been to Rachel Froke this day? The new, fresh word, with the leaven in it? "A little of it;" that was what she wanted.

Rachel took up the small red Bible that lay on the light-stand beside her.

"I'll will give thee my First-Day crumb, Desire," she said. "It may taste sweet to thee."

She turned to Revelation, seventh chapter.

"Look over with me; thee will see then where the crumb is," she said; and as Desire came near and looked over her upon the page, she read from the last two verses: —

"They shall hunger no more, neither thirst any more.

"For the *Tenderness* that is in the midst of the *Almightiness* shall feed them, and shall lead them unto living fountains of water; and God shall wipe away all tears from their eyes."

Her voice lingered over the words she put for the "Lamb" and the "Throne," so that she said "Tenderness" with its own very yearning inflection, and "Almightiness" with a strong fullness, glad in that which can never fall short or be exhausted. Then she softly laid over the cover, and sat perfectly still. It was the Quaker silence that falls upon them in their assemblies, leaving each heart to itself and that which the Spirit has given.

Desire was hushed all through; something living and real had thrilled into her thought; her restlessness quieted suddenly under it, as Mary stood quiet before the message of the angel.

When she did speak again, after a time, as Rachel Froke broke the motionless pause by laying the book gently back again upon the table, it was to say, —

"Why don't they preach like that, and leave the rest to preach itself? A Sermon means a Word; why don't they just say the word, and let it go?"

The Friend made no reply.

"I never could — quite — like that about the 'Lamb,' before," said Desire, hesitatingly. "It seemed, — I don't know, — putting Him *down*, somehow; making him tame; taking the grandness away that made the gentleness any good. But, — 'Tenderness;' that is beautiful! Does it mean so in the other place? About taking away the sins, — do you think?"

"'The Tenderness of God — the Compassion — that taketh away the sins of the world?'" Mrs. Froke repeated, half inquiringly. "Jesus Christ, God's Heart of Love toward man? I think it is so. I think, child, thee has got thy crumb also, to-day."

But not all yet.

Pretty soon, they heard the front door open, and Uncle Titus come in. Another step was behind his; and Kenneth Kincaid's voice was speaking, about some book he had called to take.

Desire's face flushed, and her manner grew suddenly flurried.

"I must go," she said, starting up; yet when she got to the door, she paused and delayed.

The voices were talking on, in the study; somehow, Desire had last words also, to say to Mrs. Froke.

She was partly shy about going past that open door, and partly afraid they might not notice her if she did. Back in her girlish thought was a secret suggestion that she was pushing at all the time with a certain self-scorn and denial, that it might happen that she and Kenneth Kincaid would go out at the same moment; if so, he would walk up the street with her, and Kenneth Kincaid was one of the few persons whom Desire Ledwith thoroughly believed in and liked. "There was no Mig about him," she said. It is hazardous when a girl of seventeen makes one of her rare exceptions in her estimate of character in favor of a man of six and twenty.

Yet Desire Ledwith hated "nonsense;" she wouldn't have anybody sending her bouquets as they did to Agatha and Florence; she had an utter contempt for lavender pantaloons and waxed moustaches; but for Kenneth Kincaid, with his honest, clear look at life, and his high strong purpose, to say friendly things, — tell her a little now and then of how the world looked to him and what it demanded, — this lifted her up; this made it seem worth while to speak and to hear.

So she was very glad when Uncle Titus saw her go down the hall, after she had made up her mind that that way lay her straight path, and that things contrived were not things worth happening, — and spoke out her name, so that she had to stop, and turn to the open doorway and reply; and Kenneth Kincaid came over and held out his hand to her. He had two books in the other, — a volume of Bunsen and a copy of "Guild Court," — and he was just ready to go.

"Not been to church to-day?" said Uncle Titus to Desire.

"I've been — to Friend's Meeting," the girl answered.

"Get anything by that?" he asked, gruffly, letting the shag down over his eyes that behind it beamed softly.

"Yes; a morsel," replied Desire. "All I wanted."

"All you wanted? Well, that's a Sunday-full!"

"Yes, sir, I think it is," said she.

When they got out upon the sidewalk, Kenneth Kincaid asked, "Was it one of the morsels that may be shared, Miss Desire? Some crumbs multiply by dividing, you know."

"It was only a verse out of the Bible, with a new word in it."

"A new word? Well, I think Bible verses often have that. I suppose it was what they were made for."

Desire's glance at him had a question in it.

"Made to look different at different times, as everything does that has life in it. Isn't that true? Clouds, trees, faces, — do they ever look twice the same?"

"Yes," said Desire, thinking especially of the faces. "I think they do, or ought to. But they may look *more*."

"I didn't say *contradictory*. To look more, there must be a difference; a fresh aspect. And that is what the world is full of; and the world is the word of God."

"The world?" said Desire, who had been taught in a dried up, mechanical sort of way, that the Bible is the word of God; and practically left to infer that, that point once settled, it might be safely shut up between its covers and not much meddled with, certainly not over freely interpreted.

"Yes. What God had to say. In the beginning was the Word, and the Word was God. Without him was not anything made that was made."

Desire's face brightened. She knew those words by heart. They were the first Sunday-school lesson she ever committed to memory, out of the New Testament; "down to 'grace and truth,'" as she recollected. What a jumble of repetitions it had been to her, then! Sentences so much alike that she could not remember them apart, or which way they came. All at once the simple, beautiful meaning was given to her.

What God had to say.

And it took a world, — millions of worlds, — to say it with.

"And the Bible, too?" she said, simply following out her own mental perception, without giving the link. It was not needed. They were upon one track.

"Yes; all things; and all *souls*. The world-word comes through things; the Bible came through souls. And it is all the more alive, and full, and deep, and changing; like a river."

"Living fountains of waters! that was part of the morsel to-day," Desire repeated impulsively, and then shyly explained.

"And the new word?"

Desire shrunk into silence for a moment; she was not used to, or fond of Bible quoting, or even Bible talk; yet she was hungering all the time for Bible truth.

Mr. Kincaid waited.

So she repeated it presently; for Desire never made a fuss; she was too really sensitive for that.

"'The Tenderness in the midst of the Almightiness shall feed them, and shall lead them to living fountains of water.'"

Mr. Kincaid recognized the "new word," and his face lit up.

"'The Lamb in the midst of the Throne,'" he said. "Out of the Heart of God, the Christ. Who was there before; the intent by which all things were made. The same yesterday, and to-day, and forever; who ever liveth to make intercession for us. Christ *had to be.* The Word, full of grace, must be made flesh. Why need people dispute about Eternity and Divinity, if they can only see that? — Was that Mrs. Froke's reading?"

"Yes; that was Rachel's sermon."

"It is an illumination."

They walked all up Orchard Street without another word.

Then Kenneth Kincaid said, —

"Miss Desire, why won't you come and teach in the Mission School?"

"I teach? Why, I've got everything to learn!"

"But as fast as you *do* learn; the morsels, you know. That is the way they are given out. That is the wonder of the kingdom of heaven. There is no need to go away and buy three hundred pennyworth before we begin, that every one may take a little; the bread given as the Master breaks it feeds them till they are filled; and there are baskets full of fragments to gather up."

Kenneth Kincaid's heart was in his Sunday work, as his sister had said. The more gladly now, that the outward daily bread was being given.

Mr. Geoffrey, — one of those busy men, so busy that they do promptly that which their hands find to do, — had put Kenneth in the way of work. It only needed a word from him, and the surveying and laying out of some new streets and avenues down there where Boston is growing so big and grand and strange, were put into his charge. Kenneth was busy now, cheerily busy, from Monday morning to Saturday night; and restfully busy on the Sunday, straightening the paths and laying out the ways for souls to walk in. He felt the harmony and the illustration between his week and his Sunday, and the one strengthening the other, as all true outward work does harmonize with and show forth, and help the spiritual doing. It could not have been so with that gold work, or any little feverish hitching on to other men's business; producing nothing, advancing nothing, only standing between to snatch what might fall, or to keep a premium for passing from hand to hand.

Our great cities are so full, — our whole country is so overrun, — with these officious middle-men whom the world does not truly want; chiffonniers of trade, who only pick up a living out of the great press and waste and overflow; and our boys are so eager to slip in to some such easy, ready-made opportunity, — to get some crossing to sweep.

What will come of it all, as the pretenses multiply?

Will there be always pennies for every little broom? Will two, and three, and six sweeps be tolerated between side and side? By and by, I think, they will have to turn to and lay pavements. Hard, honest work, and the day's pay for it; that is what we have got to go back to; that and the day's snug, patient living, which the pay achieves.

Then, as I say, the week shall illustrate the Sunday, and the Sunday shall glorify the week; and what men do and build shall stand true types, again, for the inner growth and the invisible building; so that if this outer tabernacle were dissolved, there should be seen glorious behind it, the house not made with hands, — eternal.

As Desire Ledwith met this young Kenneth Kincaid from day to day, seeing him so often at her Aunt Ripwinkley's, where he and Dorris went in and out now, almost like a son and daughter, — as she walked beside him this morning, hearing him say these things, at which the heart-longing in her burned anew toward the real and satisfying, — what wonder was it that her restlessness grasped at that in his life which was strong and full of rest; that she felt glad and proud to have him tell his thought to her; that without any silliness, — despising all silliness, — she should yet be conscious, as girls of seventeen are conscious, of something that made her day sufficient when she had so met him, — of a temptation to turn into those streets in her walks that led his way? Or that she often, with her blunt truth, toward herself as well as others, and her quick contempt of sham and subterfuge, should snub herself mentally, and turn herself round as by a grasp of her own shoulders, and make herself walk off stoutly in a far and opposite direction, when, without due need and excuse, she caught herself out in these things?

What wonder that this stood in her way, for very pleasantness, when Kenneth asked her to come and teach in the school? That she was ashamed to let herself do a thing — even a good thing, that her life needed, — when there was this conscious charm in the asking; this secret thought — that she should walk up home with him every Sunday!

She remembered Agatha and Florence, and she imagined, perhaps, more than they would really have thought of it at home; and so as they turned into Shubarton Place, — for he had kept on all the way along Bridgeley and up Dorset Street with her, — she checked her steps suddenly as they came near the door, and said brusquely, —

"No, Mr. Kincaid; I can't come to the Mission. I might learn A, and teach them that; but how do I know I shall ever learn B, myself?"

He had left his question, as their talk went on, meaning to ask it again before they separated. He thought it was prevailing with her, and that the help that comes of helping others would reach her need; it was for her sake he asked it; he was disappointed at the sudden, almost trivial turn she gave it.

"You have taken up another analogy, Miss Desire," he said. "We were talking about crumbs and feeding. The five loaves and the five thousand. 'Why reason ye because ye have no bread? How is it that ye do not understand?'"

Kenneth quoted these words naturally, pleasantly; as he might quote anything that had been spoken to them both out of a love and authority they both recognized, a little while ago.

But Desire was suddenly sharp and fractious. If it had not touched some deep, live place in her, she would not have minded so much. It was partly, too, the coming toward home. She had got away out of the pure, clear spaces where such things seemed to be fit and unstrained, into the edge of her earth atmosphere again, where, falling, they took fire. Presently she would be in that ridiculous pink room, and Glossy Megilp would be chattering about "those lovely purple poppies with the black grass," that she had been lamenting all the morning she had not bought for her chip hat, instead of the pomegranate flowers. And Agatha would be on the bed, in her cashmere sack, reading Miss Braddon.

"It would sound nice to tell them she was going down to the Mission School to give out crumbs!"

Besides, I suppose that persons of a certain temperament never utter a more ungracious "No," than when they are longing all the time to say "Yes."

So she turned round on the lower step to Kenneth, when he had asked that grave, sweet question of the Lord's, and said perversely, —

"I thought you did not believe in any brokering kind of business. It's all there, — for everybody. Why should I set up to fetch and carry?"

She did not look in his face as she said it; she was not audacious enough to do that; she poked with the stick of her sunshade between the uneven bricks of the sidewalk, keeping her eyes down, as if she watched for some truth she expected to pry up. But she only wedged the stick in so that she could not get it out; and Kenneth Kincaid making her absolutely no answer at all, she had to stand there, growing red and ashamed, held fast by her own silly trap.

"Take care; you will break it," said Kenneth, quietly, as she gave it a twist and a wrench. And he put out his hand, and took it from hers, and drew gently upward in the line in which she had thrust it in.

"You were bearing off at an angle. It wanted a straight pull."

"I never pull straight at anything. I always get into a crook, somehow. You didn't answer me, Mr. Kincaid. I didn't mean to be rude — or wicked. I didn't mean —"

"What you said. I know that; and it's no use to answer what people don't mean. That makes the crookedest crook of all."

"But I think I did mean it partly; only not contrarimindedly. I do mean that I have no business — yet awhile. It would only be — Migging at gospel!"

And with this remarkable application of her favorite illustrative expression, she made a friendly but abrupt motion of leave-taking, and went into the house.

Up into her own room, in the third story, where the old furniture was, and no "fadging," — and sat down, bonnet, gloves, sunshade, and all, in her little cane rocking-chair by the window.

Helena was down in the pink room, listening with charmed ears to the grown up young-ladyisms of her elder sisters and Glossy Megilp.

Desire sat still until the dinner-bell rang, forgetful of her dress, forgetful of all but one thought that she spoke out as she rose at last at the summons to take off her things in a hurry, —

"I wonder, — I *wonder* — if I shall ever live anything all straight out!"

XIII.

PIECES OF WORLDS.

MR. DICKENS never put a truer thought into any book, than he put at the beginning of "Little Dorrit."

That, from over land and sea, from hundreds, thousands of miles away, are coming the people with whom we are to have to do in our lives; and that, "what is set to us to do to them, and what is set for them to do to us, will all be done."

Not only from far places in this earth, over land and sea, — but from out the eternities, before and after, — from which souls are born, and into which they die, — all the lines of life are moving continually which are to meet and join, and bend, and cross our own.

But it is only with a little piece of this world, as far as we can see it in this short and simple story, that we have now to do.

Rosamond Holabird was coming down to Boston.

With all her pretty, fresh, delicate, high-lady ways, with her beautiful looks, and her sweet readiness for true things and noble living, she was coming, for a few days only, — the coöperative housekeeping was going on at Westover, and she could not be spared long, — right in among them here in Aspen Street, and Shubarton Place, and Orchard Street, and Harrisburg Square, where Mrs. Scherman lived whom she was going to stay with. But a few days may be a great deal.

Rosamond Holabird was coming for far more than she

knew. Among other things she was coming to get a lesson; a lesson right on in a course she was just now learning; a lesson of next things, and best things, and real folks.

You see how it happened, — where the links were; Miss Craydocke, and Sin Scherman, and Leslie Goldthwaite, were dear friends, made to each other one summer among the mountains. Leslie had had Sin and Miss Craydocke up at Z——, and Rosamond and Leslie were friends, also.

Mrs. Frank Scherman had a pretty house in Harrisburg Square. She had not much time for paying fashionable calls, or party-going, or party-giving. As to the last, she did not think Frank had money enough yet to "circumfuse," she said, in that way.

But she had six lovely little harlequin cups on a side-shelf in her china closet, and six different-patterned breakfast plates, with colored borders to match the cups; rose, and brown, and gray, and vermilion, and green, and blue. These were all the real china she had, and were for Frank and herself and the friends whom she made welcome, — and who might come four at once, — for day and night. She delighted in "little stays;" in girls who would go into the nursery with her, and see Sinsie in her bath; or into the kitchen, and help her mix up "little delectabilities to surprise Frank with;" only the trouble had got to be now, that the surprise occurred when the delectabilities did not. Frank had got demoralized, and expected them. She rejoiced to have Miss Craydocke drop in of a morning and come right up stairs, with her little petticoats and things to work on; and she and Frank returned these visits in a social, cosy way, after Sinsie was in her crib for the night. Frank's boots never went on with a struggle for a walk down to Orchard Street; but they were terribly impossible for Continuation Avenue.

So it had come about long ago, though I have not had a corner to mention it in, that they "knew the Muffin Man," in an Aspen Street sense; and were no strangers to the charm of Mrs. Ripwinkley's "evenings." There was always an "evening" in the "Mile Hill House," as the little family and friendly coterie had come to call it.

Rosamond and Leslie had been down together for a week once, at the Schermans; and this time Rosamond was coming alone. She had business in Boston for a day or two, and had written to ask Asenath "if she might." There were things to buy for Barbara, who was going to be married in a "navy hurry," besides an especial matter that had determined her just at this time to come.

And Asenath answered, "that the scarlet and gray, and green and blue were pining and fading on the shelf; and four days would be the very least to give them all a turn and treat them fairly; for such things had their delicate susceptibilities, as Hans Andersen had taught us to know, and might starve and suffer, — why not? being made of protoplasm, same as anybody."

Rosamond's especial errand to the city was one that just a little set her up, innocently, in her mind. She had not wholly got the better, — when it interfered with no good-will or generous dealing, — of a certain little instinctive reverence for imposing outsides and grand ways of daily doing; and she was somewhat complacent at the idea of having to go, — with kindly and needful information, — to Madam Mucklegrand, in Spreadsplendid Park.

Madam Mucklegrand was a well-born Boston lady, who had gone to Europe in her early youth, and married a Scottish gentleman with a Sir before his name. Consequently, she was quite entitled to be called "my lady;" and some people who liked the opportunity of touching their republican tongues to the salt of European dignitaries, addressed her so; but, for the most part, she assumed and received simply the style of "Madam." A queen may be called "Madam," you know. It covers an indefinite greatness. But when she spoke of her late, — very long ago, — husband, she always named him as "Sir Archibald."

Madam Mucklegrand's daughter wanted a wet-nurse for her little baby.

Up in Z——, there was a poor woman whose husband, a young brakeman on the railroad, had been suddenly killed three months ago, before her child was born. There was a sister here in Boston, who could take care of it for her if she could go to be foster-mother to some rich little baby, who was yet so poor as this — to need one. So Rosamond Holabird, who was especially interested for Mrs. Jopson, had written to Asenath, and had an advertisement put in the "Transcript," referring to Mrs. Scherman for information. And the Mucklegrand carriage had rolled up, the next day, to the house in Harrisburg Square.

They wanted to see the woman, of course, and to hear all about her, — more than Mrs. Scherman was quite able to tell; therefore when she sent a little note up to Z——, by the evening mail, Rosamond replied with her "Might she come?"

She brought Jane Jopson and the baby down with her, left them over night at Mrs. Ginnever's, in Sheafe Street, and was to go for them next morning and take them up to Spreadsplendid Park. She had sent a graceful, polite little note to Madam Mucklegrand, dated "Westover, Z——," and signed, "Rosamond Holabird," offering to do this, that there might not be the danger of Jane's losing the chance in the meanwhile.

It was certainly to accomplish the good deed that Rosamond cared the most; but it was also certainly something to accomplish it in that very high quarter. It lent a piquancy to the occasion.

She came down to breakfast very nicely and discriminatingly dressed, with the elegant quietness of a lady who knew what was simply appropriate to such an errand and the early hour, but who meant to be recognized as the lady in every unmistakable touch; and there was a carriage ordered for her at half past nine.

Sin Scherman was a cute little matron; she discerned the dash of subdued importance in Rosamond's air; and she thought it very likely, in the Boston nature of things, that it would get wholesomely and civilly toned down.

Just at this moment, Rosamond, putting on her little straw bonnet with real lace upon it, and her simple little narrow-bordered green shawl, that was yet, as far as it went, veritable cashmere, — had a consciousness, in a still, modest way, not only of her own personal dignity as Rosamond Holabird, who was the same going to see Madam Mucklegrand, or walking over to Madam Pennington's, and as much in her place with one as the other; but of the dignity of Westover itself, and Westover ladyhood, represented by her among the palaces of Boston-Appendix to-day.

She was only twenty, this fair and pleasant Rosamond of ours, and country simple, with all her native tact and grace; and she forgot, or did not know how full of impressions a life like Madam Mucklegrand's might be, and how very trifling and fleeting must be any that she might chance to make.

She drove away down to the North End, and took Jane Jopson and her baby in, — very clean and shiny, both of them, — and Jane particularly nice in the little black crape bonnet that Rosamond herself had made, and the plain black shawl that Mrs. Holabird had given her.

She stood at the head of the high, broad steps, with her mind very much made up in regard to her complete and well-bred self-possession, and the manner of her quietly assured self-introduction. She had her card all ready that should explain for her; and to the servant's reply that Madam Mucklegrand was in, she responded by moving forward with only enough of voluntary hesitation to allow him to indicate to her the reception room, at the door of which she gave him the little pasteboard, with, —

"Take that to her, if you please," and so sat down, very much as if she had been in such places frequently before, which she never had. One may be quite used to the fine, free essence of gentle living, and never in all one's life have anything to do with such solid, concrete expression of it as Rosamond saw here.

Very high, to begin with, the ceiled and paneled room was; reaching up into space as if it had really been of no consequence to the builders where they should put the cover on; and with no remotest suggestion of any reserve for further superstructure upon the same foundation.

Very dark, and polished, and deeply carved, and heavily ornamented were its wainscotings, and frames, and cornices; out of the new look of the streets, which it will take them yet a great while to outgrow, she had stepped at once into a grand, and mellow, and ancient stateliness.

There were dim old portraits on the walls, and paintings that hinted at old mastership filled whole panels; and the tall, high-backed, wonderfully wrought oaken chairs had heraldic devices in relief upon their bars and corners; and there was a great, round mosaic table, in soft, rich, dark colors, of most precious stones; these, in turn, hidden with piles of rare engravings.

The floor was of dark woods, inlaid; and sumptuous rugs were put about upon it for the feet, each one of which was wide enough to call a carpet.

And nothing of it all was *new;* there was nothing in the room but some plants in a jardiniere by the window, that seemed to have a bit of yesterday's growth upon it.

A great, calm, marble face of Jove looked down from high up, out of the shadows.

Underneath sat Rosamond Holabird, holding on to her identity and her self-confidence.

Madam Mucklegrand came in plainly enough dressed, — in black; you would not notice what she had on; but you would notice instantly the consummate usedness to the world and the hardening into the mould thereof that was set and furrowed upon eye and lip and brow.

She sailed down upon Rosamond like a frigate upon a graceful little pinnace; and brought to within a pace or two of her, continuing to stand an instant, as Rosamond rose, just long enough for the shadow of a suggestion that it might not be altogether material that she should be seated again at all.

But Rosamond made a movement backward to her chair, and laid her hand upon its arm, and then Madam Mucklegrand decided to sit down.

"You called about the nurse, I conclude, Miss — Holabird?"

"Yes, ma'am; I thought you had some questions you wished to ask, and that I had better come myself. I have her with me, in the carriage."

"Thank you," said Madam Mucklegrand, politely.

But it was rather a *de haut en bas* politeness; she exercised it also toward her footman.

Then followed inquiries about age, and health, and character. Rosamond told all she knew, clearly and sufficiently, with some little sympathetic touches that she could not help, in giving her story.

Madam Mucklegrand met her nowhere, however, on any common ground; she passed over all personal interest; instead of two women befriending a third in her need, who in turn was to give life to a little child waiting helplessly for some such ministry, it might have been the leasing of a house, or the dealing about some merchandise, that was between them.

Rosamond proposed, at last, to send Jane Jopson in.

Jane and her baby were had in, and had up-stairs; the physician and attending nurse pronounced upon her; she was brought down again, to go home and dispose of her child, and return. Rosamond, meanwhile, had been sitting under the marble Jove.

There was nothing really rude in it; she was there on business; what more could she expect? But then she knew all the time, that she too was a lady, and was taking trouble to do a kind thing. It was not so that Madam Mucklegrand would have been treated at Westover.

Rosamond was feeling pretty proud by the time Madam Mucklegrand came down stairs.

"We have engaged the young woman; the doctor quite approves; she will return without delay, I hope?"

As if Rosamond were somehow responsible all through.

"I have no doubt she will; good morning, madam."

"Good morning. I am, really, very much obliged. You have been of great service."

Rosamond turned quietly round upon the threshold.

"That was what I was very anxious to be," she said, in her perfectly sweet and musical voice, — "to the poor woman."

ROSAMOND AT MADAM MUCKLEGRAND'S. See p. 154.

Italics would indicate too coarsely the impalpable emphasis she put upon the last two words. But Mrs. Mucklegrand caught it.

Rosamond went away quite as sure of her own self-respect as ever, but very considerably cured of Spreadsplendidism.

This was but one phase of it, she knew; there are real folks, also, in Spreadsplendid Park; they are a good deal covered up, there, to be sure; but they can't help that. It is what always happens to somebody when Pyramids are built. Madam Mucklegrand herself was, perhaps, only a good deal covered up.

How lovely it was to go down into Orchard Street after that, and take tea with Miss Craydocke! How human and true it seemed, — the friendliness that shone and breathed there, among them all. How kingdom-of-heaven-like the air was, and into what pleasantness of speech it was born!

And then Hazel Ripwinkley came over, like a little spirit from another blessed society, to tell that "the picture-book things were all ready, and that it would take everybody to help."

That was Rosamond's first glimpse of Witch Hazel, who found her out instantly, — the real, Holabirdy part of her, — and set her down at once among her "folks."

It was bright and cheery in Mrs. Ripwinkley's parlor; you could hardly tell whence the cheeriness radiated, either.

The bright German lamp was cheery, in the middle of the round table; the table was cheery, covered with glossy linen cut into large, square book-sheets laid in piles, and with gay pictures of all kinds, brightly colored; and the scissors, — or scissorses, — there were ever so many shining pairs of them, — and the little mucilage bottles, and the very scrap-baskets, — all looked cozy and comfortable, and as if people were going to have a real good time among them, somehow.

And the somehow was in making great beautiful, everlasting picture-books for the little orphans in Miss Craydocke's Home, — the Home, that is, out of several blessed and similar ones that she was especially interested in, and where Hazel and Diana had been with her until they knew all the little waifs by sight and name and heart, and had their especial chosen property among them, as they used to have among the chickens and the little yellow ducks at Homesworth Farm.

Mrs. Ripwinkley was cheery; it might be a question whether all the light did not come from her first, in some way, and perhaps it did; but then Hazel was luminous, and she fluttered about with quick, happy motions, till like a little glancing taper she had shone upon and lit up everybody and everything; and Dorris was sunny with clear content, and Kenneth was blithe, and Desire was scintillant, as she always was either with snaps or smiles; and here came in beaming Miss Craydocke, and gay Asenath and her handsome husband; and our Rosa Mundi; there, — how can you tell? It was all round; and it was more every minute.

There were cutters and pasters and stitchers and binders; and every part was beautiful work, and nobody could tell which was pleasantest. Cutting out was nice, of course; who doesn't like cutting out pictures? Some were done beforehand, but there were as many left as there would be time for. And pasting, on the fine, smooth linen, making it glow out with charming groups and tints of flowers and birds and children in gay clothes, — that was delightful; and the stitchers had the pleasure of combining and arranging it all; and the binders, — Mrs. Ripwinkley and Miss Craydocke, — finished all off with the pretty ribbons and the gray covers, and theirs being the completing touch, thought *they* had the best of it.

"But I don't think finishing is best, mother," said Hazel, who was diligently snipping in and out around rose leaves or baby faces, as it happened. "I think beginning is always beautiful. I never want to end off, — anything nice, I mean."

"Well, we don't end off this," said Diana. "There's the giving, next."

"And then their little laughs and Oo's," said Hazel.

"And their delight day after day; and the comfort of them in their little sicknesses," said Miss Craydocke.

"And the stories that have got to be told about every picture," said Dorris.

"No; nothing really nice does end; it goes on and on," said Mrs. Ripwinkley.

"Of course!" said Hazel, triumphantly, turning on the Drummond light of her child-faith. "We're forever and ever people, you know!"

"Please paste some more flowers, Mr. Kincaid," said Rosamond, who sat next him, stitching. "I want to make an all-flower book of this. No, — not roses; I've a whole page already; this great white lily, I think. That's beautiful!"

"Wouldn't it do to put in this laurel bush next, with the bird's nest in it?"

"O, those lovely pink and white laurels! Yes. Where did you get such pictures, Miss Hazel?"

"O, everybody gave them to us, all summer, ever since we began. Mrs. Geoffrey gave those flowers; and mother painted some. She did that laurel. But don't call me Miss Hazel, please; it seems to send me off into a corner."

Rosamond answered by a little irresistible caress; leaning her head down to Hazel, on her other side, until her cheek touched the child's bright curls, quickly and softly. There was magnetism between those two.

Ah, the magnetism ran round!

"For a child's picture-book, Mrs. Ripwinkley?" said Mrs. Scherman, reaching over for the laurel picture. "Aren't these almost too exquisite? They would like a big scarlet poppy just as well,—perhaps better. Or a clump of cat-o'-nine-tails," she added, whimsically.

"There *is* a clump of cat-o'-nine-tails," said Mrs. Ripwinkley. "I remember how I used to delight in them as a child,—the real ones."

"Pictures are to *tell* things," said Desire, in her brief way.

"These little city refugees *must* see them, somehow," said Rosamond, gently. "I understand. They will never get up on the mountains, maybe, where the laurels grow, or into the shady swamps among the flags and the cat-o'-nine-tails. You have *picked out* pictures to give them, Mrs. Ripwinkley."

Kenneth Kincaid's scissors stopped a moment, as he looked at Rosamond, pausing also over the placing of her leaves.

Desire saw that from the other side; she saw how beautiful and gracious this girl was—this Rosamond Holabird; and there was a strange little twinge in her heart, as she felt, suddenly, that let there be ever so much that was true and kindly, or even tender, in her, it could never come up in her eyes or play upon her lips like that; she could never say it out sweetly and in due place;

everything was a spasm with her; and nobody would ever look at her just as Kenneth Kincaid looked at Rosamond then.

She said to herself, with her harsh, unsparing honesty, that it must be a "hitch inside;" a cramp or an awkwardness born in her, that set her eyes, peering and sharp, so near together, and put that knot into her brows instead of their widening placidly, like Rosamond's, and made her jerky in her speech. It was no use; she couldn't look and behave, because she couldn't *be;* she must just go boggling and kinking on, and — losing everything, she supposed.

The smiles went down, under a swift, bitter little cloud, and the hard twist came into her face with the inward pinching she was giving herself; and all at once there crackled out one of her sharp, strange questions; for it was true that she could not do otherwise; everything was sudden and crepitant with her.

"Why need all the good be done up in batches, I wonder? Why can't it be spread round, a little more even? There must have been a good deal left out somewhere, to make it come in a heap, so, upon you, Miss Craydocke!"

Hazel looked up.

"I know what Desire means," she said. "It seemed just so to me, *one* way. Why oughtn't there to be *little* homes, done-by-hand homes, for all these little children, instead of — well — machining them all up together?"

And Hazel laughed at her own conceit.

"It's nice; but then — it isn't just the way. If we were all brought up like that we shouldn't know, you see!"

"You wouldn't want to be brought up in a platoon, Hazel?" said Kenneth Kincaid. "No; neither should I."

"I think it was better," said Hazel, "to have my turn of being a little child, all to myself; *the* little child, I mean, with the rest of the folks bigger. To make much of me, you know. I shouldn't want to have missed that. I shouldn't like to be *loved* in a platoon."

"Nobody is meant to be," said Miss Craydocke.

"Then why — " began Asenath Scherman, and stopped.

"Why what, dear?"

"Revelations," replied Sin, laconically. "There are loads of people there, all dressed alike, you know; and — well — its platoony, I think, rather! And down here, such a world-full; and the sky — full of worlds. There doesn't seem to be much notion of one at a time, in the general plan of things."

"Ah, but we've got the key to all that," said Miss Craydocke. "'The very hairs of your head are all numbered.' It may be impossible with us, you know, but not with Him."

"Miss Hapsie! you always did put me down, just when I thought I was smart," said Sin Scherman.

Asenath loved to say "Miss Hapsie," now and then, to her friend, ever since she had found out what she called her "squee little name."

"But the little children, Miss Craydocke," said Mrs. Ripwinkley. "It seems to me Desire has got a right thought about it."

Mrs. Ripwinkley and Hazel always struck the same note. The same delicate instinct moved them both. Hazel "knew what Desire meant;" her mother did not let it be lost sight of that it was Desire who had led the way in this thought of the children; so that the abrupt beginning — the little flash out of the cloud — was quite forgotten presently, in the tone of hearty understanding and genuine interest with which the talk went on; and it was as if all that was generous and mindfully suggestive in it had first and truly come from her. They unfolded herself for her — these friendly ones — as she could not do; out of her bluntness grew a graciousness that lay softly over it; the cloud itself melted away and floated off; and Desire began to sparkle again more lambently. For she was not one of the kind to be meanly or enviously "put out."

"It seemed to me there must be a great many spare little corners somewhere, for all these spare little children," she said; "and that, lumped up together so, there was something they did not get."

"That is precisely the thing," said Miss Craydocke, emphatically. "I wonder, sometimes," she went on, tenderly, "if whenever God makes a little empty place in a home, it isn't really on purpose that it might be filled with one of these, — if people only thought."

"Miss Craydocke," said Hazel, "how did you begin your beehive?"

"I!" said the good lady. "I didn't. It began itself."

"Well, then, how did you *let* it begin?"

"Ah!"

The tone was admissive, and as if she had said, "*That* is another thing!" She could not contradict that she had let it be.

"I'll tell you a queer story," she said, "of what they say they used to do, in old Roman Catholic times and places, when they wanted to *keep up* a beehive that was in any danger of dwindling or growing unprofitable. I read it somewhere in a book of popular beliefs and customs about bees and other interesting animals. An old woman once went to her friend, and asked her what she did to make her hive so gainful. And this was what the old wife said; it sounds rather strange to us, but if there is anything irreverent in it, it is the word and not the meaning; 'I go,' she said, 'to the priest, and get a little round Godamighty, and put it in the hive, and then all goes well; the bees thrive, and there is plenty of honey; they always come, and stay, and work, when *that* is there."

"A little round — something awful! what *did* she mean?" asked Mrs. Scherman.

"She meant a consecrated wafer, — the Sacrament. We don't need to put the wafer in; but if we let *Him* in, you see, — just say to Him it is his house, to do with as He likes, — He takes the responsibility, and brings in all the rest."

Nobody saw, under the knitting of Desire Ledwith's brows, and the close setting of her eyes, the tenderness with which they suddenly moistened, and the earnestness with which they gleamed. Nobody knew how she thought to herself inwardly, in the same spasmodic fashion that she used for speech, —

"They Mig up their parlors with upholstery, and put rose-colored paper on their walls, and call them *their* houses; and shut the little round awfulness and goodness out! We've all been doing it! And there's no place left for what might come in."

Mrs. Scherman broke the hush that followed what Miss Hapsie said. Not hastily, or impertinently; but when it seemed as if it might be a little hard to come down into the picture-books and the pleasant easiness again.

"Let's make a Noah's Ark picture-book, — you and I," she said to Desire. "Give us all your animals, — there's a whole Natural History full over there, all painted with splendid daubs of colors; the children did that, I know, when they *were* children. Come; we'll have everything in, from an elephant to a bumble-bee!"

"We did not mean to use those, Mrs. Scherman," said Desire. "We did not think they were good enough. They are *so* daubed up."

"They're perfectly beautiful. Exactly what the young ones will like. Just divide round, and help. We'll wind up with the most wonderful book of all; the book they'll all cry for, and that will have to be given always, directly after the Castor Oil."

It took them more than an hour to do that, all working hard; and a wonderful thing it was truly, when it was done. Mrs. Scherman and Desire Ledwith directed all the putting together, and the grouping was something astonishing.

There were men and women, — the Knowers, Sin called them; she said that was what she always thought the old gentleman's name was, in the days when she first heard of him, because he knew so much; and in the backgrounds of the same sheets were their country cousins, the orangs, and the little apes. Then came the elephants, and the camels, and the whales; "for why should'nt the fishes be put in, since they must all have been swimming round sociably, if they weren't inside; and why shouldn't the big people be all kept together properly?"

There were happy families of dogs and cats and lions and snakes and little humming-birds; and in the last part were all manner of bugs, down to the little lady-bugs in blazes of red and gold, and the gray fleas and mosquitoes which Sin improvised with pen and ink, in a swarm at the end.

"And after that, I don't believe they wanted any more," she said; and handed over the parts to Miss Craydocke to be tied together. For this volume had had to be made in many folds, and Mrs. Ripwinkley's blue ribbon would by no means stretch over the back.

And by that time it was eleven o'clock, and they had worked four hours. They all jumped up in a great hurry then, and began to say good-by.

"This must not be the last we are to have of you, Miss Holabird," said Mrs. Ripwinkley, laying Rosamond's shawl across her shoulders.

"Of course not," said Mrs Scherman, "when you are all coming to our house to tea to-morrow night."

Rosamond bade the Ripwinkleys good-night with a most sweet cordiality, and thanks for the pleasure she had had, and she told Hazel and her mother that it was "neither beginning nor end, she believed; for it seemed to her that she had only found a little new piece of her world, and that Aspen Street led right out of Westover in the invisible geography, she was sure."

"Come!" said Miss Craydocke, standing on the door-steps. "It is all invisible geography out here, pretty nearly; and we've all our different ways to go, and only these two unhappy gentlemen to insist on seeing everybody home."

So first the whole party went round with Miss Hapsie; and then Kenneth and Dorris, who always went home with Desire, walked up Hanley Street with the Schermans and Rosamond, and so across through Dane Street to Shubarton Place.

But while they were on their way, Hazel Ripwinkley was saying to her mother, up in her room, where they made sometimes such long good-nights,—

"Mother! there were some little children taken away from you before we came, you know? And now we've got this great big house, and plenty of things, more than it takes for us."

"Well?"

"Don't you think it's expected that we should do something with the corners? There's room for some real good little times for somebody. I think we ought to begin a beehive."

Mrs. Ripwinkley kissed Hazel very tenderly, and said, only, —

"We can wait, and see."

Those are just the words that mothers so often put children off with! But Mrs. Ripwinkley, being one of the real folks, meant it; the very heart of it.

In that little talk, they took the consecration in; they would wait and see; when people do that, with an expectation, the beehive begins.

Up Hanley Street, the six fell into pairs.

Mrs. Scherman and Desire, Dorris and Mr. Scherman, Rosamond and Kenneth Kincaid.

It only took from Bridgeley Street up to Dane, to tell Kenneth Kincaid so much about Westover, in answer to his questions, that he too thought he had found a new little piece of his world. What Rosamond thought, I do not know; but a girl never gives a young man so much as she gave Kenneth in that little walk without having some of the blessed consciousness that comes with giving. The sun knows it shines, I dare say; or else there is a great waste of hydrogen and other things.

There was not much left for poor little Desire after they parted from the Schermans and turned the corner of Dane Street. Only a little bit of a way, in which new talk could hardly begin, and just time for a pause that showed how the talk that had come to an end was missed; or how, perhaps, it stayed in the mind, repeating itself, and keeping it full.

Nobody said anything till they had crossed B—— Street; and then Dorris said, "How beautiful,—*real* beautiful, Rosamond Holabird is!" And Kenneth answered, "Did you hear what she said to Mrs. Ripwinkley?"

They were full of Rosamond! Desire did not speak a word.

Dorris had heard and said it over. It seemed to please Kenneth to hear it again. "A piece of her world!"

"How quickly a true person springs to what belongs to—their life!" said Kenneth, using that wrong little pronoun that we shall never be able to do without.

"People don't always get what belongs, though," blurted Desire at last, just as they came to the long door-steps. "Some people's lives are like complementary colors, I think; they see blue, and live red!"

"But the colors are only accidentally—I mean temporarily—divided; they are together in the sun; and they join somewhere—beyond."

"I hate beyond!" said Desire, recklessly. "Good-night. Thank you." And she ran up the steps.

Nobody knew what she meant. Perhaps she hardly knew herself.

They only thought that her home life was not suited to her, and that she took it hard.

XIV.

"SESAME; AND LILIES."

"I'VE got a discouragement at my stomach," said Luclarion Grapp.

"What's the matter?" asked Mrs. Ripwinkley, naturally.

"Mrs. Scarup. I've been there. There ain't any bottom to it."

"Well?"

Mrs. Ripwinkley knew that Luclarion had more to say, and that she waited for this monosyllable.

"She's sick again. And Scarup, he's gone out West; spending a hundred dollars to see whether or no there's a chance anywhere for a *smart* man, — and that ain't he, so it's a double waste, — to make fifty. No girl; and the children all under foot, and Pinkie looking miserable over the dishes."

"Pinkie isn't strong."

"No. She's powerful weak. I just wish you'd seen that dirty settin'-room fire-place; looks as if it hadn't been touched since Scarup smoked his pipe there, the night before he went off a wild-gandering. And clo'es to be ironed, and the girl cleared out, because 'she'd always been used to fust-class families.' There wasn't anything to your hand, and you couldn't tell where to begin, unless you began with a cataplasm!"

Luclarion had heard, by chance, of a cataclysm, and that was what she meant.

"It wants — creation, over again! Mrs. Scarup hadn't

any fit breakfast; there was burnt toast, made out of tough bread, that she'd been trying to eat; and a cup of tea, half drunk; something the matter with that, I presume. I'd have made her some gruel, if there'd been a fire; and if there'd been any kindlings, I'd have made her a fire; but there 'twas; there wasn't any bottom to it!"

"You had better make the gruel here, Luclarion."

"That's what I come back for. But — Mrs. Ripwinkley!"

"Well?"

"Don't it appear to you it's a kind of a stump? I don't want to do it just for the satisfaction; though it *would* be a satisfaction to plough everything up thorough, and then rake it over smooth; what do you think?"

"What have you thought, Luclarion? Something, of course."

"She wants a real smart girl — for two dollars a week. She can't get her, because she ain't. And I kind of felt as though I should like to put in. Seemed to me it was a — but there! I haven't any right to stump *you*."

"Wouldn't it be rather an aggravation? I don't suppose you would mean to stay altogether?"

"Not unless — but don't go putting it into my head, Mrs. Ripwinkley. I shall feel as if I *was*. And I don't think it goes quite so far as that, yet. We ain't never stumped to more than one thing at a time. What she wants is to be straightened out. And when things once looked *my* way, she might get a girl, you see. Anyhow, 'twould encourage Pinkie, and kind of set her going. Pinkie likes things nice; but it's such a Hoosac tunnel to undertake, that she just lets it all go, and gets off upstairs, and sticks a ribbon in her hair. That's all she *can* do. I s'pose 'twould take a fortnight, maybe?"

"Take it, Luclarion," said Mrs. Ripwinkley, smiling.

Luclarion understood the smile.

"I s'pose you think it's as good as took. Well, perhaps it is — spoke for. But it wasn't me, you know. Now what'll you do?"

"Go into the kitchen and make the pudding."

"But then?"

"We are not stumped for then, you know."

"There was a colored girl here yesterday, from up in Garden Street, asking if there was any help wanted. I think she came in partially, to look at the flowers; the 'sturtiums *are* splendid, and I gave her some. She was awfully dressed up, — for colors, I mean; but she looked clean and pleasant, and spoke bright. Maybe she'd come, temporary. She seemed taken with things. I know where to find her, and I could go there when I got through with the gruel. Mrs. Scarup must have that right off."

And Luclarion hurried away.

It was not the first time Mrs. Ripwinkley had lent Luclarion; but Miss Grapp had not found a kitchen mission in Boston heretofore. It was something new to bring the fashion of simple, prompt, neighborly help down intact from the hills, and apply it here to the tangle of city living, that is made up of so many separate and unrecognized struggles.

When Hazel came home from school, she went all the way up the garden walk, and in at the kitchen door. "That was the way she took it all," she said; "first the flowers, and then Luclarion and what they had for dinner, and a drink of water; and then up-stairs, to mother."

To-day she encountered in the kitchen a curious and startling apparition of change.

A very dusky brown maiden, with a petticoat of flashing purple, and a jacket of crimson, and extremely puzzling hair tied up with knots of corn color, stood in possession over the stove, tending a fricassee, of which Hazel recognized at once the preparation and savor as her mother's; while beside her on a cricket, munching cold biscuit and butter with round, large bites of very white little teeth, sat a small girl of five of the same color, gleaming and twinkling as nothing human ever does gleam and twinkle but a little darkie child.

"Where is Luclarion?" asked Hazel, standing still in the middle of the floor, in her astonishment.

"I don't know. I'm Damaris, and this one's little Vash. Don't go for callin' me Dam, now; the boys did that in my last place, an' I left, don' yer see? I ain't goin' to be swore to, anyhow!"

"And Damaris glittered at Hazel, with her shining teeth and her quick eyes, full of fun and good humor, and enjoyed her end of the joke extremely.

"Have you come to *stay?*" asked Hazel.

"'Course. I don' mostly come for to go."

"What does it mean, mother?" Hazel asked, hurrying up into her mother's room.

And then Mrs. Ripwinkley explained.

"But what *is* she? Black or white? She's got straight braids and curls at the back of her head, like everybody's" —

"'Course," said a voice in the doorway. "An' wool on top,—place where wool ought to grow,—same 's everybody, too."

Damaris had come up, according to orders, to report a certain point in the progress of the fricassee.

"They all pulls the wool over they eyes, now-days, an' sticks the straight on behind. Where's the difference?"

Mrs. Ripwinkley made some haste to rise and move toward the doorway, to go down stairs, turning Damaris from her position, and checking further remark. Diana and Hazel stayed behind, and laughed. "What fun!" they said.

It was the beginning of a funny fortnight; but it is not the fun I have paused to tell you of; something more came of it in the home-life of the Ripwinkleys; that which they were "waiting to see."

Damaris wanted a place where she could take her little sister; she was tired of leaving her "shyin' round," she said. And Vash, with her round, fuzzy head, her bright eyes, her little flashing teeth, and her polished mahogany skin, — darting up and down the house "on Aarons," or for mere play, — dressed in her gay little scarlet flannel shirt-waist, and black and orange striped petticoat, — was like some "splendid, queer little fire-bug," Hazel said, and made a surprise and a picture wherever she came. She was "cute," too, as Damaris had declared beforehand; she was a little wonder at noticing and remembering, and for all sorts of handiness that a child of five could possibly be put to.

Hazel dressed rag babies for her, and made her a soap-box baby-house in the corner of the kitchen, and taught her her letters; and began to think that she should hate to have her go when Luclarion came back.

Damaris proved clever and teachable in the kitchen; and had, above all, the rare and admirable disposition to keep things scrupulously as she had found them; so that Luclarion, in her afternoon trips home, was comforted greatly to find that while she was "clearing and ploughing" at Mrs. Scarup's, her own garden of neatness was not being turned into a howling wilderness; and she observed, as is often done so astutely, that "when you *do* find a neat, capable, colored help, it's as good help as you can have." Which you may notice is just as true without the third adjective as with.

Luclarion herself was having a splendid time.

The first thing she did was to announce to Mrs. Scarup that she was out of her place for two weeks, and would like to come to her at her wages; which Mrs. Scarup received with some such awed and unbelieving astonishment as she might have done the coming of a legion of angels with Gabriel at their head. And when one strong, generous human will, with powers of brain and body under it sufficient to some good work, comes down upon it as Luclarion did upon hers, there *is* what Gabriel and his angels stand for, and no less sent of God.

The second thing Luclarion did was to clean that "settin'-room fire-place," to restore the pleasant brown color of its freestone hearth and jambs, to polish its rusty brasses till they shone like golden images of gods, and to lay an ornamental fire of chips and clean little sticks across the irons. Then she took a wet broom and swept the carpet three times, and dusted everything with a damp duster; and then she advised Mrs. Scarup, whom the gruel had already cheered and strengthened, to be "helped down, and sit there in the easy-chair, for a change, and let her take her room in hand." And no doctor ever prescribed any change with better effect. There are a good many changes that might be made for people, without sending them beyond their own doors. But it isn't the doctors who always know *what* change, or would dare to prescribe it if they did.

Mrs. Scarup was "helped down," it seemed, — really up, rather, — into a new world. Things had begun all over again. It was worth while to get well, and take courage. Those brasses shone in her face like morning suns.

"Well, I do declare to Man, Miss Grapp!" she exclaimed; and breath and expression failed together, and that was all she could say.

Up-stairs, Luclarion swept and rummaged. She found the sheet and towel drawers, and made everything white and clean. She laid fresh napkins over the table and bureau tops, and set the little things — boxes, books, what not, — daintily about on them. She put a clean spread on the bed, and gathered up things for the wash she meant to have, with a recklessness that Mrs. Scarup herself would never have dared to use, in view of any "help" she ever expected to do it.

And then, with Pinkie to lend feeble assistance, Luclarion turned to in the kitchen.

It was a "clear treat," she told Mrs. Ripwinkley afterward. "Things had got to that state of mussiness, that you just began at one end and worked through to the other, and every inch looked new made over after you as you went along."

She put the children out into the yard on the planks, and gave them tin pans and clothes-pins to keep house with, and gingerbread for their dinner. She and Pinkie had cups of tea, and Mrs. Scarup had her gruel, and went up to bed again; and that was another new experience, and a third stage in her treatment and recovery.

When it came to the cellar, Luclarion got the choreman in; and when all was done, she looked round on the renovated home, and said within herself, "If Scarup, now, will only break his neck, or get something to do, and stay away with his pipes and his boots and his contraptions!"

And Scarup did. He found a chance in some freight-house, and wrote that he had made up his mind to stay out there all winter; and Mrs. Scarup made little excursions about the house with her returning strength, and every journey was a pleasure-trip, and the only misery was that at the end of the fortnight Miss Grapp was going away, and then she should be "all back in the swamp again."

"No, you won't," said Luclarion; "Pinkie's waked up, and she's going to take pride, and pick up after the children. She can do that, now; but she couldn't shoulder everything. And you'll have somebody in the kitchen. See if you don't. I've 'most a mind to say I'll stay till you do."

Luclarion's faith was strong; she knew, she said, that "if she was doing at her end, Providence wasn't leaving off at his. Things would come round."

This was how they did come round.

It only wanted a little sorting about. The pieces of the puzzle were all there. Hazel Ripwinkley settled the first little bit in the right place. She asked her mother one night, if she didn't think they might begin their beehive with a fire-fly? Why couldn't they keep little Vash?

"And then," said Diana, in her quiet way, slipping one of the big three-cornered pieces of the puzzle in, "Damaris might go to Mrs. Scarup for her two dollars a week. She is willing to work for that, if she can get Vash taken. And this would be all the same, and better."

Desire was with them when Luclarion came in, and heard it settled.

"How is it that things always fall right together for you, so? How *came* Damaris to come along?"

"You just take hold of something and try," said Luclarion. "You'll find there's always a working alongside. Put up your sails, and the wind will fill 'em."

Uncle Titus wanted to know "what sort of use a thing like that could be in a house?"

He asked it in his very surliest fashion. If they had had any motives of fear or favor, they would have been disconcerted, and begun to think they had made a mistake.

But Hazel spoke up cheerily, —

"Why, to wait on people, uncle. She's the nicest little fetch-and-carrier you ever saw!"

"Humph! who wants to be waited on, here? You girls, with feet and hands of your own? Your mother doesn't, I know."

"Well, to wait *on*, then," says Hazel, boldly. "I'm making her a baby-house, and teaching her to read; and Diana is knitting scarlet stockings for her, to wear this winter. We like it."

"O, if you like it! That's always a reason. I only want to have people give the real one."

And Uncle Titus walked off, so that nobody could tell whether *he* liked it or not.

Nobody told him anything about the Scarups. But do you suppose he didn't know? Uncle Titus Oldways was as sharp as he was blunt.

"I guess I know, mother," said Hazel, a little while after this, one day, "how people write stories."

"Well?" asked her mother, looking up, ready to be amused with Hazel's deep discovery.

"If they can just begin with one thing, you see, that makes the next one. It can't help it, hardly. Just as it does with us. What made me think of it was, that it seemed to me there was another little piece of our bee-hive story all ready to put on; and if we went and did it, — I wonder if you wouldn't, mother? It fits exactly."

"Let me see."

"That little lame Sulie at Miss Craydocke's Home, that we like so much. Nobody adopts her away, because she *is* lame; her legs are no use at all, you know, and she just sits all curled up in that great round chair that Mrs. Geoffrey gave her, and sews patchwork, and makes paper dolls. And when she drops her scissors, or her thread, somebody has to come and pick it up. She wants waiting on; she just wants a little lightning-bug, like Vash, to run round for her all the time. And we don't, you see; and we've got Vash! And Vash — likes paper dolls."

Hazel completed the circle of her argument with great triumph.

"An extra piece of bread to finish your too much butter," said Diana.

"Yes. Doesn't it just make out?" said Hazel, abating not a jot of her triumph, and taking things literally, as nobody could do better than she, upon occasion, for all her fancy and intuition.

"I wonder what Uncle Oldways would say to that," said Diana.

"He'd say 'Faugh, faugh!' But he doesn't mean faugh, faugh, half the time. If he does, he doesn't stick to it. Mother," she asked rather suddenly, "do you think Uncle Oldways feels as if we oughtn't to do — other things — with his money?"

"What other things?"

"Why, *these* others. Vash, and Sulie, perhaps. Wouldn't he like it if we turned his house into a Beehive?"

"It isn't his house," said Mrs. Ripwinkley. "He has given it to me."

"Well, — do you feel 'obligated,' as Luclarion says?"

"In a certain degree, — yes. I feel bound to consider

his comfort and wishes, as far as regards his enjoyment with us, and fulfilling what he reasonably looked for when he brought us here."

"Would that interfere?"

"Suppose you ask him, Hazel?"

"Well, I could do that."

"Hazel wouldn't mind doing anything!" said Diana, who, to tell the truth was a little afraid of Uncle Titus, and who dreaded of all things, being snubbed.

"Only," said Hazel, to whom something else had just occurred, "wouldn't he think — wouldn't it be — *your* business?"

"It is all your plan, Hazel. I think he would see that."

"And you are willing, if he doesn't care?"

"I did not quite say that. It would be a good deal to think of."

"Then I'll wait till you've thought," said clear-headed little Hazel.

"But it fits right on. I can see that. And Miss Craydocke said things would, after we had begun."

Mrs. Ripwinkley took it into her thoughts, and carried it about with her for days, and considered it; asking herself questions.

Was it going aside in search of an undertaking that did not belong to her?

Was it bringing home a care, a responsibility, for which they were not fitted, — which might interfere with the things they were meant, and would be called, to do?

There was room and opportunity, doubtless, for them to do something; Mrs. Ripwinkley had felt this; she had not waited for her child to think of it for her; she had only waited, in her new, strange sphere, for circumstances to guide the way, and for the Giver of all circumstance to guide her thought. She chose, also, in the things that would affect her children's life and settle duties for them, to let them grow also to those duties, and the perception of them, with her. To this she led them, by all her training and influence; and now that in Hazel, her child of quick insight and true instincts, this influence was bearing fruit and quickening to action, she respected her first impulses; she believed in them; they had weight with her, as argument in themselves. These impulses, in young, true souls, freshly responding, are, she knew, as the proof-impressions of God's Spirit.

Yet she would think; that was her duty; she would not do a thing hastily, or unwisely.

Sulie Praile had been a good while, now, at the Home.

A terrible fall, years ago, had caused a long and painful illness, and resulted in her present helplessness. But above those little idle, powerless limbs, that lay curled under the long, soft skirt she wore, like a baby's robe, were a beauty and a brightness, a quickness of all possible motion, a dexterous use of hands, and a face of gentle peace and sometimes glory, that were like a benediction on the place that she was in; like the very Holy Ghost in tender form like a dove, resting upon it, and abiding among them who were there.

In one way, it would hardly be so much a giving as a taking, to receive her in. Yet there was care to assume, the continuance of care to promise or imply; the possibility of conflicting plans in much that might be right and desirable that Mrs. Ripwinkley should do for her own. Exactly what, if anything, it would be right to undertake in this, was matter for careful and anxious reflection.

The resources of the Home were not very large; there

were painful cases pressing their claims continually; as fast as a little place was vacated it could be filled; was wanted, ten times over; and Sulie Praile had been there a good while. If somebody would only take her, as people were very ready to take — away to happy, simple, comfortable country homes, for mere childhood's sake — the round, rosy, strong, and physically perfect ones! But Sulie must be lifted and tended; she must keep somebody at home to look after her; no one could be expected to adopt a child like that.

Yet Hazel Ripwinkley thought they could be; thought, in her straightforward, uncounting simplicity, that it was just the natural, obvious, beautiful thing to do, to take her home — into a real home — into pleasant family life; where things would not crowd; where she could be mothered and sistered, as girls ought to be, when there are so many nice places in the world, and not so many people in them as there might be. When there could be so much visiting, and spare rooms kept always in everybody's house, why should not somebody who needed to, just come in and stay? What were the spare places made for?

"We might have Sulie for this winter," said Mrs. Ripwinkley, at last. "They would let her come to us for that time; and it would be a change for her, and leave a place for others. Then if anything made it impossible for us to do more, we should not have raised an expectation to be disappointed. And if we can and ought to do more, it will be shown us by that time more certainly."

She asked Miss Craydocke about it, when she came home from Z—— that fall. She had been away a good deal lately; she had been up to Z—— to two weddings, — Leslie Goldthwaite's and Barbara Holabird's. Now she was back again, and settled down.

Miss Craydocke thought it a good thing wisely limited.

"Sulie needs to be with older girls; there is no one in the Home to be companion to her; the children are almost all little. A winter here would be a blessing to her!"

"But the change again, if she should have to make it?" suggested Mrs. Ripwinkley.

"Good things don't turn to bad ones because you can't have them any more. A thing you're not fit for, and never ought to have had, may; but a real good stays by; it overflows all the rest. Sulie Praile's life could never be so poor again, after a winter here with you, as it might be if she had never had it. If you'd like her, let her come, and don't be a bit afraid. We're only working by inches, any of us; like the camel's-hair embroiderers in China. But it gets put together; and it is beautiful, and large, and whole, somewhere."

"Miss Craydocke always knows," said Hazel.

Nobody said anything again, about Uncle Titus. A winter's plan need not be referred to him. But Hazel, in her own mind, had resolved to find out what was Uncle Titus's, generally and theoretically; how free they were to be, beyond winter plans and visits of weeks; how much scope they might have with this money and this house, that seemed so ample to their simple wants, and what they might do with it and turn it into, if it came into their heads or hearts or consciences.

So one day she went in and sat down by him in the study, after she had accomplished some household errand with Rachel Froke.

Other people approached him with more or less of strategy, afraid of the tiger in him; Desire Ledwith faced him courageously; only Hazel came and nestled up beside him, in his very cage, as if he were no wild beast, after all.

Yet he pretended to growl, even at her, sometimes; it was so funny to see her look up and chirp on after it, like some little bird to whom the language of beasts was no language at all, and passed by on the air as a very big sound, but one that in no wise concerned it.

"We've got Sulie Praile to spend the winter, Uncle Titus," she said.

"Who's Sulie Praile?"

"The lame girl, from the Home. We wanted somebody for Vash to wait on, you know. She sits in a round chair, that twists, like yours; and she's — just like a lily in a vase!" Hazel finished her sentence with a simile quite unexpected to herself.

There was something in Sulie's fair, pale, delicate face, and her upper figure, rising with its own peculiar lithe, easily swayed grace from among the gathered folds of the dress of her favorite dark green color, that reminded — if one thought of it, and Hazel turned the feeling of it into a thought at just this moment — of a beautiful white flower, tenderly and commodiously planted.

"Well, I suppose it's worth while to have a lame girl to sit up in a round chair, and look like a lily in a vase, is it?"

"Uncle Titus, I want to know what you think about some things."

"That is just what I want to know myself, sometimes. To find out what one thinks about things, is pretty much the whole finding, isn't it?"

"Don't be very metaphysical, please, Uncle Titus. Don't turn your eyes round into the back of your head. That isn't what I mean."

"What do you mean?"

"Just plain looking."

"O!"

"Don't you think, when there are places, all nice and ready, — and people that would like the places and haven't got 'em, — that the people ought to be put into the places?"

"'The shirtless backs put into the shirts?'"

"Why, yes, of course. What are shirts made for?"

"For some people to have thirty-six, and some not to have any," said Mr. Oldways.

"No," said Hazel. "Nobody wants thirty-six, all at once. But what I mean is, rooms, and corners, and pleasant windows, and seats at the table; places where people come in visiting, and that are kept saved up. I can't bear an empty box; that is, only for just one pleasant minute, while I'm thinking what I can put into it."

"Where's your empty box, now?"

"Our house, *was* rather empty-boxy. Uncle Titus, do you mind how we fill it up, — because you gave it to us, you know?"

"No. So long as you don't crowd yourselves out."

"Or you, Uncle Titus. We don't want to crowd you out. Does it crowd you any to have Sulie and Vash there, and to have us 'took up' with them, as Luclarion says?"

How straight Witch Hazel went to her point!

"Your catechism crowds me just a little, child," said Uncle Titus. "I want to see you go your own way. That is what I gave you the house for. Your mother knows that. Did she send you here to ask me?"

"No. I wanted to know. It was I that wanted to begin a kind of a Beehive — like Miss Craydocke's.

Would you care if it was turned quite into a Beehive, finally?"

Hazel evidently meant to settle the furthest peradventure, now she had begun.

"Ask your mother to show you the deed. 'To Frances Ripwinkley, her heirs and assigns,' — that's you and Diana, — 'for their use and behoof, forever.' I've no more to do with it."

"'Use, and behoof,'" said Hazel, slowly. And then she turned the leaves of the great Worcester that lay upon the study table, and found "Behoof."

"'Profit, — gain, — benefit;' then that's what you meant; that we should make as much more of it as we could. That's what I think, Uncle Titus. I'm glad you put 'behoof' in."

"They always put it in, child!"

"Do they? Well, then, they don't always work it out!" and Hazel laughed.

At that, Mr. Oldways pulled off his spectacles, looked sharp at Hazel with two sharp, brown eyes, — set near together, Hazel noticed for the first time, like Desire's, — let the keenness turn gradually into a twinkle, suffered the muscles that had held his lips so grim to relax, and laughed too; his peculiar, up-and-down shake of a laugh, in which head and shoulders made the motions, as if he were a bottle, and there were a joke inside of him which was to be well mixed up to be thoroughly enjoyed.

"Go home to your mother, jade-hopper!" he said, when he had done; "and tell her I'm coming round to-night, to tea, amongst your bumble-bees and your lilies!"

XV.

WITH ALL ONE'S MIGHT.

LET the grapes be ever so sweet, and hang in plenty ever so low, there is always a fair bunch out of reach.

Mrs. Ledwith longed, now, to go to Europe.

At any rate, she was eager to have her daughters go. But, after just one year, to take what her Uncle Oldways had given her, in return for her settling herself near him, and *un*settle herself, and go off to the other side of the world! Besides, what he had given her would not do it. That was the rub, after all. What was two thousand a year, now-a-days? Nothing is anything, now-a-days. And it takes everything to do almost nothing.

The Ledwiths were just as much pinched now as they were before they ever heard from Uncle Oldways. People with unlimited powers of expansion always are pinched; it is good for them; one of the saving laws of nature that keeps things decently together.

Yet, in the pink room of a morning, and in the mellow-tinted drawing-room of an evening, it was getting to be the subject oftenest discussed. It was that to which they directed the combined magnetism of the family will; everything was brought to bear upon it; Bridget's going away on Monday morning, leaving the clothes in the tubs, the strike-price of coal, and the overcharge of the grocer; Florence's music, Helena's hopeless distress over French and German; even Desire's listlessness and fidgets; most of all Mrs. Megilp's plans, which were ripening towards this long coveted end. She and Glossy really thought they should go this winter.

"It is a matter of economy now; everybody's going. The Fargo's and the Fayerwerses, and the Hitherinyons have broken all up, and are going out to stay indefinitely. The Fayerwerses have been saving up these four years to get away, there are so many of them, you know; the passage money counts, and the first travelling; but after you *are* over, and have found a place to settle down in," — then followed all the usual assertions as to cheap delights and inestimable advantages, and emancipation from all American household ills and miseries.

Uncle Oldways came up once in a while to the house in Shubarton Place, and made an evening call. He seemed to take apricot-color for granted, when he got there, as much as he did the plain, old, unrelieved brown at Mrs. Ripwinkley's; he sat quite unconcernedly in the grand easy chair that Laura wheeled out for him; indeed, it seemed as if he really, after a manner, indorsed everything by his acceptance without demur of what he found. But then one must sit down on something; and if one is offered a cup of coffee, or anything on a plate, one cannot easily protest against sea-green china. We do, and we have, and we wear, and we say, a great many things, and feel ourselves countenanced and confirmed, somehow, — perhaps excused, — because nobody appears surprised or says anything. But what should they say; and would it be at all proper that they should be surprised? If we only thought of it, and once tried it, we might perhaps find it quite as easy and encouraging, on the same principle, *not* to have apricot rep and sea-green china.

One night Mr. Oldways was with them when the talk turned eastwardly over the water. There were new names in the paper, of people who had gone out in the *Aleppo*, and a list of Americans registered at Bowles Brothers,' among whom were old acquaintance.

"I declare, how they all keep turning up there!" said Mrs. Ledwith.

"The war doesn't seem to make much difference," said her husband.

"To think how lucky the Vonderbargens were, to be in Paris just at the edge of the siege!" said Glossy Megilp. "They came back from Como just in time; and poor Mr. Washburne had to fairly hustle them off at last. They were buying silks, and ribbons, and gloves, up to the last minute, for absolutely nothing. Mrs. Vonderbargen said it seemed a sin to come away and leave anything. I'm sure I don't know how they got them all home; but they did."

Glossy had been staying lately with the Vonderbargens in New York. She stayed everywhere, and picked up everything.

"You have been abroad, Mrs. Scherman?" said Mrs. Ledwith, inquiringly, to Asenath, who happened to be calling, also, with her husband, and was looking at some photographs with Desire.

"No, ma'am," answered Mrs. Scherman, very promptly, not having spoken at all before in the discussion. "I do not think I wish to go. The syphon has been working too long."

"The Syphon?"

Mrs. Ledwith spoke with a capital S in her mind; but was not quite sure whether what Mrs. Scherman meant might be a line of Atlantic steamers or the sea-serpent.

"Yes, ma'am. The emptying back and forth. There is'nt much that is foreign over there, now, nor very much that is native here. The hemispheres have got miserably mixed up. I think when I go 'strange countries for to see,' it will have to be Patagonia or Independent Tartary."

Uncle Oldways turned round with his great chair, so as to face Asenath, and laughed one of his thorough fun-digesting laughs, his keen eyes half shut with the enjoyment, and sparkling out through their cracks at her.

But Asenath had resumed her photographs with the sweetest and quietest unconsciousness.

Mrs. Ledwith let her alone after that; and the talk rambled on to the schools in Munich, and the Miracle Plays at Oberammergau.

"To think of *that* invasion!" said Asenath, in a low tone to Desire, "and corrupting *that* into a show, with a run of regular performances! I do believe they have pulled down the last unprofaned thing now, and trampled over it."

"If we go," said Mrs. Megilp," we shall join the Fayerwerses, and settle down with them quietly in some nice place; and then make excursions. We shall not try to do all Europe in three months; we shall choose, and take time. It is the only way really to enjoy or acquire; and the quiet times are so invaluable for the lessons and languages."

Mrs. Megilp made up her little varnishes with the genuine gums of truth and wisdom; she put a beautiful shine even on to her limited opportunities and her enforced frugalities.

"Mrs. Ledwith, you *ought* to let Agatha and Florence go too. I would take every care of them; and the expense would be so divided — carriages, and couriers, and everything — that it would be hardly anything."

"It is a great opportunity," Mrs. Ledwith said, and

sighed. "But it is different with us from what it is with you. We must still be a family here, with nearly the same expenses. To be sure Desire has done with school, and she doesn't care for gay society, and Helena is a mere child yet; if it ever could" —

And so it went on between the ladies, while Mr. Oldways and Mr. Ledwith and Frank Scherman got into war talk, and Bismarck policy, and French poss — no, *im*-possibilities.

"I don't think Uncle Oldways minded much," said Mrs. Ledwith to Agatha, and Mrs. Megilp, up-stairs, after everybody had gone who was to go.

"He never minds anything," said Agatha.

"I don't know," said Mrs. Megilp, slowly. "He seemed mightily pleased with what Asenath Scherman said."

"O, she's pretty, and funny; it makes no difference what she says; people are always pleased."

"We might dismiss one girl this winter," said Mrs. Ledwith, "and board in some cheap country place next summer. I dare say we could save it in the year's round; the difference, I mean. When you weren't actually travelling, it wouldn't cost more than to have you here, — dress and all.

"They wouldn't need to have a new thing," said Glossy.

"Those people out at Z—— want to buy the house. I've a great mind to coax Grant to sell, and take a slice right out, and send them," said Mrs. Ledwith, eagerly. She was always eager to accomplish the next new thing for her children; and, to say the truth, did not much consider herself. And so far as they had ever been able, the Ledwiths had always been rather easily given to "taking the slice right out."

The Megilps had had a little legacy of two or three thousand dollars, and were quite in earnest in their plans, this time, which had been talk with them for many years.

"Those poor Fayerwerses!" said Asenath to her husband, walking home. "Going out now, after the cheap European living of a dozen years ago! The ghost always goes over on the last load. I wonder at Mrs. Megilp. She generally knows better."

"She'll do," said Frank Scherman. "If the Fayerwerses stick anywhere, as they probably will, she'll hitch on to the Fargo's, and turn up at Jerusalem. And then there are to be the Ledwiths, and their 'little slice.'"

"O, dear! what a mess people do make of living!" said Asenath.

Uncle Titus trudged along down Dorset Street with his stick under his arm.

"Try 'em! Find 'em out!" he repeated to himself. "That's what Marmaduke said. Try 'em with this,—try 'em with that; a good deal, or a little; having and losing, and wanting. That's what the Lord does with us all; and I begin to see He has a job of it!"

The house was sold, and Agatha and Florence went.

It made home dull for poor Desire, little as she found of real companionship with her elder sisters. But then she was always looking for it, and that was something. Husbands and wives, parents and children, live on upon that, through years of repeated disappointments, and never give up the expectation of that which is somewhere, and which these relations represent to them, through all their frustrated lives.

That is just why. It *is* somewhere.

It turned out a hard winter, in many ways, for Desire Ledwith. She hated gay company, and the quiet little circle that she had become fond of at her Aunt Ripwinkley's was broken somewhat to them all, and more to Desire than, among what had grown to be her chronic discontents, she realized or understood, by the going away for a time of Kenneth Kincaid.

What was curious in the happening, too, he had gone up to "And" to build a church. That had come about through the Marchbankses' knowledge of him, and this, you remember, through their being with the Geoffreys when the Kincaids were first introduced in Summit Street.

The Marchbankses and the Geoffreys were cousins. A good many Boston families are.

Mr. Roger Marchbanks owned a good deal of property in And. The neighborhood wanted a church; and he interested himself actively and liberally in behalf of it, and gave the land,—three lots right out of the middle of Marchbanks Street, that ran down to the river.

Dorris kept her little room, and was neighborly as heretofore; but she was busy with her music, and had little time but her evenings; and now there was nobody to walk home with Desire to Shubarton Place, if she stayed in Aspen Street to tea. She came sometimes, and stayed all night; but that was dreary for Helena, who never remembered to shut the piano or cover up the canary, or give the plants in the bay window their evening sprinkle, after the furnace heat had been drying them all day.

Kenneth Kincaid came down for his Sundays with Dorris, and his work at the Mission; a few times he called in at Uncle Oldways' after tea, when the family was all together; but they saw him very seldom; he gave those Sunday evenings mostly to needed rest, and to quiet talk with Dorris.

Desire might have gone to the Mission this winter, easily

enough, after all. Agatha and Florence and Glossy Megilp were not by to make wondering eyes, or smile significant smiles; but there was something in herself that prevented; she knew that it would be more than half to *get*, and she still thought she had so little to give! Besides, Kenneth Kincaid had never asked her again, and she could not go to him and say she would come.

Desire Ledwith began to have serious question of what life was ever going to be for her. She imagined, as in our early years and our first gray days we are all apt to imagine, that she had found out a good deal that it was *not* going to be.

She was not going to be beautiful, or accomplished, or even, she was afraid, agreeable; she found that such hard work with most people. She was not ever — and that conclusion rested closely upon these foregoing — to be married, and have a nice husband and a pretty house, and go down stairs and make snow-puddings and ginger-snaps of a morning, and have girls staying with her, and pleasant people in to tea; like Asenath Scherman. She couldn't write a book, — that, perhaps, was one of her premature decisions, since nobody knows till they try, and the books are lying all round, in leaves, waiting only to be picked up and put together, — or paint a picture; she couldn't bear parties, and clothes were a fuss, and she didn't care to go to Europe.

She thought she should rather like to be an old maid, if she could begin right off, and have a little cottage out of town somewhere, or some cosy rooms in the city. At least, she supposed that was what she had got to be, and if that were settled, she did not see why it might not be begun young, as well as married life. She could not endure waiting, when a thing was to be done.

"Aunt Frances," she said one day, "I wish I had a place of my own. What is the reason I can't? A girl can go in for Art, and set up a studio; or she can go to Rome, and sculp, and study; she can learn elocution, and read, whether people want to be read to or not; and all that is Progress and Woman's Rights; why can't she set up a *home?*"

"Because, I suppose, a house is not a home; and the beginning of a home is just what she waits for. Meanwhile, if she has a father and a mother, she would not put a slight on *their* home, or fail of her share of the duty in it."

"But nobody would think I failed in my duty if I were going to be married. I'm sure mamma would think I was doing it beautifully. And I never shall be married. Why can't I live something out for myself, and have a place of my own? I have got money enough to pay my rent, and I could do sewing in a genteel way, or keep a school for little children. I'd rather — take in back stairs to wash," she exclaimed vehemently, "than wait round for things, and be nothing! And I should like to begin young, while there might be some sort of fun in it. You'd like to come and take tea with me, wouldn't you, Aunt Frank?"

"If it were all right that you should have separate teas of your own."

"And if I had waffles. Well, I should. I think, just now, there's nothing I should like so much as a little kitchen of my own, and a pie-board, and a biscuit-cutter, and a beautiful baking oven, and a Japan tea-pot."

"The pretty part. But brooms, and pails, and wash-tubs, and the back stairs?"

"I specified back stairs in the first place, of my own accord. I wouldn't shirk. Sometimes I think that real good old-fashioned hard work is what I do want. I should like to find the right, honest thing, and do it, Aunt Frank."

She said it earnestly, and there were tears in her eyes.

"I believe you would," said Mrs. Ripwinkley. "But perhaps the right, honest thing, just now, is to wait patiently, with all your might."

"Now, that's good," said Desire, "and cute of you, too, that last piece of a sentence. If you had stopped at '*patiently*,' as people generally do! That's what exasperates; when you want to do something with all your might. It almost seems as if I could, when you put it so."

"It is a 'stump,' Luclarion would say."

"Luclarion is a saint and a philosopher. I feel better," said Desire.

She stayed feeling better all that afternoon; she helped Sulie Praile cut out little panels from her thick sheet of gray painting-board, and contrived her a small easel with her round lightstand and a book-rest; for Sulie was advancing in the fine arts, from painting dollies' paper faces in cheap water colors, to copying bits of flowers and fern and moss, with oils, on gray board; and she was doing it very well, and with exquisite delight.

To wait, meant something to wait for; something coming by and by; that was what comforted Desire to-day, as she walked home alone in the sharp, short, winter twilight; that, and the being patient with all one's might. To be patient, is to be also strong; this she saw, newly; and Desire coveted, most of all, to be strong.

Something to wait for. "He does not cheat," said Desire, low down in her heart, to herself. For the child had faith, though she could not talk about it.

Something; but very likely not the thing you have

seen, or dreamed of; something quite different, it may be, when it comes; and it may come by the way of losing, first, all that you have been able yet, with a vague, whispering hope, to imagine.

The things we do not know! The things that are happening, — the things that are coming; rising up in the eastward of our lives below the horizon that we can yet see; it may be a star, it may be a cloud!

Desire Ledwith could not see that out at Westover, this cheery winter night, it was one of dear Miss Pennington's "Next Thursdays;" she could not see that the young architect, living away over there in the hundred-year-old house on the side of East Hill, a boarder with old Miss Arabel Waite, had been found, and appreciated, and drawn into their circle by the Haddens and the Penningtons and the Holabirds and the Inglesides; and that Rosamond was showing him the pleasant things in their Westover life, — her "swan's nest among the reeds," that she had told him of, — that early autumn evening, when they had walked up Hanley Street together.

XVI.

SWARMING.

SPRING came on early, with heavy rains and freshets in many parts of the country.

It was a busy time at Z——.

Two things had happened there that were to give Kenneth Kincaid more work, and would keep him where he was all summer.

Just before he went to Z——, there had been a great fire at West Hill. All Mr. Roger Marchbanks's beautiful place was desolate. House, conservatories, stables, lovely little vine-covered rustic buildings, exquisitely tended shrubbery, — all swept over in one night by the red flames, and left lying in blackness and ashes.

For the winter, Mr. Marchbanks had taken his family to Boston; now he was planning eagerly to rebuild. Kenneth had made sketches; Mr. Marchbanks liked his ideas; they had talked together from time to time. Now, the work was actually in hand, and Kenneth was busy with drawings and specifications.

Down at the river, during the spring floods, a piece of the bridge had been carried away, and the dam was broken through. There were new mill buildings, too, going up, and a block of factory houses. All this business, through Mr. Marchbanks directly or indirectly, fell also into Kenneth's hands.

He wrote blithe letters to Dorris; and Dorris, running in and out from her little spring cleanings that Hazel was helping her with, told all the letters over to the Ripwinkleys.

"He says I must come up there in my summer vacation and board with his dear old Miss Waite. Think of Kentie's being able to give me such a treat as that! A lane, with ferns and birches, and the woods, — *pine* woods!—and a hill where raspberries grow, and the river!"

Mrs. Ledwith was thinking of her summer plans at this time, also. She remembered the large four-windowed room looking out over the meadow, that Mrs. Megilp and Glossy had at Mrs. Prendible's, for twelve dollars a week, in And. She could do no better than that, at country boarding, anywhere; and Mr. Ledwith could sleep at the house in Shubarton Place, getting his meals down town during the week, and come up and spend his Sundays with them. A bedroom, in addition, for six dollars more, would be all they would want.

The Ripwinkleys were going up to Homesworth by and by for a little while, and would take Sulie Praile with them. Sulie was ecstatically happy. She had never been out of the city in all her life. She felt, she said, "as if she was going to heaven without dying." Vash was to be left at Mrs. Scarup's with her sister.

Miss Craydocke would be away at the mountains; all the little life that had gathered together in the Aspen Street neighborhood, seemed about to be broken up.

Uncle Titus Oldways never went out of town, unless on business. Rachel Froke stayed, and kept his house; she sat in the gray room, and thought over the summers she had had.

"Thee never loses anything out of thy life that has been in," she said. "Summer times are like grains of musk; they keep their smell always, and flavor the shut-up places they are put away in."

For you and me, reader, we are to go to Z—— again. I hope you like it.

But before that, I must tell you what Luclarion Grapp has done.

Partly from the principle of her life, and partly from the spirit of things which she would have caught at any rate, from the Ripwinkley home and the Craydocke "Beehive," — for there is nothing truer than that the kingdom of heaven is like leaven, — I suppose she had been secretly thinking for a good while, that she was having too easy a time here, in her first floor kitchen and her garden bedroom; that this was not the life meant for her to live right on, without scruple or question; and so began in her own mind to expect some sort of "stump;" and even to look about for it.

"It isn't as it was when Mrs. Ripwinkley was a widow, and poor, — that is, comparative; and it took all her and my contrivance to look after the place and keep things going, and paying, up in Homesworth; there was something to buckle to, then; but now, everything is eased and flatted out, as it were; it makes me res'less, like a child put to bed in the daytime."

Luclarion went down to the North End with Miss Craydocke, on errands of mercy; she went in to the new Mission, and saw the heavenly beauty of its intent, and kindled up in her soul at it; and she came home, time after time, and had thoughts of her own about these things, and the work in the world there was to do.

She had cleaned up and set things going at Mrs. Scarup's; she learned something in doing that, beyond what she knew when she set about it; her thoughts began to shape themselves to a theory; and the theory took to itself a text and a confirmation and a command.

"Go down and be a neighbor to them that have fallen among thieves."

Luclarion came to a resolution in this time of May, when everybody was making plans and the spring-cleaning was all done.

She came to Mrs. Ripwinkley one morning, when she was folding away winter clothes, and pinning them up in newspapers, with camphor-gum; and she said to her, without a bit of preface, — Luclarion hated prefaces, —

"Mrs. Ripwinkley, I'm going to swarm!"

Mrs. Ripwinkley looked up in utter surprise; what else could she do?

"Of course 'm, when you set up a Beehive, you must have expected it; it's the natural way of things; they ain't good for much unless they do. I've thought it all over; I'll stay and see you all off, first, if you want me to, and then — I'll swarm."

"Well," said Mrs. Ripwinkley, assenting in full faith, beforehand; for Mrs. Ripwinkley, if I need now to tell you of it, was not an ordinary woman, and did not take things in an ordinary selfish way, but grasped right hold of the inward right and truth of them, and believed in it; sometimes before she could quite see it; and she never had any doubt of Luclarion Grapp. "Well! And now tell me all about it."

"You see," said Luclarion, sitting down in a chair by the window, as Mrs. Ripwinkley suspended her occupation and took one by the bedside, "there's places in this town that folks leave and give up. As the Lord might have left and give up the world, because there was dirt and wickedness in it; only He didn't. There's places where it ain't genteel, nor yet respectable, to live; and so those places grow more disrespectable and miserable every day. They're left to themselves. What I think is, they hadn't ought to be. There's one clean spot down there,

"MRS. RIPWINKLEY, I'M GOING TO SWARM!" See p. 198.

now, in the very middle of the worst dirt. And it ain't bad to live in. *That's* started. Now, what I think is, that somebody ought to start another, even if its only a little one. Somebody ought to just go there and *live*, and show 'em how, just as I took and showed Mrs. Scarup, and she's been living ever since, instead of scratching along. If some of them folks had a clean, decent neighbor to go to see, — to drink tea with, say, — and was to catch an idea of her fixings and doings, why, I believe there'd be more of 'em, — cleaned up, you know. They'd get some kind of an ambition and a hope. Tain't enough for ladies — though I bless 'em in my soul for what I've seen 'em do — to come down there of a Fridays, and teach and talk awhile, and then go home to Summit Street and Republic Avenue, and take up *their* life again where they left it off, that is just as different as heaven is from 'tother place; somebody's got to come right down *out* of heaven, and bring the life in, and live it amongst them miserable folks, as the Lord Jesus Christ came and did! And it's borne in upon me, strong and clear, that that's what's got to be before all's righted. And so — for a little piece of it, and a little individual stump — I'm going to swarm, and settle, and see what'll come."

Mrs. Ripwinkley was looking very intently at Luclarion. Her breath went and came hurriedly, and her face turned pale with the grand surprise of such a thought, such a plan and purpose, so simply and suddenly declared. Her eyes were large and moist with feeling.

"Do you *know*, Luclarion," she exclaimed at last, "do you realize what this is that you are thinking of; what a step it would be to take, — what a work it would be to even hope to begin to do? Do you know how strange it is, — how almost impracticable, — that it is not even safe?"

"'Twasn't *safe* for Him — when He came into the world," Luclarion answered.

"Not to say I think there's any comparison," she began again, presently, "or that I believe there's anything to be really scared of, — except dirt; and you *can* clean a place round you, as them Mission people have done. Why, there ain't a house in Boston nicer, or sweeter, or airier even, than that one down in Arctic Street, with beautiful parlors and bedrooms, and great clean galleries leading round, and skylighted, — *sky* lighted! for you see the blue heaven is above all, and you *can* let the skylight in, without any corruption coming in with it; and if twenty people can do that much, or a hundred, — one can do something. 'Taint much, either, to undertake; only to be willing to go there, and make a clean place for yourself, and a home; and live there, instead of somewheres else that's ready made; and let it spread. And you know I've always looked forrud to some kind of a house-keep of my own, finally."

"But, Luclarion, I don't understand! All alone? And you couldn't use a whole house, you know. Your neighbors would be *inmates*. Why, it seems to me perfectly crazy!"

"Now, ma'am, did you ever know me to go off on a tangent, without some sort of a string to hold on to? I ain't goin' to swarm all alone! I never heard of such a thing. Though if I couldn't *swarm*, and the thing was to be done, I say I'd try it. But Savira Golding is going to be married to Sam Gallilee, next month; and he's a stevedore, and his work is down round the wharves; he's class-leader in our church, and a first-rate, right-minded man, or else Savira wouldn't have him; for if Savira ain't a clear Christian, and a doing woman, there ain't one this side of

Paradise. Now, you see, Sam Gallilee makes money; he runs a gang of three hundred men. He can afford a good house, and a whole one, if he wants; but he's going in for a big one, and neighbors. They mean to live nice, — he and Savira; and she has pretty, tasty ways; there'll be white curtains, and plants blooming in her windows, you may make sure; she's always had 'em in that little up-stairs dress-making room of hers; and boxes of mignonette and petunias on the ledges; and birds singing in a great summer cage swung out against the wall. She's one of the kind that reaches out, and can't be kept in; and she knows her gifts, and is willing to go and let her light shine where it will help others, and so glorify; and Sam, he's willing too, and sees the beauty of it. And so, — well, that's the swarm."

"And the 'little round Godamighty in the middle of it,'" said Mrs. Ripwinkley, her face all bright and her eyes full of tears.

"*Ma'am!*"

Then Mrs. Ripwinkley told her Miss Craydocke's story.

"Well," said Luclarion, "there's something dear and right-to-the-spot about it; but it does sound singular; and it certainly ain't a thing to say careless."

Desire Ledwith grew bright and excited as the summer came on, and the time drew near for going to Z——. She could not help being glad; she did not stop to ask why; summer-time was reason enough, and after the weariness of the winter, the thought of Z—— and the woods and the river, and sweet evenings and mornings, and gardens and orchards, and road-side grass, was lovely to her.

"It is *so* pleasant up there!" she would keep saying to Dorris; and somehow she said it to Dorris oftener than to anybody else.

There was something fitful and impetuous in her little outbursts of satisfaction; they noticed it in her; the elder ones among them noticed it with a touch of anxiety for her.

Miss Craydocke, especially, read the signs, matching them with something that she remembered far back in the life that had closed so peacefully, with white hairs and years of a serene content and patience, over all unrest and disappointment, for herself. She was sorry for this young girl, for whom she thought she saw an unfulfilled dream of living that should go by her like some bright cloud, just near enough to turn into a baptism of tears.

She asked Desire, one day, if she would not like to go with her, this summer, to the mountains.

Desire put by the suggestion hastily.

"O, no, thank you, Miss Craydocke, I must stay with mamma and Helena. And besides," she added, with the strict, full truth she always demanded of herself, "I *want* to go to Z——."

"Yes," said Miss Craydocke.

There was something tender, like a shade of pity, in her tone.

"But you would enjoy the mountains. They are full of strength and rest. One hardly understands the good the hills do one. David did, looking out into them from Jerusalem. 'I will look to the hills, from whence cometh my strength.'"

"Some time," said Desire. "Some time I shall need the hills, and — be ready for them. But this summer — I want a good, gay, young time. I don't know why, except that I shall be just eighteen this year, and it seems as if, after that, I was going to be old. And I want to be with people I know. I *can* be gay in the country; there is something to be gay about. But I can't dress and dance in the city. That is all gas-light and get-up."

"I suppose," said Miss Craydocke, slowly, "that our faces are all set in the way we are to go. Even if it is—" She stopped. She was thinking of one whose face had been set to go to Jerusalem. Her own words had led her to something she had not foreseen when she began.

Nothing of such suggestion came to Desire. She was in one of her rare moods of good cheer.

"I suppose so," she said, heedlessly. And then, taking up a thought of her own suddenly, — "Miss Craydocke! Don't you think people almost always live out their names? There's Sin Scherman; there'll always be a little bit of mischief and original naughtiness in her, — with the harm taken out of it; and there's Rosamond Holabird, — they couldn't have called her anything better, if they'd waited for her to grow up; and Barb *was* sharp; and our little Hazel is witchy and sweet and wild-woodsy; and Luclarion, — isn't that shiny and trumpety, and doesn't she do it? And then — there's me. I shall always be stiff and hard and unsatisfied, except in little bits of summer times that won't come often. They might as well have christened me Anxiety. I wonder why they didn't."

"That would have been very different. There is a nobleness in Desire. You will overlive the restless part," said Miss Craydocke.

"Was there ever anything restless in your life, Miss Craydocke? And how long did it take to overlive it? It doesn't seem as if you had ever stubbed your foot against anything; and I'm *always* stubbing."

"My dear, I have stubbed along through fifty-six years; and the years had all three hundred and sixty-five days in them. There were chances, — don't you think so?"

"It looks easy to be old after it is done," said Desire. "Easy and comfortable. But to be eighteen, and to think of having to go on to be fifty-six; I beg your pardon, — but I wish it was over!"

And she drew a deep breath, heavy with the days that were to be.

"You are not to take it all at once, you know," said Miss Craydocke.

"But I do, every now and then. I can't help it. I am sure it is the name. If they had called me 'Hapsie,' like you, I should have gone along jolly, as you do, and not minded. You see you have to *hear* it all the time; and it tunes you up to its own key. You can't feel like a Dolly, or a Daisy, when everybody says — De-sire!"

"I don't know how I came to be called 'Hapsie,'" said Miss Craydocke. "Somebody who liked me took it up, and it seemed to get fitted on. But that wasn't when I was young."

"What was it, then?" asked Desire, with a movement of interest.

"Keren-happuch," said Miss Craydocke, meekly. "My father named me, and he always called me so, — the whole of it. He was a severe, Old-Testament man, and *his* name was Job."

Desire was more than half right, after all. There was a good deal of Miss Craydocke's story hinted in those few words and those two ancient names.

"But I turned into 'Miss Craydocke' pretty soon, and settled down. I suppose it was very natural that I should," said the sweet old maid, serenely.

XVII.

QUESTIONS AND ANSWERS.

THE evening train came in through the little bend in the edge of the woods, and across the bridge over the pretty rapids, and slid to its stopping-place under the high arches of the other bridge that connected the main street of Z—— with its continuation through "And."

There were lights twinkling in the shops, where they were making change, and weighing out tea and sugar, and measuring calico, although outside it was not yet quite dark.

The train was half an hour late; there had been a stoppage at some draw or crossing near the city.

Mr. Prendible was there, to see if his lodgers were come, and to get his evening paper; the platform was full of people. Old Z—— acquaintances, many of them, whom Desire and her mother were pleased, and Helena excited to see.

"There's Kenneth Kincaid!" she exclaimed, quite loudly, pulling Desire's sleeve.

"Hush!" said Desire, twitching away. "How can you, Helena?"

"He's coming, — he heard me!" cried Helena, utterly impenitent.

"I should think he might!" And Desire walked off a little, to look among the trunks that were being tumbled from the baggage car.

She had seen him all the time; he had been speaking to Ruth Holabird, and helping her up the steps with her parcels. Mr. Holabird was there with the little Westover carryall that they kept now; and Kenneth put her in, and then turned round in time to hear Helena's exclamation and to come down again.

"Can I help you? I'm very glad you are come," he said, cordially.

Well; he might have said it to anybody. Again, well; it was enough to say to anybody. Why should Desire feel cross?

He took Helena's bag; she had a budget beside; Mr. Prendible relieved Mrs. Ledwith; Desire held on valiantly to her own things. Kenneth walked over the bridge with them, and down the street to Mr. Prendible's door; there he bade them good-by and left them.

It was nice to be in Z——; it was very sweet here under the blossoming elms and locusts; it was nice to see Kenneth Kincaid again, and to think that Dorris was coming by and by, and that the lanes were green and full of ferns and vines, and that there was to be a whole long summer; but there were so many people down there on the platform, — there was such a muss always; Ruth Holabird was a dear little thing, but there were always so many Ruths about! and there was only one cross, stiff, odd, uncomfortable Desire!

But the very next night Kenneth came down and stayed an hour; there was a new moon glistening through the delicate elm-tips, and they sat out on the piazza and breathed in such an air as they had not had in their nostrils for months and months.

The faint, tender light from the golden west in which the new moon lay, showed the roof and tower of the little church, Kenneth's first beautiful work; and Kenneth told them how pleasant it was up at Miss Arabel's, and of the tame squirrels that he fed at his window, and of the shady pasture-path that led away over the brook from the very door, and up among pines and into little still nooks where dry mossy turf and warm gray rocks were sheltered in by scraggy cedars and lisping birches, so that they were like field-parlors opening in and out from each other with all sorts of little winding and climbing passages, between clumps of bayberry bushes and tall ferns; and that the girls from Z—— and Westover made morning picnics there, since Lucilla Waters had grown intimate with Delia Waite and found it out; and that Delia Waite and even Miss Arabel carried their dressmaking down there sometimes in a big white basket, and stayed all day under the trees. They had never used to do this; they had stayed in the old back sitting room with all the litter round, and never thought of it till those girls had come and showed them how.

"I think there is the best and sweetest neighborliness and most beautiful living here in Z——, that I ever knew in any place," said Kenneth Kincaid; "except that little piece of the same thing in Aspen Street."

Kenneth had found out how Rosamond Holabird recognized Aspen Street as a piece of her world.

Desire hated, as he spoke, her spitefulness last night; what she had said to herself of "so many Ruths;" why could not she not be pleased to come into this beautiful living and make a little part of it?

She was pleased; she would be; she found it very easy when Kenneth said to her in that frank intimate way,—"I wish you and your mother would come over and see what Dorris will want, and help me a little about that room of hers. I told Miss Waite not to bother; just to let the old things stand,—I knew Dorris would like them,—and anything else I would get for her myself. I mean Dolly shall take a long vacation this year; from June right through to September; and its 'no end of jolly,' as those English fellows say, that you have come too!"

Kenneth Kincaid was fresher and pleasanter and younger himself, than Desire had ever seen him before; he seemed to have forgotten that hard way of looking at the world; he had found something so undeniably good in it. I am afraid Desire had rather liked him for his carping, which was what he least of all deserved to be liked for. It showed how high and pure his demands were; but his praise and admissions were better; it is always better to discern good than to fret at the evil.

"I shall see you every day," he said, when he shook hands at parting; "and Helena, if you want a squirrel to keep in your pocket next winter, I'll begin training one for you at once."

He had taken them right to himself, as if they belonged to him; he spoke as if he were very glad that he should see them every day.

Desire whistled over her unpacking; she could not sing, but she could whistle like a blackbird. When her father came up on Saturday night, he said that her eyes were brighter and her cheeks were rounder, for the country air; she would take to growing pretty instead of strong-minded, if she didn't look out.

Kenneth came round on Monday, after tea, to ask them to go over to Miss Waite's and make acquaintance.

"For you see," he said, "you will have to be very intimate there, and it is time to begin. It will take one call to be introduced, and another, at least, to get up-stairs and see that beautiful breezy old room that can't be lived in in winter, but is to be a delicious sort of camping-out for Dolly, all summer. It is all windows and squirrel-holes and doors that wont shut. Everything comes in but the rain; but the roof is tight on that corner. Even the woodbine has got tossed in through a broken upper pane, and I wouldn't have it mended on any account. There are swallows' nests in the chimneys, and wrens under the gable, and humming-birds in the honeysuckle. When Dolly gets there, it will be perfect. It just wants her to take it all right into her heart and make one piece of it. *They* don't know, — the birds and the squirrels, — it takes the human. There has to be an Adam in every garden of Eden."

Kenneth really chattered, from pure content and delight.

It did not take two visits to get up-stairs. Miss Arabel met them heartily. She had been a shy, timid old lady, from long neglect and humble living; but lately she had "come out in society," Delia said. Society had come after her, and convinced her that she could make good times for it.

She brought out currant wine and gave them, the first thing; and when Kenneth told her that they were his and Dorris's friends, and were coming next week to see about getting ready for her, she took them right round through all four of the ground rooms, to the queer corner staircase, and up into the "long west chamber," to show them what a rackety old place it was, and to see whether they supposed it could be made fit.

"Why it's like the Romance of the Forest!" said Helena, delighted. "I wish *we* had come here. Don't you have ghosts, or robbers, or something, up and down those stairs, Miss Waite?" For she had spied a door that led directly out of the room, from beside the chimney, up into the rambling old garret, smelling of pine boards and penny-royal.

"No; nothing but squirrels and bees, and sometimes a bat," answered Miss Arabel.

"Well, it doesn't want fixing. If you fix it, you will spoil it. I shall come here and sleep with Dorris, — see if I don't."

The floor was bare, painted a dark, marbled gray. In the middle was a great braided rug, of blue and scarlet and black. The walls were pale gray, with a queer, stencilled scroll-and-dash border of vermilion and black paint.

There was an old, high bedstead, with carved frame and posts, bare of drapery; an antiquated chest of drawers; and a half-circular table with tall, plain, narrow legs, between two of the windows. There was a corner cupboard, and a cupboard over the chimney. The doors of these, and the high wainscot around the room, were stained in old-fashioned "imitation mahogany," very streaky and red. The wainscot was so heavily finished that the edge running around the room might answer for a shelf.

"Just curtains, and toilet covers, and a little low rocking chair," said Mrs. Ledwith. "That is all you want."

"But the windows are so high," suggested Desire. "A low chair would bury her up, away from all the pleasantness. I'll tell you what I would have, Mr. Kincaid. A kind of dais, right across that corner, to take in two windows; with a carpet on it, and a chair, and a little table."

"Just the thing!" said Kenneth. "That is what I wanted you for, Miss Desire," he said in a pleased, gentle way, lowering his tone to her especial hearing, as he stood beside her in the window.

And Desire was very happy to have thought of it.

Helena was spurred by emulation to suggest something.

"I'd have a — hammock — somewhere," she said.

"Good," said Kenneth. "That shall be out under the great butternut."

The great butternut walled in one of the windows with a wilderness of green, and the squirrels ran chattering up and down the brown branches, and peeping in all day. In the autumn, when the nuts were ripe, they would be scrambling over the roof, and in under the eaves, to hide their stores in the garret, Miss Arabel told them.

"Why doesn't everbody have an old house, and let the squirrels in?" cried Helena, in a rapture.

In ten days more, — the first week of June, — Dorris came.

Well, — "That let in all the rest," Helena said, and Desire, may be, thought. "We shan't have it to ourselves any more."

The girls could all come down and call on Dorris Kincaid, and they did.

But Desire and Helena had the first of it; nobody else went right up into her room; nobody else helped her unpack and settle. And she was so delighted with all that they had done for her.

The dais was large enough for two or three to sit upon at once, and it was covered with green carpet of a small, mossy pattern, and the window was open into the butternut on one side, and into the honeysuckle on the other, and it was really a bower.

"I shall live ten hours in one," said Dorris.

"And you'll let me come and sleep with you some night, and hear the bats," said Helena.

The Ledwiths made a good link; they had known the Kincaids so well; if it had been only Dorris, alone, with her brother there, the Westover girls might have been shy of coming often. Since Kenneth had been at Miss Waite's, they had already grown a little less free of the beautiful woods that they had just found out and begun fairly to enjoy last autumn.

But the Ledwiths made a strong party; and they lived close by; there were plans continually.

Since Leslie Goldthwaite and Barbara Holabird were married and gone, and the Roger Marchbankses were burned out, and had been living in the city and travelling, the Hobarts and the Haddens and Ruth and Rosamond and Pen Pennington had kept less to their immediate Westover neighborhood than ever; and had come down to Lucilla's, and to Maddy Freeman's, and the Inglesides, as often as they had induced them to go up to the Hill.

Maud Marchbanks and the Hendees were civil and neighborly enough at home, but they did not care to "ramify." So it came to pass that they were left a good deal to themselves. Olivia and Adelaide, when they came up to Westover, to their uncle's, wondered "that papa cared to build again; there really wasn't anything to come for; West Hill was entirely changed."

So it was; and a very good thing.

I came across the other day, reading over Mr. Kingsley's "Two Years Ago," a true word as to social needs in England, that reminded me of this that the Holabirds and the Penningtons and the Inglesides have been doing, half unconsciously, led on from "next" to next, in Z——.

Mr. Kingsley, after describing a Miss Heale, and others of her class, — the middle class, with no high social opportunities, and with time upon their hands, wasted often in false dreams of life and unsatisfied expectations, "bewildering heart and brain with novels," for want of a nobler companionship, says this: "Till in country villages, the ladies who interest themselves about the poor will recollect that the farmers' and tradesmens' daughters are just as much in want of their influence as the charity children, and will yield a far richer return for their labor, so long will England be full of Miss Heales."

If a kindly influence and fellowship are the duty of the aristocratic girls of England toward their "next," below, how far more false are American girls to the spirit of their country, and the blessed opportunities of republican sympathies and equalities, when they try to draw invisible lines between themselves and those whose outer station differs by but so little, and whose hearts and minds, under the like culture with their own, crave, just as they do, the best that human intercourse can give. Social science has something to do, before — or at least simultaneously with — reaching down to the depths where all the wrongs and blunders and mismanagements of life have precipitated their foul residuum. A master of one of our public schools, speaking of the undue culture of the brain and imagination, in proportion to the opportunities offered socially for living out ideas thus crudely gathered, said that his brightest girls were the ones who in after years, impatient of the little life gave them to satisfy the capacities and demands aroused and developed during the brief period of school life, and fed afterwards by their own ill-judged and ill-regulated reading, were found fallen into lives of vice. Have our women, old or young, who make and circumscribe the opportunities of social intercourse and enjoyment, nothing to search out here, and help, as well, or as soon as, to get their names put on committee lists, and manage these public schools themselves, which educate and stimulate up to the point of possible fierce temptation, and then have nothing more that they can do?

It was a good thing for Desire Ledwith to grow intimate, as she did, with Rosamond Holabird. There were identical points of character between the two. They were both so real.

"You don't want to *play* anything," Barbara Holabird had said to Rosamond once, in some little discussion of social appearances and pretensions. "And that's the beauty of you!"

It was the beauty of Desire Ledwith also; only, with Rosamond, her ambitions had clothed themselves with a grace and delicateness that would have their own perfect and thorough as far as it went; and with Desire, the same demands of true living had chafed into an impatience with shams and a blunt disregard of and resistance to all conventionalisms.

"You are a good deal alike, you two," Kenneth Kincaid said to them one day, in a talk they all three happened to have together.

And he had told Rosamond afterward that there was "something grand in Desire Ledwith; only grand things almost always have to grow with struggles."

Rosamond had told this again to Desire.

It was not much wonder that she began to be happier; to have a hidden comfort of feeling that perhaps the "waiting with all her might" was nearly over, and the "by and by" was blossoming for her, though the green leaves of her own shy sternness with herself folded close down about the sweetening place, and she never parted them aside to see where the fragrance came from.

They were going to have a grand, large, beautiful supper party in the woods.

Mrs. Holabird and Mrs. Hobart were the matrons, and gave out the invitations.

"I don't think I could possibly spend a Tuesday afternoon with a little 't,'" said Mrs. Lewis Marchbanks, laughing, and tossing down poor, dear, good Mrs. Hobart's note upon her table. "It is *rather* more than is to be expected!"

"Doctor and Mrs. Hautayne are here, and Dakie Thayne is home from West Point. It will be rather a nice party."

"The Holabirds seem to have got everything into their own hands," said Mrs. Marchbanks, haughtily. "It is always a pity when people take the lead who are not exactly qualified. Mrs. Holabird *will* not discriminate!"

"I think the Holabirds are splendid," spoke up Lily, "and I don't think there's any fun in sticking up by ourselves! I can't bear to be judicious!"

Poor little Lily Marchbanks had been told a tiresome many times that she must be "judicious" in her intimacies.

"You can be *pleasant* to everybody," said mother and elder sister, with a salvo of Christian benignity.

But it is so hard for little children to be pleasant with fence and limitation.

"Where must I stop?" Lily had asked in her simplicity. "When they give me a piece of their luncheon, or when they walk home from school, or when they say they will come in a little while?"

But there came a message back from Boston by the eleven o'clock train on the morning of the Tuesday with a little "t," from Mr. Marchbanks himself, to say that his brother and Mr. Geoffrey would come up with him to dinner, and to desire that carriages might be ready afterward for the drive over to Waite's grove.

Mrs. Marchbanks marveled, but gave her orders. Arthur came out early, and brought with him his friend Archie Mucklegrand; and these two were bound also for the merry-making.

Now Archie Mucklegrand was the identical youth of the lavender pantaloons and the waxed moustache, whom Desire, as "Miss Ledwith," had received in state a year and a half ago.

So it was an imposing cavalcade, after all, from West Hill, that honored the very indiscriminate pleasure party, and came riding and driving in at about six o'clock. There were the barouche and the coupé for the ladies and elder gentlemen, and the two young men accompanied them on horseback.

Archie Mucklegrand had been at West Hill often before. He and Arthur had just graduated at Harvard, and the Holabirds had had cards to their grand spread on Class Day. Archie Mucklegrand had found out what a pretty girl — and a good deal more than merely pretty — Rosamond Holabird was; and although he might any day go over to his big, wild Highland estate, and take upon himself the glory of "Sir Archibald" there among the hills and moors, — and though any one of a good many pretty girls in Spreadsplendid Park and Republic Avenue might be induced, perhaps, if he tried, to go with him, — all this did not hinder him from perceiving that up here in Z—— was just the most bewitching companionship he had ever fallen in with, or might ever be able to choose for himself for any going or abiding; that Rosamond Holabird was just the brightest, and sweetest, and most to his mind of any girl that he had ever seen, and most like "the woman" that a man might dream of. I do not know that he quite said it all to himself in precisely that way; I am pretty sure that he did not, as yet; but whatever is offhand and young-mannish and modern enough to express to one's self without "sposhiness" an admiration and a preference like that, he undoubtedly did say. At any rate, after his Christmas at Z—— with Arthur, and some charade parties they had then at Westover, and after Class Day, when everybody had been furious to get an introduction, and all the Spreadsplendid girls and their mothers had been wondering who that Miss Holabird was and where she came from, and Madam Mucklegrand herself — not having the slightest recollection of her as the Miss Holabird of that early-morning business call, whose name she had just glanced at and dropped into an Indian china scrap-jar before she went down-stairs — had asked him the same questions, and pronounced that she was "an exceedingly graceful little person, certainly," — after all this, Archie had made up his — mind, shall I say? at least his inclination, and his moustache — to pursue the acquaintance, and be as irresistible as he could.

But Rosamond had learned — things do so play into our lives in a benign order — just before that Christmas time and those charades, in one of which Archie Mucklegrand had sung to her, so expressively, the "Birks of Aberfeldy," — that Spreadsplendid Park was not, at least his corner of it, — a "piece of her world;" and she did not believe that Aberfeldy would be, either, though Archie's voice was beautiful, and —

"Bonnie lassie, will ye go?"

sounded very enticing — in a charade.

So she was quite calm when the Marchbanks party came upon the ground, and Archie Mucklegrand, with white trousers and a lavender tie, and the trim, waxed moustache, looking very handsome in spite of his dapperness, found her out in the first two minutes, and attached himself to her forthwith in a most undetachable and determined manner, which was his way of being irresistible.

They were in the midst of their tea and coffee when

the West Hill party came. Miss Arabel was busy at the coffee-table between the two oaks, pouring out with all her might, and creaming the fragrant cups with a rich lavishness that seemed to speak of milky mothers without number or limit of supply; and Rosamond, as the most natural and hospitable thing to do, conducted the young gentleman as soon as she could to that lady, and commended him to her good offices.

These were not to be resisted; and as soon as he was occupied, Rosamond turned to attend to others coming up; and the groups shifting, she found herself presently a little way off, and meanwhile Mrs. Marchbanks and her son had reached the table and joined Archie.

"I say, Arthur! O, Mrs. Marchbanks! You never got such coffee as this, I do believe! The open air has done something to it, or else the cream comes from some supernal cows! Miss Holabird!"

Rosamond turned round.

"I don't see, — Mrs. Marchbanks ought to have some of this coffee, but where is your good woman gone?" For Miss Arabel had stepped round behind the oak-tree for a moment, to see about some replenishing.

In her prim, plain dress, utterly innocent of style or *bias*, and her zealous ministry, good Miss Arabel might easily be taken for some comfortable, superior old servant; but partly from a sudden sense of fun, — Mrs. Marchbanks standing there in all her elegant dignity, — and partly from a jealous chivalry of friendship, Rosamond would not let it pass so.

"Good woman? Hush! she is one of our hostesses; the owner of the ground, and a dear friend of mine. Here she is. Miss Waite, let me introduce Mr. Archibald Mucklegrand. Mrs. Marchbanks will like some coffee, please."

Which Mrs. Marchbanks took with a certain look of amazement, that showed itself subtilely in a slight straightening of the lips and an expansion of the nostrils. She did not *sniff*; she was a great deal too much a lady; she was Mrs. Marchbanks, but if she had been Mrs. Higgin, and had felt just so, she would have sniffed.

Somebody came up close to Rosamond on the other side.

"That was good," said Kenneth Kincaid. "Thank you for that, Miss Rosamond."

"Will you have some more?" asked Rosamond, cunningly, pretending to misunderstand, and reaching her hand to take his empty cup.

"One mustn't ask for all one would like," said Kenneth, relinquishing the cup, and looking straight in her eyes.

Rosamond's eyes fell; she had no rejoinder ready; it was very well that she had the cup to take care of, and could turn away, for she felt a very foolish color coming up in her face.

She made herself very busy among the guests. Archie Mucklegrand stayed by, and spoke to her every time he found a chance. At last, when people had nearly done eating and drinking, he asked her if she would not show him the path down to the river.

"It must be beautiful down there under the slope," he said.

She called Dorris and Desire, then, and Oswald Megilp, who was with them. He was spending a little time here at the Prendibles, with his boat on the river, as he had used to do. When he could take an absolute vacation, he was going away with a pedestrian party, among the mountains. There was not much in poor Oswald Megilp, but Desire and Rosamond were kind to him now that his mother was away.

As they all walked down the bank among the close evergreens, they met Mr. Geoffrey and Mr. Marchbanks, with Kenneth Kincaid, coming up. Kenneth came last, and the two parties passed each other single file, in the narrow pathway.

Kenneth paused as he came close to Rosamond, holding back a bough for her.

"I have something very nice to tell you," he whispered, "by and by. But it is a secret, as yet. Please don't stay down there very long."

Nobody heard the whisper but Rosamond; if they could have done so, he would not have whispered. Archie Mucklegrand was walking rather sulkily along before; he had not cared for a party to be made up when he asked Rosamond to go down to the river with him. Desire and Dorris had found some strange blossom among the underbrush, and were stopping for it; and Oswald Megilp was behind them. For a few seconds, Kenneth had Rosamond quite to himself.

The slight delay had increased the separation between her and Archie Mucklegrand, for he had kept steadily on in his little huff.

"I do not think we shall be long," said Rosamond, glancing after him, and looking up, with her eyes bright. She was half merry with mischief, and half glad with a quieter, deeper pleasure, at Kenneth's words.

He would tell her something in confidence; something that he was glad of; he wanted her to know it while it was yet a secret; she had not the least guess what it could be; but it was very "nice" already. Rosamond always did rather like to be told things first; to have her friends confide in and consult with her, and rely upon her sympathy; she did not stop to separate the old feeling which she was quite aware of in herself, from something new that made it especially beautiful that Kenneth Kincaid should so confide and rely.

Rosamond was likely to have more told her to-night than she quite dreamed of.

"Desire!"

They heard Mrs. Ledwith's voice far back among the trees.

Desire answered.

"I want you, dear!"

"Something about shawls and baskets, I suppose," said Desire, turning round, perhaps a little the more readily that Kenneth was beside her now, going back also.

Dorris and Oswald Megilp, finding there was a move to return, and being behind Desire in the pathway, turned also, as people will who have no especial motive for going one way rather than another; and so it happened that after all Rosamond and Archie Mucklegrand walked on down the bank to the river together, by themselves.

Archie's good humor returned quickly.

"I am glad they are gone; it was such a fuss having so many," he said.

"We shall have to go back directly; they are beginning to break up," said Rosamond.

And then, coming out to the opening by the water, she began to talk rather fast about the prettiness of the view, and to point out the bridge, and the mills, and the shadow of East Hill upon the water, and the curve of the opposite shore, and the dip of the shrubs and their arched reflections. She seemed quite determined to have all the talk to herself.

Archie Mucklegrand played with his stick, and twisted the end of his moustache. Men never ought to allow themselves to learn that trick. It always comes back upon them when it makes them look most foolish.

Archie said nothing, because there was so much he wanted to say, and he did not know how to begin.

He knew his mother and sister would not like it, — as long as they could help it, certainly, — therefore he had suddenly made up his mind that there should be no such interval. He could do as he pleased; was he not Sir Archibald? And there was his Boston grandfather's property, too, of which a large share had been left outright to him; and he had been twenty-one these six months. There was nothing to hinder; and he meant to tell Rosamond Holabird that he liked her better than any other girl in the world. Somebody else would be telling her so, if he didn't; he could see how they all came round her; perhaps it might be that tall, quiet, cheeky looking fellow, — that Kincaid. He would be before him, at any rate.

So he stood and twisted his moustache, and said nothing, — nothing, I mean, except mere little words of assent and echo to Rosamond's chatter about the pretty view.

At last, — "You are fond of scenery, Miss Holabird?"

Rosamond laughed.

"O yes, I suppose I am; but we don't call this scenery. It is just pleasantness, — beauty. I don't think I quite like the word 'scenery.' It seems artificial, — got up for outside effect. And the most beautiful things do not speak from the outside, do they? I never travelled, Mr. Mucklegrand. I have just lived here, until I have lived *into* things, or they into me. I rather think it is travelling, skimming about the world in a hurry, that makes people talk about 'scenery.' Isn't it?"

"I dare say. I don't care for skimming, myself. But I like to go to nice places, and stay long enough to get into them, as you say. I mean to go to Scotland next year. I've a place there among the hills and lochs, Miss Rosamond."

"Yes. I have heard so. I should think you would wish to go and see it."

"I'll tell you what I wish, Miss Holabird!" he said suddenly, letting go his moustache, and turning round with sufficient manfulness, and facing her. "I suppose there is a more gradual and elegant way of saying it; but I believe straightforward is as good as any. I wish you cared for me as I care for you, and then you would go with me."

Rosamond was utterly confounded. She had not imagined that it could be hurled at her, this fashion; she thought she could parry and put aside, if she saw anything coming. She was bewildered and breathless with the shock of it; she could only blindly, and in very foolish words, hurl it back.

"O, dear, no!" she exclaimed, her face crimson. "I mean — I don't — I couldn't! I beg your pardon, Mr. Mucklegrand; you are very good; I am very sorry; but I wish you hadn't said so. We had better go back."

"No," said Archie Mucklegrand, "not yet. I've said it now. I said it like a moon calf, but I mean it like a man. Won't you — can't you — be my wife, Rosamond? I must know that."

"No, Mr. Mucklegrand," answered Rosamond, quite steadily now and gently. "I could not be. We were never meant for each other. You will think so yourself next year, — by the time you go to Scotland."

"I shall never think so."

Of course he said that; young men always do; they mean it at the moment, and nothing can persuade them otherwise.

"I told you I had lived right here, and grown into these things, and they into me," said Rosamond, with a sweet slow earnestness, as if she thought out while she explained it; and so she did; for the thought and meaning of her life dawned upon her with a new perception, as she stood at this point and crisis of it in the responsibility of her young womanhood. "And these, and all the things that have influenced me, have given my life its direction; and I can see clearly that it was never meant to be your way. I do not know what it will be; but I know yours is different. It would be wrenching mine to turn it so."

"But I would turn mine for you," said Archie.

"You couldn't. Lives *grow* together. They join beforehand, if they join at all. You like me, perhaps, — just what you see of me; but you do not know me, nor I you. If it — this — were meant, we should."

"Should what?"

"Know. Be sure."

"I am sure of what I told you."

"And I thank you very much; but I do not — I never could — belong to you."

What made Rosamond so wise about knowing and belonging?

She could not tell, herself; she had never thought it out before; but she seemed to see it very clearly now. She did not belong to Archie Mucklegrand, nor he to her; he was mistaken; their lives had no join; to make them join would be a force, a wrenching.

Archie Mucklegrand did not care to have it put on such deep ground. He liked Rosamond; he wanted her to like him; then they should be married, of course, and go to Scotland, and have a good time; but this quiet philosophy cooled him somewhat. As they walked up the bank together, he wondered at himself a little that he did not feel worse about it. If she had been coquettish, or perverse, she might have been all the more bewitching to him. If he had thought she liked somebody else better, he might have been furiously jealous; but "her way of liking a fellow would be a slow kind of a way, after all." That was the gist of his thought about it; and I believe that to many very young men, at the age of waxed moustaches and German dancing, that "slow kind of a way" in a girl is the best possible insurance against any lasting damage that their own enthusiasm might suffer.

He had not been contemptible in the offering of his love; his best had come out at that moment; if it does not come out then, somehow, — through face and tone, in some plain earnestness or simple nobleness, if not in fashion of the spoken word as very well it may not, — it must be small best that the man has in him.

Rosamond's simple saying of the truth, as it looked to her in that moment of sure insight, was the best help she could have given him. Truth is always the best help. He did not exactly understand the wherefore, as she understood it; but the truth touched him nevertheless, in the way that he could perceive. They did not "belong" to each other.

And riding down in the late train that evening, Archie Mucklegrand said to himself, drawing a long breath, — "It would have been an awful tough little joke, after all, telling it to the old lady!"

"Are you too tired to walk home?" Kenneth Kincaid asked of Rosamond, helping her put the baskets in the carriage.

Dakie Thayne had asked Ruth the same question five minutes before, and they two had gone on already. Are girls ever too tired to walk home after a picnic, when the best of the picnic is going to walk home with them? Of course Rosamond was not too tired; and Mrs. Holabird had the carryall quite to herself and her baskets.

They took the River Road, that was shady all the way, and sweet now with the dropping scents of evening; it was a little longer, too, I think, though that is one of the local questions that have never yet been fully decided.

"How far does Miss Waite's ground run along the river?" asked Kenneth, taking Rosamond's shawl over his arm.

"Not far; it only just touches; it runs back and broadens toward the Old Turnpike. The best of it is in those woods and pastures."

"So I thought. And the pastures are pretty much run out."

"I suppose so. They are full of that lovely gray crackling moss."

"Lovely for picnics. Don't you think Miss Waite would like to sell?"

"Yes, indeed, if she could. That is her dream; what she has been laying up for her old age: to turn the acres into dollars, and build or buy a little cottage, and settle down safe. It is all she has in the world, except her dressmaking."

"Mr. Geoffrey and Mr. Marchbanks want to buy. They will offer her sixteen thousand dollars. That is the secret, — part of it."

"O, Mr. Kincaid! How glad, — how *sorry*, I can't help being, too! Miss Waite to be so comfortable! And never to have her dear old woods to picnic in any more! I suppose they want to make streets and build it all up."

"Not all. I'll tell you. It is a beautiful plan. Mr. Geoffrey wants to build a street of twenty houses, — ten on a side, — with just a little garden plot for each, and leave the woods behind for a piece of nature for the general good, — a real Union Park; a place for children to play in, and grown folks to rest and walk and take tea in, if they choose; but for nobody to change or meddle with any further. And these twenty houses to be let to respectable persons of small means, at rents that will give him seven per cent. for his whole outlay. Don't you see? Young people, and people like Miss Waite herself, who don't want *much* house-room, but who want it nice and comfortable, and will keep it so, and who *do* want a little of God's world-room to grow in, that they can't get in the crowded town streets, where the land is selling by the foot to be all built over with human packing-cases, and where they have to pay as much for being shut up and smothered, as they will out here to live and breathe. That Mr. Geoffrey is a glorious man, Rosamond! He is doing just this same thing in the edges of three or four other towns, buying up the land just before it gets too dear, to save for people who could not save it for themselves. He is providing for a class that nobody seems to have thought of, — the nice, narrow-pursed people, and the young beginners, who get married and take the world in the old-fashioned way."

He had no idea he had called her "Rosamond," till he saw the color shining up so in her face verifying the name. Then it flashed out upon him as he sent his thought back through the last few sentences that he had spoken.

"I beg your pardon," he said, suddenly. "But I was so full of this beautiful doing, — and I always think of you so! Is there a sin in that?"

Rosamond colored deeper yet, and Kenneth grew more bold. He had spoken it without plan; it had come of itself.

"I can't help it now. I shall say it again, unless you tell me not! Rosamond! I shall have these houses to build. I am getting ever so much to do. Could you begin the world with me, Rosamond?"

Rosamond did not say a word for a full minute. She only walked slowly by his side, her beautiful head inclined gently, shyly; her sweet face all one bloom, as faces never bloom but once.

Then she turned toward him and put out her hand.

"I will begin the world with you," she said.

And their world — that was begun for them before they were born — lifted up its veil and showed itself to them, bright in the eternal morning.

Desire Ledwith walked home all alone. She left Dorris at Miss Waite's, and Helena had teased to stay with her. Mrs. Ledwith had gone home among the first, taking a seat offered her in Mrs. Tom Friske's carriage to East Square; she had a headache, and was tired.

Desire felt the old, miserable questions coming up, tempting her.

Why?

Why was she left out, — forgotten? Why was there nothing, very much, in any of this, for her?

Yet underneath the doubting and accusing, something lived — stayed by — to rebuke it; rose up above it finally, and put it down, though with a thrust that hurt the heart in which the doubt was trampled.

Wait. Wait — with all your might!

Desire could do nothing very meekly; but she could even *wait* with all her might. She put her foot down with a will, at every step.

"I was put here to be Desire Ledwith," she said, relentlessly, to herself; "not Rosamond Holabird, nor even Dolly. Well, I suppose I can stay put, and *be!* If things would only *let* me be!"

But they will not. Things never do, Desire.

They are coming, now, upon you. Hard things, — and all at once.

XVIII.

ALL AT ONCE.

THERE was a Monday morning train going down from Z——.

Mr. Ledwith and Kenneth Kincaid were in it, reading the morning papers, seated side by side.

It was nearly a week since the picnic, but the engagement of Rosamond and Kenneth had not transpired. Mr. Holabird had been away in New York. Of course nothing was said beyond Mrs. Holabird and Ruth and Dolly Kincaid, until his return. But Kenneth carried a happy face about with him, in the streets and in the cars and about his work; and his speech was quick and bright with the men he met and had need to speak to. It almost told itself; people might have guessed it, if they had happened, at least to see the *two* faces in the same day, and if they were alive to sympathetic impressions of other people's pain or joy. There are not many who stop to piece expressions, from pure sympathy, however; they are, for the most part, too busy putting this and that together for themselves.

Desire would have guessed it in a minute; but she saw little of either in this week. Mrs. Ledwith was not well, and there was a dress to be made for Helena.

Kenneth Kincaid's elder men friends said of him, when they saw him in these days, "That's a fine fellow; he is doing very well." They could read that; he carried it in his eye and in his tone and in his step, and it was true.

It was a hot morning; it would be a stifling day in the

city. They sat quiet while they could, in the cars, taking the fresh air of the fields and the sea reaches, reading the French news, and saying little.

They came almost in to the city terminus, when the train stopped. Not at a station. There were people to alight at the last but one; these grew impatient after a few minutes, and got out and walked.

The train still waited.

Mr. Ledwith finished a column he was reading, and then looked up, as the conductor came along the passage.

"What is the delay?" he asked of him.

"Freight. Got such a lot of it. Takes a good while to handle."

Freight outward bound. A train making up.

Mr. Ledwith turned to his newspaper again.

Ten minutes went by. Kenneth Kincaid got up and went out, like many others. They might be kept there half an hour.

Mr. Ledwith had read all his paper, and began to grow impatient. He put his head out at the window, and looked and listened. Half the passengers were outside. Brakemen were walking up and down.

"Has he got a flag out there?" says the conductor to one of these.

"Don't know. Can't see. Yes, he has; I heard him whistle brakes."

Just then, their own bell sounded, and men jumped on board. Kenneth Kincaid came back to his seat.

Behind, there was a long New York train coming in.

Mr. Ledwith put his head out again, and looked back. All right; there had been a flag; the train had slackened just beyond a curve.

But why will people do such things? What is the use

of asking? Mr. Ledwith still looked out; he could not have told you why.

A quicker motion; a darkening of the window; a freight car standing upon a siding, close to the switch, as they passed by; a sudden, dull blow, half unheard in the rumble of the train. Women, sitting behind, sprang up, — screamed; one dropped, fainting: they had seen a ghastly sight; warm drops of blood flew in upon them; the car was in commotion.

Kenneth Kincaid, with an exclamation of horror, clutched hold of a lifeless body that fell — was thrust — backward beside him; the poor head fractured, shattered, against the fatal window frame.

The eleven o'clock train came out.

People came up the street, — a group of gentlemen, three or four, — toward Mr. Prendible's house.

Desire sat in a back window behind the blinds, busy. Mrs. Ledwith was lying on the bed.

Steps came in at the house door.

There was an exclamation; a hush. Mr. Prendible's voice, Kenneth Kincaid's, Mr. Dimsey's, the minister's.

"O! How?" — Mrs. Prendible's voice, now.

"Take care!"

"Where are they?"

Mrs. Ledwith heard.

"What is the matter?" — springing up, with a sudden instinct of precognition.

Desire had not seen or heard till now. She dropped her work.

"What is it, mother?"

Mrs. Ledwith was up, upon the floor; in the doorway; out in the passage; trembling; seized all over with a horrible dread and vague knowledge.

"*Tell* me what it is!" she cried, to those down below.

They were all there upon the staircase; Mrs. Prendible furthest up.

"O, Mrs. Ledwith!" she cried. "*Don't* be frightened! *Don't* take on! Take it easy, — do!"

Desire rushed down among them; past Mrs. Prendible, past the minister, straight to Kenneth Kincaid.

Kenneth took her right in his arms, and carried her into a little room below.

"There could have been no pain," he said, tenderly. "It was the accident of a moment. Be strong, — be patient, dear!"

There had been tender words natural to his lips lately. It was not strange that in his great pity he used them now.

"My father!" gasped Desire.

"Yes; your father. It was our Father's will."

"Help me to go to my mother!"

She took his hand, half blind, almost reeling.

And then they all, somehow, found themselves upstairs.

There were moans of pain; there were words of prayer. We have no right there. It is all told.

"Be strong, — be patient, dear!"

It came back, in the midst of the darkness, the misery; it helped her through those days; it made her strong for her mother. It comforted her, she hardly knew how much; but O, how cruel it seemed afterward!

They went directly down to Boston. Mr. Ledwith was buried from their own house. It was all over; and now, what should they do? Uncle Titus came to see them. Mrs. Ripwinkley came right back from Homesworth.

[illegible]

[illegible]

[illegible]

[illegible]

[illegible]

[illegible]

[illegible]

— before the letters came, bringing back the first terribleness in the first reception of and response to it, of her elder children.

It was so awful to have them away, — on the other side of the world! If they were only once all together again! Families ought not to separate. But then, it had been for their good; how could she have imagined? She supposed she should have done the same again, under the same circumstances.

And then came Mrs. Megilp's letter, delayed a mail, as she would have delayed entering the room, if they had been rejoined in their grief, until the family had first been gathered together with their tears and their embraces.

Then she wrote, — as she would have come in; and her letter, as her visit would have been, was after a few words of tender condolence, — and they were very sweet and tender, for Mrs. Megilp knew how to lay phrases like illuminating gold-leaf upon her meaning, — eminently practical and friendly, full of judicious, not to say mitigating, suggestions.

It was well, she thought, that Agatha and Florence were with her. They had been spared so much; and perhaps if all this had happened first, they might never have come. As to their return, she thought it would be a pity; "it could not make it really any better for you," she said; "and while your plans are unsettled, the fewer you are, the more easily you will manage. It seems hard to shadow their young lives more than is inevitable; and new scenes and interests are the very best things for them; their year of mourning would be fairly blotted out at home, you know. For yourself, poor friend, of course you cannot care; and Desire and Helena are not much come forward; but it would be a dead blank and stop to them, so much lost, right out; and I feel as if it were a kind Providence for the dear girls that they should be just where they are. We are living quietly, inexpensively; it will cost no more to come home at one time than at another;" etc.

There are persons to whom the pastime of life is the whole business of it; sickness and death and misfortune, — to say nothing of cares and duties — are the interruptions, to be got rid of as they may.

The next week came more letters; they had got a new idea out there. Why should not Mrs. Ledwith and the others come and join them? They were in Munich, now; the schools were splendid; would be just the thing for Helena; and "it was time for mamma to have a rest."

This thought, among the dozen others, had had its turn in Mrs. Ledwith's head. To break away, and leave everything, that is the impulse of natures like hers when things go hard and they cannot shape them. Only to get off; if she could do that!

Meanwhile, it was far different with Desire.

She was suffering with a deeper pain; not with a sharper loss, for she had seen so little of her father; but she looked in and back, and thought of what she *ought* to miss, and what had never been.

She ought to have known her father better; his life ought to have been more to her; was it her fault, or, harder yet, had it been his? This is the sorest thrust of grief; when it is only shock, and pity, and horror, and after these go by, not grief enough!

The child wrestled with herself, as she always did, questioning, arraigning. If she could make it all right, in the past, and now; if she could feel that all she had to do was to be tenderly sorry, and to love on through the darkness, she would not mind the dark; it would be only a phase of the life, — the love. But to have lived her life so far, to have had the relations of it, and yet *not* to have lived it, not to have been real child, real sister, not to be real stricken daughter now, tasting the suffering just as God made it to be tasted, — was she going through all things, even this, in a vain shadow? *Would* not life touch her?

She went away back, strangely, and asked whether she had had any business to be born? Whether it were a piece of God's truth at all, that she and all of them should be, and call themselves a household, — a home? The depth, the beauty of it were so unfulfilled! What was wrong, and how far back? Living in the midst of superficialities; in the noontide of a day of shams; putting her hands forth and grasping, almost everywhere, nothing but thin, hard surface, — she wondered how much of the world was real; how many came into the world where, and as, God meant them to come. What it was to "climb up some other way into the sheepfold," and to be a thief and a robber, even of life!

These were strange thoughts. Desire Ledwith was a strange girl.

But into the midst there crept one comfort; there was one glimpse out of the darkness into the daylight.

Kenneth Kincaid came in often to see them, — to inquire; just now he had frequent business in the city; he brought ferns and flowers, that Dorris gathered and filled into baskets, fresh and damp with moss.

Dorris was a dear friend; she dwelt in the life and the brightness; she reached forth and gathered, and turned and ministered again. The ferns and flowers were messages; leaves out of God's living Word, that she read, found precious, and sent on; apparitions, they seemed, standing forth to sense, and making sweet, true signs from the inner realm of everlasting love and glory.

And Kenneth, — Desire had never lost out of her heart those words, — "Be strong, — be patient, dear!"

He did not speak to her of himself; he could not demand congratulation from her grief; he let it be until she should somehow learn, and of her own accord, speak to him.

So everybody let her alone, poor child, to her hurt.

The news of the engagement was no Boston news; it was something that had occurred, quietly enough, among a few people away up in Z——. Of the persons who came in, — the few remaining in town, — nobody happened to know or care. The Ripwinkleys did, of course; but Mrs. Ripwinkley remembered last winter, and things she had read in Desire's unconscious, undisguising face, and aware of nothing that could be deepening the mischief now, thinking only of the sufficient burden the poor child had to bear, thought kindly, "better not."

Meanwhile Mrs. Ledwith was dwelling more and more upon the European plan. She made up her mind, at last, to ask Uncle Titus. When all was well, she would not seem to break a compact by going away altogether, so soon, to leave him; but now, — he would see the difference; perhaps advise it. She would like to know what he would advise. After all that had happened, — everything so changed, — half her family abroad, — what could she do? Would it not be more prudent to join them, than to set up a home again without them, and keep them out there? And all Helena's education to provide for, and everything so cheap and easy there, and so dear and difficult here?

"Now, tell me, truly, uncle, should you object? Should you take it at all hard? I never meant to have left you, after all you have done; but you see I have to break up, now poor Grant is gone; we cannot live as we did before, even with what you do; and — for a little while — it is cheaper there; and by and by we can come back and make some other plan. Besides, I feel sometimes as if I *must* go off; as if there weren't anything left here for me."

Poor woman! poor *girl*, still, — whose life had never truly taken root!

"I suppose," said Uncle Titus, soberly, "that God shines all round. He's on this side as much as He is on that."

Mrs. Ledwith looked up out of her handkerchief, with which at that moment she had covered her eyes.

"I never knew Uncle Titus was pious!" she said to herself. And her astonishment dried her tears.

He said nothing more that was pious, however; he simply assured her, then and in conversations afterward, that he should take nothing "hard;" he never expected to bind her, or put her on parole; he chose to come to know his relatives, and he had done so; he had also done what seemed to him right, in return for their meeting him half way; they were welcome to it all, to take it and use it as they best could, and as circumstances and their own judgment dictated. If they went abroad, he should advise them to do it before the winter.

These words implied consent, approval. Mrs. Ledwith went up-stairs after them with a heart so much lightened that she was very nearly cheerful. There would be a good deal to do now, and something to look forward to; the old pulses of activity were quickened. She could live with those faculties that had been always vital in her, as people breathe with one live lung; but trouble and change had wrought in her no deeper or further capacity; had wakened nothing that had never been awake before.

The house and furniture were to be sold; they would sail in September.

When Desire perceived that it was settled, she gave way; she had said little before; her mother had had many plans, and they amused her; she would not worry her with opposition; and besides, she was herself in a secret dream of a hope half understood.

It happened that she told it to Kenneth Kincaid herself; she saw almost every one who came, instead of her mother; Mrs. Ledwith lived in her own room chiefly. This was the way in which it had come about, that nobody noticed or guessed how it was with Desire, and what aspect Kenneth's friendship and kindness, in the simple history of those few weeks, might dangerously grow to bear with her.

Except one person. Luclarion Grapp, at last, made up her mind.

Kenneth heard what Desire told him, as he heard all she ever had to tell, with a gentle interest; comforted her when she said she could not bear to go, with the suggestion that it might not be for very long; and when she looked up in his face with a kind of strange, pained wonder, and repeated, —

"But I cannot *bear*, — I tell you, I cannot *bear* to go!" he answered, —

"One can bear all that is right; and out of it the good will come that we do not know. All times go by. I am sorry — very sorry — that you must go; but there will be the coming back. We must all wait for that."

She did not know what she looked for; she did not

know what she expected him to mean; she expected nothing; the thought of his preventing it in any way never entered into her head; she knew, if she *had* thought, how he himself was waiting, working. She only wanted him to *care*. Was this caring? Much? She could not tell.

"We never can come *back*," she said, impetuously. "There will be all the time — everything — between."

He almost spoke to her of it, then; he almost told her that the everything might be more, not less; that friendships gathered, multiplied; that there would be one home, he hoped, in which, by and by, she would often be; in which she would always be a dear and welcome comer.

But she was so sad, so tried; his lips were held; in his pure, honest kindness, he never dreamt of any harm that his silence might do; it only seemed so selfish to tell her how bright it was with him.

So he said, smiling, —

"And who knows what the 'everything' may be?" And he took both her hands in his as he said good-by, — for his little stops were of minutes on his way, always, — and held them fast, and looked warmly, hopefully into her face.

It was all for her, — to give her hope and courage; but the light of it was partly kindled by his own hope and gladness that lay behind; and how could she know that, or read it right? It was at once too much, and not enough, for her.

Five minutes after, Luclarion Grapp went by the parlor door with a pile of freshly ironed linen in her arms, on her way up-stairs.

Desire lay upon the sofa, her face down upon the pillow; her arms were thrown up, and her hands clasped upon the sofa-arm; her frame shook with sobs.

Luclarion paused for the time of half a step; then she went on. She said to herself in a whisper, as she went, —

"It is a stump; a proper hard one! But there's nobody else; and I have got to tell her!"

That evening, under some pretense of clean towels, Luclarion came up into Desire's room.

She was sitting alone, by the window, in the dark.

Luclarion fussed round a little; wiped the marble slab and the basin; set things straight; came over and asked Desire if she should not put up the window-bars, and light the gas.

"No," said Desire. "I like this best."

So did Luclarion. She had only said it to make time.

"Desire," she said, — she never put the "Miss" on, she had been too familiar all her life with those she was familiar with at all, — "the fact is I've got something to say, and I came up to say it."

She drew near — came close, — and laid her great, honest, faithful hand on the back of Desire Ledwith's chair, put the other behind her own waist, and leaned over her.

"You see, I'm a woman, Desire, and I know. You needn't mind me, I'm an old maid; that's the way I do know. Married folks, even mothers, half the time forget. But old maids never forget. I've had my stumps, and I can see that you've got yourn. But you'd ought to understand; and there's nobody, from one mistake and another, that's going to tell you. It's awful hard; it will be a trouble to you at first," — and Luclarion's strong voice trembled tenderly with the sympathy that her old maid heart had in it, after, and because of, all those years, — "but Kenneth Kincaid" —

"*What!*" cried Desire, starting to her feet, with a sudden indignation.

"Is going to be married to Rosamond Holabird," said Luclarion, very gently. "There! you ought to know, and I have told you."

"What makes you suppose that that would be a trouble to me?" blazed Desire. "How do you dare"—

"I didn't dare; but I had to!" sobbed Luclarion, putting her arms right round her.

And then Desire — as she would have done at any rate, for that blaze was the mere flash of her own shame and pain — broke down with a moan.

"All at once! All at once!" she said piteously, and hid her face in Luclarion's bosom.

And Luclarion folded her close; hugged her, the good woman, in her love that was sisterly and motherly and all, because it was the love of an old maid, who had endured, for a young maid upon whom the endurance was just laid, — and said, with the pity of heaven in the words, —

"Yes. All at once. But the dear Lord stands by. Take hold of His hand, — and bear with all your might!"

XIX.

INSIDE.

"DO you think, Luclarion," said Desire, feebly, as Luclarion came to take away her bowl of chicken broth, — "that it is my *duty* to go with mamma?"

"I don't know," said Luclarion, standing with the little waiter in her right hand, her elbow poised upon her hip, — "I've thought of that, and I *don't* know. There's most generally a stump, you see, one way or another, and that settles it, but here there's one both ways. I've kinder lost my road: come to two blazes, and can't tell which. Only, it ain't my road, after all. It lays between the Lord and you, and I suppose He means it shall. Don't you worry; there'll be some sort of a sign, inside or out. That's His business, you've just got to keep still, and get well."

Desire had asked her mother, before this, if she would care very much, — no, she did not mean that, — if she would be disappointed, or disapprove, that she should stay behind.

"Stay behind? Not go to Europe? Why, where *could* you stay? What would you do?"

"There would be things to do, and places to stay," Desire had answered, constrainedly. "I could do like Dorris."

"Teach music!"

"No. I don't know music. But I might teach something I do know. Or I could — rip," she said, with an odd smile, remembering something she had said one day, so long ago; the day the news came up to Z—— from Uncle Oldways. "And I might make out to put together, for other people, and for a real business. I never cared to do it just for myself."

"It is perfectly absurd," said Mrs Ledwith. "You couldn't be left to take care of yourself. And if you could, how it would look! No; of course you must go with us."

"But do you *care?*"

"Why, if there were any proper way, and if you really hate so to go, — but there isn't," said Mrs. Ledwith, not very grammatically or connectedly.

"She *doesn't* care," said Desire to herself, after her mother had left her, turning her face to the pillow, upon which two tears ran slowly down. "And that is my fault, too, I suppose. I have never been *anything!*"

Lying there, she made up her mind to one thing. She would get Uncle Titus to come, and she would talk to him.

"He won't encourage me in any notions," she said to herself. "And I mean now, if I can find it out, to do the thing God means; and then I suppose, — I *believe,* — the snarl will begin to unwind."

Meanwhile, Luclarion, when she had set a nice little bowl of tea-muffins to rise, and had brought up a fresh pitcher of ice-water into Desire's room, put on her bonnet and went over to Aspen Street for an hour.

Down in the kitchen, at Mrs. Ripwinkley's, they were having a nice time.

Their girl had gone. Since Luclarion left, they had fallen into that Gulf-stream which nowadays runs through everybody's kitchen. Girls came, and saw, and conquered in their fashion; they muddled up, and went away. The nice times were in the intervals when they *had* gone away.

Mrs. Ripwinkley did not complain; it was only her end of the "stump;" why should she expect to have a Luclarion Grapp to serve her all her life?

This last girl had gone as soon as she found out that Sulie Praile was "no relation, and didn't anyways belong there, but had been took in." She "didn't go for to come to work in an *Insecution.* She had always been used to first-class private families."

Girls will not stand any added numbers, voluntarily assumed, or even involuntarily befalling; they will assist in taking up no new responsibilities; to allow things to remain as they are, and cannot help being, is the depth of their condescension, — the extent of what they will put up with. There must be a family of some sort, of course, or there would not be a "place;" that is what the family is made for; but it must be established, no more to fluctuate; that is, you may go away, some of you, if you like, or you may die; but nobody must come home that has been away, and nobody must be born. As to anybody being "took in!" Why, the girl defined it; it was not being a family, but an *Insecution.*

So the three — Diana, and Hazel, and Sulie — were down in the kitchen; Mrs. Ripwinkley was busy in the dining-room close by; there was a berry-cake to be mixed up for an early tea. Diana was picking over the berries, Hazel was chopping the butter into the flour, and Sulie on a low cushioned seat in a corner — there was one kept ready for her in every room in the house, and Hazel and Diana carried her about in an "arm-chair," made of their own clasped hands and wrists, wherever they all wanted to go, — Sulie was beating eggs.

Sulie did that so patiently; you see she had no temptation to jump up and run off to anything else. The eggs turned, under her fingers, into thick, creamy, golden froth, fine to the last possible divisibility of the little air-bubbles.

They could not do without Sulie now. They had had her for "all winter;" but in that winter she had grown into their home.

"Why," said Hazel to her mother, when they had the few words about it that ended in there being no more words at all, — "that's the way children are *born* into houses, isn't it? They just come; and they're new and strange at first, and seem so queer. And then after a while you can't think how the places were, and they not in them. Sulie belongs, mother!"

So Sulie beat eggs, and darned stockings, and painted her lovely little flower-panels and racks and easels, and did everything that could be done, sitting still in her round chair, or in the cushioned corners made for her; and was always in the kitchen, above all, when any pretty little cookery was going forward.

Vash ran in and out from the garden, and brought balsamine blossoms, from which she pulled the little fairy slippers, and tried to match them in pairs; and she picked off the "used-up and puckered-up" morning glories, which she blew into at the tube-end, and "snapped" on the back of her little brown hand.

Wasn't that being good for anything, while berry-cake was making? The girls thought it was; as much as the balsamine blossoms were good for anything, or the brown butterflies with golden spots on their wings, that came and lived among them. The brown butterflies were a "piece of the garden;" little brown Vash was a piece of the house. Besides, she would eat some of the berry-cake when it was made; wasn't that worth while? She would have a "little teenty one" baked all for herself in a tin pepper-pot cover. Isn't that the special pleasantness of making cakes where little children are?

Vash was always ready for an "Aaron," too; they could not do without her, any more than without Sulie. Pretty soon, when Diana should have left school, and Vash should be a little bigger, they meant to "coöperate," as the Holabirds had done at Westover.

Of course, they knew a great deal about the Holabirds by this time. Hazel had stayed a week with Dorris at Miss Waite's; and one of Witch Hazel's weeks among "real folks" was like the days or hours in fairy land, that were years on the other side. She found out so much and grew so close to people.

Hazel and Ruth Holabird were warm friends. And Hazel was to be Ruth's bridesmaid, by and by!

For Ruth Holabird was going to be married to Dakie Thayne.

"That seemed so funny," Hazel said. "Ruth didn't *look* any older than she did; and Mr. Dakie Thayne was such a nice boy!"

He was no less a man, either; he had graduated among the first three at West Point; he was looking earnestly for the next thing that he should do in life with his powers and responsibilities; he did not count his marrying a *separate* thing; that had grown up alongside and with the rest; of course he could do nothing without Ruth; that was just what he had told her; and she, — well Ruth was always a sensible little thing, and it was just as plain to her as it was to him. Of course she must help him think and plan; and when the plans were made, it would take two to carry them out; why, yes, they must be married. What other way would there be?

That wasn't what she *said*, but that was the quietly

natural and happy way in which it grew to be a recognized thing in her mind, that pleasant summer after he came straight home to them with his honors and his lieutenant's commission in the Engineers; and his hearty, affectionate taking-for-granted; and it was no surprise or question with her, only a sure and very beautiful "rightness," when it came openly about.

Dakie Thayne was a man; the beginning of a very noble one; but it is the noblest men that always keep a something of the boy. If you had not seen anything more of Dakie Thayne until he should be forty years old, you would then see something in him which would be precisely the same that it was at Outledge, seven years ago, with Leslie Goldthwaite, and among the Holabirds at Westover, in his first furlough from West Point.

Luclarion came into the Ripwinkley kitchen just as the cakes — the little pepper-pot one and all — were going triumphantly into the oven, and Hazel was baring her little round arms to wash the dishes, while Diana tended the pans.

Mrs. Ripwinkley heard her old friend's voice, and came out.

"That girl ought to be here with you; or somewheres else than where she is, or is likely to be took," said Luclarion, as she looked round and sat down, and untied her bonnet-strings.

Miss Grapp hated bonnet-strings; she never endured them a minute longer than she could help.

"Desire?" asked Mrs. Ripwinkley, easily comprehending.

"Yes; Desire. I tell you she has a hard row to hoe, and she wants comforting. She wants to know if it is her duty to go to Yourup with her mother. Now it may be her duty to be *willing* to go; but it ain't anybody's else duty to let her. That's what came to me as I was coming along. I couldn't tell *her* so, you see, because it would interfere with her part; and that's all in the tune as much as any; only we've got to chime in with our parts at the right stroke, the Lord being Leader. Ain't that about it, Mrs. Ripwinkley?"

"If we are sure of the score, and can catch the sign," said Mrs. Ripwinkley, thoughtfully.

"Well, I've sung mine; it's only one note; I may have to keep hammering on it; that's according to how many repeats there are to be. Mr. Oldways, he ought to know, for one. Amongst us, we have got to lay our heads together, and work it out. She's a kind of an odd chicken in that brood; and my belief is she's like the ugly duck Hazel used to read about. But she ought to have a chance; if she's a swan, she oughtn't to be trapesed off among the weeds and on the dry ground. 'Tisn't even ducks she's hatched with; they don't take to the same element."

"I'll speak to Uncle Titus, and I will think," said Mrs. Ripwinkley.

But before she did that, that same afternoon by the six o'clock penny post, a little note went to Mr. Oldways:—

"DEAR UNCLE TITUS,—

"I want to talk with you a little. If I were well, I should come to see you in your study. Will you come up here, and see me in my room?

"Yours sincerely, DESIRE LEDWITH."

Uncle Titus liked that. It counted upon something in him which few had the faith to count upon; which, truly, he gave few people reason to expect to find.

He put his hat directly on, took up his thick brown stick, and trudged off, up Borden Street to Shubarton Place.

When Luclarion let him in, he told her with some careful emphasis, that he had come to see Desire.

"Ask her if I shall come up," he said. "I'll wait down here."

Helena was practicing in the drawing-room. Mrs. Ledwith lay, half asleep, upon a sofa. The doors into the hall were shut, — Luclarion had looked to that, lest the playing should disturb Desire.

Luclarion was only gone three minutes. Then she came back, and led Mr. Oldways up three flights of stairs.

"It's a long climb, clear from the door," she said.

"I can climb," said Mr. Oldways, curtly.

"I didn't expect it was going to stump *you*," said Luclarion, just as short in her turn. "But I thought I'd be polite enough to mention it."

There came a queer little chuckling wheeze from somewhere, like a whispered imitation of the first few short pants of a steam-engine: that was Uncle Titus, laughing to himself.

Luclarion looked down behind her, out of the corner of her eyes, as she turned the landing. Uncle Titus's head was dropped between his shoulders, and his shoulders were shaking up and down. But he kept his big stick clutched by the middle, in one hand, and the other just touched the rail as he went up. Uncle Titus was not out of breath. Not he. He could laugh and climb.

Desire was sitting up for a little while, before going to bed again for the night. There was a low gas-light burning by the dressing-table, ready to turn up when the twilight should be gone; and a street lamp, just lighted, shone across into the room. Luclarion had been sitting with her, and her gray knitting-work lay upon the chair that she offered when she had picked it up, to Mr. Oldways. Then she went away and left them to their talk.

"Mrs. Ripwinkley has been spry about it," she said to herself, going softly down the stairs. "But she always was spry."

"You're getting well, I hope," said Uncle Titus, seating himself, after he had given Desire his hand.

"I suppose so," said Desire, quietly. "That was why I wanted to see you. I want to know what I ought to do when I am well."

"How can I tell?" asked Uncle Titus, bluntly.

"Better than anybody I can ask. The rest are all too sympathizing. I am afraid they would tell me as I wish they should."

"And I don't sympathize? Well, I don't think I do much. I haven't been used to it."

"You have been used to think what was right; and I believe you would tell me truly. I want to know whether I ought to go to Europe with my mother."

"Why not? Doesn't she want you to go?" — and Uncle Titus was sharp this time.

"I suppose so; that is, I suppose she expects I will. But I don't know that I should be much except a hindrance to her. And I think I could stay and do something here, in some way. Uncle Titus, I hate the thought of going to Europe! Now, don't you suppose I ought to go?"

"*Why* do you hate the thought of going to Europe?" asked Uncle Titus, regarding her with keenness.

"Because I have never done anything real in all my life!" broke forth Desire. "And this seems only plaster-

UNCLE TITUS AND DESIRE. See p. 253.

ing and patching what can't be patched. I want to take hold of something. I don't want to float round any more. What is there left of all we have ever tried to do, all these years? Of all my poor father's work, what is there to show for it now? It has all melted away as fast as it came, like snow on pavements; and now his life has melted away; and I feel as if we had never been anything real to each other! Uncle Titus, I can't tell you *how* I feel!"

Uncle Titus sat very still. His hat was in one hand, and both together held his cane, planted on the floor between his feet. Over hat and cane leaned his gray head, thoughtfully. If Desire could have seen his eyes, she would have found in them an expression that she had never supposed could be there at all.

She had not so much spoken *to* Uncle Titus, in these last words of hers, as she had irresistibly spoken *out* that which was in her. She wanted Uncle Titus's good common sense and sense of right to help her decide; but the inward ache and doubt and want, out of which grew her indecisions, — these showed themselves forth at that moment simply because they must, with no expectation of a response from him. It might have been a stone wall that she cried against; she would have cried all the same.

Then it was over, and she was half ashamed, thinking it was of no use, and he would not understand; perhaps that he would only set the whole down to nerves and fidgets and contrariness, and give her no common sense that she wanted, after all.

But Uncle Titus spoke, slowly; much as if he, too, were speaking out involuntarily, without thought of his auditor. People do so speak, when the deep things are stirred; they speak into the deep that answereth unto itself, — the deep that reacheth through all souls, and all living, whether souls feel into it and know of it or not.

"The real things are inside," he said. "The real world is the inside world. *God* is not up, nor down, but in the *midst.*"

Then he looked up at Desire.

"What is real of your life is living inside you now. That is something. Look at it and see what it is."

"Discontent. Misery. Failure."

"*Sense* of failure. Well. Those are good things. The beginning of better. Those are *live* things, at any rate."

Desire had never thought of that.

Now *she* sat still awhile.

Then she said, — "But we can't *be* much, without doing it. I suppose we are put into a world of outsides for something."

"Yes. To find out what it means. That's the inside of it. And to help make the outside agree with the in, so that it will be easier for other people to find out. That is the 'kingdom come and will be done, on earth as it is in heaven.' Heaven is the inside, — the truth of things."

"Why, I never knew" — began Desire, astonished. She had almost finished aloud, as her mother had done in her own mind. She never knew that Uncle Oldways was "pious."

"Never knew that was what it meant? What else can it mean? What do you suppose the resurrection was, or is?"

Desire answered with a yet larger look of wonder, only in the dim light it could not be wholly seen.

"The raising up of the dead; Christ coming up out of the tomb."

"The coming out of the tomb was a small part of it; just what could not help being, if the rest was. Jesus Christ rose out of dead *things*, I take it, into these very real ones that we are talking of, and so lived in them. The resurrection is a man's soul coming alive to the soul of creation — God's soul. *That* is eternal life, and what Jesus of Nazareth was born to show. Our coming to that is our being 'raised with Him;' and it begins, or ought to, a long way this side the tomb. If people would only read the New Testament, expecting to get as much common sense and earnest there as they do among the new lights and little 'progressive-thinkers' that are trying to find it all out over again, they might spare these gentlemen and themselves a great deal of their trouble."

The exclamation rose half-way to her lips again, — "I never knew you thought like this. I never heard you talk of these things before!"

But she held it back, because she would not stop him by reminding him that he *was* talking. It was just the truth that was saying itself. She must let it say on, while it would.

"Un —"

She stopped there, at the first syllable. She would not even call him "Uncle Titus" again, for fear of recalling him to himself, and hushing him up.

"There is something — isn't there — about those who *attain* to that resurrection; those who are *worthy?* I suppose there must be some who are just born to this world, then, and never — 'born again?'"

"It looks like it, sometimes; who can tell?"

"Uncle Oldways," — it came out this time in her earnestness, and her strong personal appeal, — "do you think there are some people — whole families of people —

who have no business in the reality of things to be at all? Who are all a mistake in the world, and have nothing to do with its meaning? I have got to feeling sometimes lately, as if — *I* — had never had any business to be."

She spoke slowly — awe-fully. It was a strange speech for a girl in her nineteenth year. But she was a girl in this nineteenth century, also; and she had caught some of the thoughts and questions of it, and mixed them up with her own doubts and unsatisfactions which they could not answer.

"The world is full of mistakes; mistakes centuries long; but it is full of salvation and setting to rights, also. 'The kingdom of heaven is like leaven, which a woman hid in three measures of meal till the whole was leavened.' You have been *allowed* to be, Desire Ledwith. And so was the man that was born blind. And I think there is a colon put into the sentence about him, where a comma was meant to be."

Desire did not ask him, then, what he meant; but she turned to the story after he had gone, and found this: —

"Neither hath this man sinned, nor his parents, but that the works of God should be manifest in him."

You can see, if you look also, where she took the colon out, and put the comma in.

Were all the mistakes — the sins, even — for the very sake of the pure blessedness and the more perfect knowledge of the setting right?

Desire began to think that Uncle Oldways' theology might help her.

What she said to him now was, —

"I want to do something. I should like to go and live with Luclarion, I think, down there in Neighbor Street. I should like to take hold of some other lives, — little children's, perhaps," — and here Desire's voice softened, — "that don't seem to have any business to be, either, and see if I could help or straighten anything. Then I feel as if I should know."

"Then — according to the Scripture — you *would* know. But — that's undertaking a good deal. Luclarion Grapp has got there; but she has been fifty-odd years upon the road. And she has been doing real things all the time. That's what has brought her there. You can't boss the world's hard jobs till you've been a journeyman at the easy ones."

"And I've missed my apprenticeship!" said Desire, with changed voice and face, falling back into her disheartenment again.

"No!" Uncle Oldways almost shouted. "Not if you come to the Master who takes in the eleventh hour workers. And it isn't the eleventh hour with you, — *child!*"

He dwelt on that word "child," reminding her of her short mistaking and of the long retrieval. Her nineteen years and the forever and ever contrasted themselves before her suddenly, in the light of hope.

She turned sharply, though, to look at her duty. Her journeyman's duty of easy things.

"Must I go to Europe with my mother?" she asked again, the conversation coming round to just that with which it had begun.

"I'll talk with your mother," said Uncle Oldways, getting up and looking into his hat, as a man always does when he thinks of putting it on presently. "Good-night. I suppose you are tired enough now. I'll come again and see you."

Desire stood up and gave him her hand.

"I thank you, Uncle Titus, with all my heart."

He did not answer her a word; but he knew she meant it.

He did not stop that night to see his niece. He went home, to think it over. But as he walked down Borden Street, swinging his big stick, he said to himself, —

"Next of kin! Old Marmaduke Wharne was right. But it takes more than the Family Bible to tell you which it is!"

Two days after, he had a talk with Mrs. Ledwith which relieved both their minds.

From the brown-and-apricot drawing-room, — from among the things that stood for nothing now, and had never stood for home, — he went straight up, without asking, and knocked at Desire's third-story door.

"Come in!" she said, without a note of expectation in her voice.

She had had a dull morning. Helena had brought her a novel from Loring's that she could not read. Novels, any more than life, cannot be read with very much patience, unless they touch something besides surface. Why do critics — some of them — make such short, smart work, — such cheerful, confident despatch, nowadays, of a story with religion in it, as if it were an abnormity, — a thing with sentence of death in itself, like a calf born with two heads, — that needs not their trouble, save to name it as it is? Why, that is, if religion stand for the relation of things to spirit, which I suppose it should? Somebody said that somebody had written a book made up of "spiritual struggles and strawberry short-cake." That was bright and funny; and it seemed to settle the matter; but, taking strawberry short-cake representatively, what else is human experience on earth made up of? And are novels to be pictures of human experience, or not?

This has nothing to do with present matters, however, except that Desire found nothing real in her novel, and so had flung it aside, and was sitting rather listlessly with her crochet which she never cared much for, when Uncle Oldways entered.

Her face brightened instantly as he came in. He sat down just where he had sat the other night. Mr. Oldways had a fashion of finding the same seat a second time when he had come in once; he was a man who took up most things where he left them off, and this was an unconscious sign of it.

"Your mother has decided to sell the house on the 23d, it seems," he said.

"Yes; I have been out twice. I shall be able to go away by then; I suppose that is all she has waited for."

"Do you think you could be contented to come and live with me?"

"Come and *live?*"

"Yes. And let your mother and Helena go to Europe."

"O, Uncle Oldways! I think I could *rest* there! But I don't want only to rest, you know. I must do something. For myself, to begin with. I have made up my mind not to depend upon my mother. Why should I, any more than a boy? And I am sure I cannot depend on anybody else."

These were Desire Ledwith's thanks; and Mr. Oldways liked them. She did not say it to please him; she thought it seemed almost ungrateful and unwilling; but she was so intent on taking up life for herself.

"You must have a place to do in,—or from," said Mr. Oldways. "And it is better you should be under some protection. You must consent to that for your mother's sake. How much money have you got?"

"Two hundred and fifty dollars a year. Of my own."

This was coming to business and calculation and common sense. Desire was encouraged. Uncle Oldways did not think her quite absurd.

"That will clothe you, — without much fuss and feathers?"

"I have done with fuss and feathers," — Desire said with a grave smile, glancing at her plain white wrapper and the black shawl that was folded around her.

"Then come where is room for you and a welcome, and do as much more as you please, and can, for yourself, or for anybody else. I won't give you a cent; you shall have something to do for me, if you choose. I am an old man now, and want help. Perhaps what I want as much as anything is what I've been all my life till lately, pretty obstinate in doing without."

Uncle Oldways spoke short, and drew his breath in and puffed it out between his sentences, in his bluff way; but his eyes were kind, as he sat looking at the young girl over his hat and cane.

She thought of the still, gray parlor; of Rachel Froke and her face of peace; and the Quaker meeting and the crumbs last year; of Uncle Oldways' study, and his shelves rich with books; of the new understanding that had begun between herself and him, and the faith she had found out, down beneath his hard reserves; of the beautiful neighborhood, Miss Craydocke's Beehive, Aunt Franks' cheery home and the ways of it, and Hazel's runnings in and out. It seemed as if the real things had opened for her, and a place been made among them in which she should have "business to be," and from which her life might make a new setting forth.

"And mamma knows?" she said, inquiringly, after that long pause.

"Yes. I told you I would talk with her. That is what we came to. It is only for you to say, now."

"I will come. I shall be glad to come!" And her face was full of light as she looked up and said it.

Desire never thought for a moment of what her mother could not help thinking of; of what Mrs. Megilp thought and said, instantly, when she learned it three weeks later.

It is wonderful how abiding influence is, — even influence to which we are secretly superior, — if ever we have been subjected to, or allowed ourselves to be swayed by it. The veriest tyranny of discipline grows into one's conscience, until years after, when life has got beyond the tyranny, conscience, — or something superinduced upon it, — keeps up the echo of the old mandates, and one can take no comfort in doing what one knows all the time one has a perfect right, besides sound reason, to do. It was a great while before our grandmothers' daughters could peaceably stitch and overcast a seam, instead of over-sewing and felling it. I know women who feel to this moment as if to sit down and read a book of a week-day, in the daytime, were playing truant to the needle, though all the sewing-machines on the one hand, and all the demand and supply of mental culture on the other, of this present changed and bettered time, protest together against the absurdity.

Mrs. Ledwith had heard the Megilp precepts and the Megilp forth-putting of things, until involuntarily everything showed itself to her in a Megilp light. The Megilp "sense of duty," therefore, came up as she unhesitatingly assented to Uncle Oldways' proposal and request. He wanted Desire; of course she could not say a word; she owed him something, which she was glad she could so make up; and secretly there whispered in her mind the suggestion which Mrs. Megilp, on the other side of the water, spoke right out.

"If he wants her, he must mean something by her. He is an old man; he might not live to give her back into her mother's keeping; what would she do there, in that old house of his, if he should die, unless — he *does* mean something? He has taken a fancy to her; she is odd, as he is; and he isn't so queer after all, but that his crotchets have a good, straightforward sense of justice in them. Uncle Titus knows what he is about; and what's more, just what he ought to be about. It is a good thing to have Desire provided for; she is uncomfortable and full of notions, and she isn't likely ever to be married."

So Desire was given up, easily, she could not help feeling; but she knew she had been a puzzle and a vexation to her mother, and that Mrs. Ledwith had never had the least idea what to do with her; least of all had she now, what she should do with her abroad.

"It was so much better for her that Uncle Titus had taken her home." With these last words Mrs. Ledwith reassured herself and cheered her child.

Perhaps it would have been the same — it came into Desire's head, that would conceive strange things — if the angels had taken her.

Mrs. Ledwith went to New York; she stayed a few days with Mrs. Macmichael, who wanted her to buy lace for her in Brussels and Bohemian glass in Prague; then a few days more with her cousin, Geraldine Raxley; and then the *City of Antwerp* sailed.

XX.

NEIGHBORS AND NEXT OF KIN.

"I'LL tell you what to do with them, Luclarion," said Hazel briskly. "Teach them to play."

"Music! Pianners!" exclaimed Luclarion, dismayed.

"No. Games. Teach them to have good times. That was the first thing ever we learnt, wasn't it, Dine? And we never could have got along without it."

"It takes *you!*" said Luclarion, looking at Hazel with delighted admiration.

"Does it? Well I don't know but it does. May I go, mother? Luclarion, haven't you got a great big empty room up at the top of the house?"

Luclarion had.

"That's just what it's for, then. Couldn't Mr. Gallilee put up a swing? And a 'flying circle' in the middle? You see they can't go out on the roofs; so they must have something else that will seem kind of flighty. And *I'll* tell you how they'll learn their letters. Sulie and I will paint 'em; great big ones, all colors; and hang 'em up with ribbons, and every child that learns one, so as to know it everywhere, shall take it down and carry it home. Then we will have marbles for numbers; and they shall play addition games, and multiplication games, and get the sums for prizes; the ones that get to the head, you know. Why, you don't understand *objects*, Luclarion!"

Luclarion had been telling them of the wild little folk of Neighbor Street, and worse, of Arctic Street. She wanted to do something with them. She had tried to get them in with gingerbread and popcorn; they came in fast enough for those; but they would not stay. They were digging in the gutters and calling names; learning the foul language of the places into which they were born; chasing and hiding in alley-ways; filching, if they could, from shops; going off begging with lies on their lips. It was terrible to see the springs from which the life of the city depths was fed.

"If you could stop it *there!*" Luclarion said, and said with reason.

"Will you let me go?" asked Hazel of her mother, in good earnest.

"'Twon't hurt her," put in Luclarion. "Nothing's catching that you haven't got the seeds of in your own constitution. And so the catching will be the other way."

The seeds of good, — to catch good; that was what Luclarion Grapp believed in, in those dirty little souls, — no, those clean little *souls*, overlaid with all outward mire and filth of body, clothing, speech, and atmosphere, for a mile about; through which they could no more grope and penetrate, to reach their own that was hidden from them in the clearer life beyond, than we can grope and reach to other stars.

"I will get Desire," quoth Hazel, inspired as she always was, both ways.

Running in at the house in Greenley Street the next Thursday, she ran against Uncle Titus coming out.

"What now?" he demanded.

"Desire," said Hazel. "I've come for her. We're wanted at Luclarion's. We've got work to do."

"Humph! Work? What kind?"

"Play," said Hazel, laughing. She delighted to bother and mystify Uncle Titus, and imagined that she did.

"I thought so. Tea parties?"

"Something like," said Hazel. "There are children down there that don't know how to grow up. They haven't any comfortable sort of fashion of growing up. Somebody has got to teach them. They don't know how to play 'Grand Mufti,' and they never heard of 'King George and his troops.' Luclarion tried to make them sit still and learn letters; but of course they wouldn't a minute longer than the gingerbread lasted, and they are eating her out of house and home. It will take young folks, and week-days, you see; so Desire and I are going." And Hazel ran up the great, flat-stepped staircase.

"Lives that have no business to be," said Uncle Titus to himself, going down the brick walk. "The Lord has His own ways of bringing lives together. And His own business gets worked out among them, beyond their guessing. When a man grows old, he can stand still now and then, and see a little."

It was a short cross street that Luclarion lived in, between two great thoroughfares crowded with life and business, bustle, drudgery, idleness, and vice. You will not find the name I give it, — although you may find one that will remind you of it, — in any directory or on any city map. But you can find the places without the names; and if you go down there with the like errands in your heart, you will find the work, as she found it, to do.

She heard the noise of street brawls at night, voices of men and women quarreling in alley-ways, and up in wretched garrets; flinging up at each other, in horrible words, all the evil they knew of in each other's lives, — "away back," Luclarion said, "to when they were little children."

"And what is it," she would say to Mrs. Ripwinkley,

telling her about it, "that *flings* it up, and can call it a shame, after all the shames of years and years? Except just *that* that the little children *were*, underneath, when the Lord let them — He knows why — be born so? I tell you, ma'am, it's a mystery; and the nigher you come to it, the more it is; it's a piece of hell and a piece of heaven; it's the wrastle of the angel and the dragon; and it's going on at one end, while they're building up their palaces and living soft and sweet and clean at the other, with everything hushed up that can't at least *seem* right and nice and proper. I know there's good folks there, in the palaces; *beautiful* folks; there, and all the way down between; with God's love in them, and His hate, that is holy, against sin; and His pity, that is *prayers* in them, for all people and places that are dark; but if they would *come down* there, and take hold! I think it's them that would, that might have part in the first resurrection, and live and reign the thousand years."

Luclarion never counted herself among them, — those who were to have thrones and judgments; she forgot, even, that she had gone down and taken hold; her words came burning-true, out of her soul; and in the heat of truth they were eloquent.

But I meant to tell you of her living.

In the daytime it was quiet; the gross evils crept away and hid from the sunshine; there was labor to take up the hours, for those who did labor; and you might not know or guess, to go down those avenues, that anything worse gathered there than the dust of the world's traffic that the lumbering drays ground up continually with their wheels, and the wind, — that came into the city from far away country places of green sweetness, and over hills and ponds and streams and woods, — flung into the little children's faces.

Luclarion had taken a house, — one of two, that fronted upon a little planked court; aside, somewhat, from Neighbor Street, as that was a slight remove from the absolute terrible contact of Arctic Street. But it was in the heart of that miserable quarter; she could reach out her hands and touch and gather in, if it would let her, the wretchedness. She had chosen a place where it was possible for her to make a nook of refuge, not for herself only, or so much, as for those to whom she would fain be neighbor, and help to a better living.

It had been once a dwelling of some well-to-do family of the days gone by; of some merchant, whose ventures went out and came in at those wharves below, whence the air swept up pure, then, with its salt smell, into the streets. The rooms were fairly large; Luclarion spent money out of her own little property, that had been growing by care and saving till she could spare from it, in doing her share toward having it all made as sweet and clean as mortar and whitewash and new pine-boards and paint and paper could make it. All that was left of the old, they scoured with carbolic soap; and she had the windows opened, and in the chimneys that had been swept of their soot she had clear fires made and kept burning for days.

Then she put her new, plain furnishings into her own two down-stairs rooms; and the Gallilees brought in theirs above; and beside them, she found two decent families, — a German paper-hanger's, and that of a carpenter at one of the theatres, whose wife worked at dressmaking, — to take the rest. Away up, at the very top, she had the wide, large room that Hazel spoke of, and a smaller one to which she climbed to sleep, for the sake of air as near heaven as it could be got.

One of her lower rooms was her living and housekeeping room; the other she turned into a little shop, in which she sold tapes and needles and cheap calicoes and a few ribbons; and kept a counter on the opposite side for bread and yeast, gingerbread, candy, and the like. She did this partly because she must do something to help out the money for her living and her plans, and partly to draw the women and children in. How else could she establish any relations between herself and them, or get any permanent hold or access? She had "turned it all over in her mind," she said; "and a tidy little shop with fair, easy prices, was the very thing, and a part of just what she came down there to do."

She made real, honest, hop-raised bread, of sweet flour that she gave ten dollars a barrel for; it took a little more than a pint, perhaps, to make a tea loaf; that cost her three cents; she sold her loaf for four, and it was better than they could get anywhere else for five. Then, three evenings in a week, she had hot muffins, or crumpets, home-made; (it was the subtle home touch and flavor that she counted on, to carry more than a good taste into their mouths, even a dim notion of home sweetness and comfort into their hearts;) these first,—a quart of flour at five cents, two eggs at a cent apiece, and a bit of butter, say three cents more, with three cents worth of milk, made an outlay of fifteen cents for a dozen and a half; so she sold them for ten cents a dozen, and the like had never been tasted or dreamed of in all that region round about; no, nor I dare almost to say, in half the region round about Republic Avenue either, where they cannot get Luclarion Grapps to cook.

The crumpets were cheaper; they were only bread-sponge, baked on a griddle; they were large, and light and tender; a quart of flour would make ten; she gave the ten for seven cents.

And do you see, putting two cents on every quart of her flour, for her labor, she *earned*, not *made*, — that word is for speculators and brokers, — with a barrel of one hundred and ninety six pounds or quarts, three dollars and ninety-two cents? The beauty of it was, you perceive, that she did a small business; there was an eager market for all she could produce, and there was no waste to allow a margin for.

I am not a bit of a political economist myself; but I have a shrewd suspicion that Luclarion Grapp was, besides having hit upon the initial, individual idea of a capital social and philanthropic enterprise.

This was all she tried to do at first; she began with bread; the Lord from heaven began with that; she fed as much of the multitude as she could reach; they gathered about her for the loaves; and they got, consciously or unconsciously, more than they came or asked for.

They saw her clean-swept floor; her netted windows that kept the flies out, the clean, coarse white cotton shades, — tacked up, and rolled and tied with cord, country-fashion, for Luclarion would not set any fashions that her poor neighbors might not follow if they would; — and her shelves kept always dusted down; they could see her way of doing that, as they happened in at different times, when she whisked about, lightly and nicely, behind and between her jars and boxes and parcels with the little feather duster that she kept hanging over her table where she made her change and sat at her sewing.

They grew ashamed by degrees, — those coarse women, — to come in in their frowsy rags, to buy her delicate muffins or her white loaves; they would fling on the cleanest shawl they had or could borrow, to "cut round to Old Maid Grapp's," after a cent's worth of yeast, — for her yeast, also, was like none other that could be got, and would *almost* make her own beautiful bread of itself.

Back of the shop was her house-room; the cheapest and cleanest of carpet, — a square, bound round with bright-striped carpet-binding, — laid in the middle of a clean dark yellow floor; a plain pine table, scoured white, standing in the middle of that; on it, at tea-time, common blue and white crockery cups and plates, and a little black teapot; a napkin, coarse, but fresh from the fold, laid down to save, and at the same time to set off, with a touch of delicate neatness, the white table; a wooden settee, with a home-made calico-covered cushion and pillows, set at right angles with the large, black, speckless stove; a wooden rocking-chair, made comfortable in like manner, on the other side; the sink in the corner, clean, freshly rinsed, with the bright tin basin hung above it on a nail.

There was nothing in the whole place that must not be, in some shape, in almost the poorest; but all so beautifully ordered, so stainlessly kept. Through that open door, those women read a daily sermon.

And Luclarion herself, — in a dark cotton print gown, a plain strip of white about the throat, — even that was cotton, not linen, and two of them could be run together in ten minutes for a cent, — and a black alpacca apron, never soiled or crumpled, but washed and ironed when it needed, like anything else, — her hair smoothly gathered back under a small white half-handkerchief cap, plain-hemmed, — was the sermon alive; with the soul of it, the inner sweetness and purity, looking out at them from clear pleasant eyes, and lips cheery with a smile that lay behind them.

She had come down there just to do as God told her: to be a neighbor, and to let her light shine. He would see about the glorifying.

She did not try to make money out of her candy, or her ginger-nuts; she kept those to entice the little children in; to tempt them to come again when they had once done an errand, shyly, or saucily, or hang-doggedly, — it made little difference which to her, — in her shop.

"I'll tell you what it's like," Hazel said, when she came in and up-stairs the first Saturday afternoon with Desire, and showed and explained to her proudly all Luclarion's ways and blessed inventions. "It's like your mother and mine throwing crumbs to make the pigeons come, when they were little girls, and lived in Boston, — I mean *here!*"

Hazel waked up at the end of her sentence, suddenly, as we all do sometimes, out of talking or thinking, to the consciousness that it was *here* that she had mentally got round to.

Desire had never heard of the crumbs or the pigeons. Mrs. Ledwith had always been in such a hurry, living on, that she never stopped to tell her children the sweet old tales of how she *had* lived. Her child-life had not ripened in her as it had done in Frank.

Desire and Hazel went up-stairs and looked at the empty room. It was light and pleasant; dormer windows opened out on a great area of roofs, above which was blue sky; upon which, poor clothes fluttered in the wind, or cats walked and stretched themselves safely and lazily in the sun.

"I always *do* like roofs!" said Hazel. "The nicest thing in "Mutual Friend" is Jenny Wren up on the Jew's roof, being dead. It seems like getting up over the world, and leaving it all covered up and put away."

"Except the old clothes," said Desire.

"They're *washed*," answered Hazel, promptly; and never stopped to think of the meaning.

Then she jumped down from the window, along under which a great beam made a bench to stand on, and looked about the chamber.

"A swing to begin with," she said. "Why what is that? Luclarion's got one!"

Knotted up under two great staples that held it, was the long loop of clean new rope; the notched board rested against the chimney below.

"It's all ready! Let's go down and catch one! Luclarion, we've come to tea," she announced, as they reached the sitting-room. "There's the shop bell!"

In the shop was a woman with touzled hair and a gown with placket split from gathers to hem, showing the ribs of a dirty skeleton skirt. A child with one garment on, — some sort of woolen thing that had never been a clean color, and was all gutter-color now, — the woman holding the child by the hand here, in a safe place, in a way these mothers have who turn their children out in the street dirt and scramble without any hand to hold. No wonder, though, perhaps; in the strangeness and unfitness of the safe, pure place, doubtless they feel an uneasy instinct that the poor little vagabonds have got astray, and need some holding.

"Give us a four-cent loaf!" said the woman, roughly, her eyes lowering under crossly furrowed brows, as she flung two coins upon the little counter.

Luclarion took down one, looked at it, saw that it had a pale side, and exchanged it for another.

"Here is a nice crusty one," she said pleasantly, turning to wrap it in a sheet of paper.

"None o' yer gammon! Give it here; there's your money; come along, Crazybug!" And she grabbed the loaf without a wrapper, and twitched the child.

Hazel sat still. She knew there was no use. But Desire with her point-black determination, went right at the boy, took hold of his hand, dirt and all; it was disagreeable, therefore she thought she must do it.

"Don't you want to come and swing?" she said.

"—— yer swing! and yer imperdence! Clear out! He's got swings enough to home! Go to ——, and be ——, you —— —— ——!"

Out of the mother's mouth poured a volley of horrible words, like a hailstorm of hell.

Desire fell back, as from a blinding shock of she knew not what.

Luclarion came round the counter, quite calmly.

"Ma'am," she said, "those words won't hurt *her*. She don't know the language. But you've got God's daily bread in your hand; how can you talk devil's Dutch over it?"

The woman glared at her. But she saw nothing but strong, calm, earnest asking in the face; the asking of God's own pity.

She rebelled against that, sullenly; but she spoke no more foul words. I think she could as soon have spoken them in the face of Christ; for it was the Christ in Luclarion Grapp that looked out at her.

"You needn't preach. You can order me out of your shop, if you like. I don't care."

"I don't order you out. I'd rather you would come again. I don't think you will bring that street-muck with you, though."

There was both confidence and command in the word; like the "Neither do I condemn thee: go, and sin no more." It detached the street-muck from the woman. It was not *she;* it was defilement she had picked up, when perhaps she could not help it. She could scrape her shoes at the door, and come in clean.

"You know a darned lot about it, I suppose!" were the last words of defiance; softened down, however, you perceive, to that which can be printed.

Desire was pale, with a dry sob in her throat, when the woman had gone and Luclarion turned round.

"The angels in heaven know; why shouldn't you?" said Luclarion. "That's what we've got to help."

A child came in afterwards, alone; with an actual clean spot in the middle of her face, where a ginger-nut or an acid drop might go in. This was a regular customer of a week past. The week had made that clean spot; with a few pleasant and encouraging hints from Luclarion, administered along with the gingerbread.

Now it was Hazel's turn.

The round mouth and eyes, with expectation in them, were like a spot of green to Hazel, feeling with her witch-wand for a human spring. But she spoke to Desire, looking cunningly at the child.

"Let us go back and swing," she said.

The girl's head pricked itself up quickly.

"We've got a swing up-stairs," said Hazel, passing close by, and just pausing. "A new one. I guess it goes pretty high; and it looks out of top windows. Wouldn't you like to come and see?"

The child lived down in a cellar.

"Take up some ginger-nuts, and eat them there," said Luclarion to Hazel.

If it had not been for that, the girl would have hung back, afraid of losing her shop treat.

Hazel knew better than to hold out her hand, at this first essay; she would do that fast enough when the time came. She only walked on, through the sitting-room, to the stairs.

The girl peeped, and followed.

Clean stairs. She had never trodden such before. Everything was strange and clean here, as she had never seen anything before in all her life, except the sky and the white clouds overhead. Heaven be thanked that they are held over us, spotless, always!

Hazel heard the little feet, shuffling, in horrible, distorted shoes, after her, over the steps; pausing, coming slowly; but still starting again, and coming on.

Up on the high landing, under the skylight, she opened the door wide into the dormer-windowed room, and went in; she and Desire, neither of them looking round.

Hazel got into the swing. Desire pushed; after three vibrations they saw the ragged figure standing in the doorway, watching, turning its head from side to side as the swing passed.

"Almost!" cried Hazel, with her feet up at the window. "There!" She thrust them out at that next swing; they looked as if they touched the blue.

"I can see over all the chimneys, and away off, down the water! Now let the old cat die."

Out again, with a spring, as the swinging slackened, she still took no notice of the child, who would have run, like a wild kitten, if she had gone after her. She called Desire, and plunged into a closet under the eaves.

"I wonder what's here!" she exclaimed.

"Rats!"

The girl in the doorway saw the dark, into which the low door opened; she was used to rats in the dark.

"I don't believe it," says Hazel; "Luclarion has a cat, a great big buff one with green eyes. She came in over the roofs, and she runs up here nights. I shouldn't wonder if there might be kittens, though, — one of these days, at any rate. Why! what a place to play 'Dare' in! It goes way round, I don't know where! Look here, Desire!"

She sat on the threshold, that went up a step, over the beam, and so leaned in. She had one eye toward the girl all the time, out of the shadow. She beckoned and nodded, and Desire came.

At the same moment, the coast being clear, the girl gave a sudden scud across, and into the swing. She began to scuff with her slipshod, twisted shoes, pushing herself.

Hazel gave another nod behind her to Desire. Desire stood up, and as the swing came back, pushed gently, touching the board only.

The girl laughed out with the sudden thrill of the motion. Desire pushed again.

Higher and higher, till the feet reached up to the window.

"There!" she cried; and kicked an old shoe off, out over the roof. "I've lost my shoe!"

"Never mind; it'll be down in the yard," said Hazel.

Thereupon the child, at the height of her sweep again, kicked out the other one.

Desire and Hazel, together, pushed her for a quarter of an hour.

"Now let's have ginger-cakes," said Hazel, taking them out of her pocket, and leaving the "cat" to die.

Little Barefoot came down at that, with a run; hanging to the rope at one side, and dragging, till she tumbled in a sprawl upon the floor.

"You ought to have waited," said Desire.

"Poh! I don't never wait!" cried the ragamuffin, rubbing her elbows. "I don't care."

"But it isn't nice to tumble round," suggested Hazel.

"I *ain't* nice," answered the child, and settled the subject.

"Well, these ginger-nuts are," said Hazel. "Here!"

"Have you had a good time?" she asked when the last one was eaten, and she led the way to go down-stairs.

"Good time! That ain't nothin'! I've had a reg'lar bust! I'm comin' agin'; it's bully. Now I must get my loaf and my shoes, and go along back and take a lickin'."

That was the way Hazel caught her first child.

She made her tell her name, — Ann Fazackerley, — and promise to come on Saturday afternoon, and bring two more girls with her.

"We'll have a party," said Hazel, "and play Puss in the Corner. But you must get leave," she added. "Ask your mother. I don't want you to be punished when you go home."

"Lor! you're green! I ain't got no mother. An' I always hooks jack. I'm licked reg'lar when I gets back, anyway. There's half a dozen of 'em. When 'tain't one, it's another. That's Jane Goffey's bread; she's been a swearin' after it this hour, you bet. But I'll come, — see if I don't!"

Hazel drew a hard breath as she let the girl go. Back to her crowded cellar, her Jane Goffeys, the swearings, and the lickings. What was one hour at a time, once or twice a week, to do against all this?

But she remembered the clean little round in her face, out of which eyes and mouth looked merrily, while she talked rough slang; the same fun and daring, — nothing worse, — were in this child's face, that might be in another's saying prettier words. How could she help her words, hearing nothing but devil's Dutch around her all the time? Children do not make the language they are born into. And the face that could be simply merry, telling such a tale as that, — what sort of bright little immortality must it be the outlook of?

Hazel meant to try her hour.

This is one of my last chapters. I can only tell you how they began, — these real folks, — the work their real living led them up to. Perhaps some other time we may follow it on. If I were to tell you now a finished story of it, I should tell a story ahead of the world.

I can show you what six weeks brought it to. I can show you them fairly launched in what may grow to a beautiful private charity, — an "Insecution," — a broad social scheme, — a millennium; at any rate, a life work, change and branch as it may, for these girls who have found out, in their girlhood, that there is genuine living, not mere "playing pretend," to be done in the world. But you cannot, in little books of three hundred pages, see things through. I never expected or promised to do that. The threescore years and ten themselves, do not do it.

It turned into regular Wednesday and Saturday afternoons. Three girls at first, then six, then less again, — sometimes only one or two; until they gradually came up to and settled at, an average of nine or ten.

The first Saturday they took them as they were. The next time they gave them a stick of candy each, the first thing; then Hazel's fingers were sticky, and she proposed the wash-basin all round, before they went up-stairs. The bright tin bowl was ready in the sink, and a clean round towel hung beside; and with some red and white soap-balls, they managed to fascinate their dirty little visitors into three clean pairs of hands, and three clean faces as well.

The candy and the washing grew to be a custom; and in three weeks' time, watching for a hot day and having it luckily on a Saturday, they ventured upon instituting a whole bath, in big round tubs, in the back shed-room, where a faucet came in over a wash bench, and a great boiler was set close by.

They began with a foot-paddle, playing pond, and sailing chips at the same time; then Luclarion told them they might have tubs full, and get in all over and duck, if they liked; and children who may hate to be washed, nevertheless are always ready for a duck and a paddle. So Luclarion superintended the bath-room; Diana helped her; and Desire and Hazel tended the shop. Luclarion invented a shower-bath with a dipper and a colander; then the wet, tangled hair had to be combed, — a climax which she had secretly aimed at with a great longing, from the beginning; and doing this, she contrived with carbolic soap and a separate suds, and a bit of sponge, to give the neglected little heads a most salutary dressing.

Saturday grew into bath-day; soap-suds suggested bubbles; and the ducking and the bubbling were a frolic altogether.

Then Hazel wished they could be put into clean clothes each time; wouldn't it do, somehow?

But that would cost. Luclarion had come to the limit of her purse; Hazel had no purse, and Desire's was small.

"But you see they've *got* to have it," said Hazel; and so she went to her mother, and from her straight to Uncle Oldways.

They counted up, — she and Desire, and Diana: two little common suits, of stockings, underclothes, and calico gowns, apiece; somebody to do a washing once a week, ready for the change; and then — "those horrid shoes!"

"I don't see how you can do it," said Mrs. Ripwinkley. "The things will be taken away from them, and sold. You would have to keep doing, over and over, to no purpose, I am afraid."

"I'll see to that," said Luclarion, facing her "stump." "We'll do for them we can do for; if it ain't ones, it will be tothers. Those that don't keep their things, can't have 'em; and if they're taken away, I won't sell bread to the women they belong to, till they're brought back. Besides, the *washing* kind of sorts 'em out, beforehand. 'Taint the worst ones that are willing to come, or to send, for that. You always have to work in at an edge, in anything, and make your way as you go along. It'll regulate. I'm *living* there right amongst 'em; I've got a clew, and a hold; I can follow things up; I shall have a 'circle;' there's circles everywhere. And in all the wheels there's a moving *spirit;* you ain't got to depend just on yourself. Things work; the Lord sees to it; it's *His* business as much as yours."

Hazel told Uncle Titus that there were shoes and stockings and gowns wanted down in Neighbor Street; things for ten children; they must have subscriptions. And so she had come to him.

The Ripwinkleys had never given Uncle Titus a Christmas or a birthday present, for fear they should seem to establish a mutual precedent. They had never talked of their plans which involved calculation, before him; they were terribly afraid of just one thing with him, and only that one, — of anything most distantly like what Desire Ledwith called "a Megilp bespeak." But now Hazel went up to him as bold as a lion. She took it for granted he was like other people, — "real folks;" that he would do — what must be done.

"How much will it cost?"

"For clothes and shoes for each child, about eight dollars for three months, we guess," said Hazel. "Mother's going to pay for the washing!"

"*Guess?* Haven't you calculated?"

"Yes, sir. 'Guess' and 'calculate' mean the same thing in Yankee," said Hazel, laughing.

Uncle Titus laughed in and out, in his queer way, with his shoulders going up and down.

Then he turned round, on his swivel chair, to his desk, and wrote a check for one hundred dollars.

"There. See how far you can make that go."

"That's good," said Hazel, heartily, looking at it; "that's splendid!" and never gave him a word of personal thanks. It was a thing for mutual congratulations, rather, it would seem; the "good" was just what they all wanted, and there it was. Why should anybody in particular be thanked, as if anybody in particular had asked for anything? She did not say this, or think it; she simply did not think about it at all.

And Uncle Oldways — again — liked it.

There! I shall not try, now, to tell you any more; their experiences, their difficulties, their encouragements, would make large material for a much larger book. I want you to know of the idea, and the attempt. If they fail, partly, — if drunken fathers steal the shoes, and the innocent have to forfeit for the guilty, — if the bad words still come to the lips often, though Hazel tells them they are not "nice," — and beginning at the outside, they are in a fair way of learning the niceness of being nice, — if some children come once or twice, and get dressed up, and then go off and live in the gutters again until the clothes are gone, — are these real failures? There is a bright, pure place down there in Neighbor Street, and twice a week some little children have there a bright, pure time. Will this be lost in the world? In the great Ledger of God will it always stand unbalanced on the debit side?

If you are afraid it will fail, — will be swallowed up in the great sink of vice and misery, like a single sweet, fresh drop, sweet only while it is falling, — go and do likewise; rain down more; make the work larger, stronger; pour the sweetness in faster, till the wide, grand time of full refreshing shall have come from the presence of the Lord!

Ada Geoffrey went down and helped. Miss Craydocke is going to knit scarlet stockings all winter for them; Mr. Geoffrey has put a regular bath-room in for Luclarion, with half partitions, and three separate tubs; Mrs. Geoffrey has furnished a dormitory, where little homeless ones can be kept to sleep. Luclarion has her hands full, and has taken in a girl to help her, whose board and wages Rachel Froke and Asenath Scherman pay. A thing like that spreads every way; you have only to be among, and one of — Real Folks.

Desire, besides her work in Neighbor Street, has gone into the Normal School. She wants to make herself fit for any teaching; she wants also to know and to become a companion of earnest, working girls.

She told Uncle Titus this, after she had been with him a month, and had thought it over; and Uncle Titus agreed, quite as if it were no real concern of his, but a very proper and unobjectionable plan for her, if she liked it.

One day, though, when Marmaduke Wharne — who had come this fall again to stay his three days, and talk over their business, — sat with him in his study, just where they had sat two years and a little more ago, and Hazel and Desire ran up and down stairs together, in and out upon their busy Wednesday errands, — Marmaduke said to Titus, —

"Afterwards is a long time, friend; but I mistrust you have found the comfort, as well as the providence, of 'next of kin?'"

"Afterwards *is* a long time," said Titus Oldways, gravely; "but the Lord's line of succession stretches all the way through."

And that same night he had his other old friend, Miss Craydocke, in; and he brought two papers that he had ready, quietly out to be signed, each with four names: "Titus Oldways," by itself, on the one side; on the other, —

"RACHEL FROKE,
MARMADUKE WHARNE,
KEREN-HAPPUCH CRAYDOCKE."

And one of those two papers — which are no further part of the present story, seeing that good old Uncle Titus is at this moment alive and well, as he has a perfect right, and is heartily welcome to be, whether the story ever comes to a regular winding up or not — was laid safely away in a japanned box in a deep drawer of his study table; and Marmaduke Wharne put the other in his pocket.

He and Titus knew. I myself guess, and perhaps you do; but neither you nor I, nor Rachel, nor Keren-happuch, know for certain; and it is no sort of matter whether we do or not.

The "next of kin" is a better and a deeper thing than any claim of law or register of bequest can show. Titus

Oldways had found that out; and he had settled in his mind, to his restful and satisfied belief, that God, to the last moment of His time, and the last particle of His created substance, can surely care for and order and direct His own.

Is that end and moral enough for a two years' watchful trial, and a two years' simple tale?

XXI.

THE HORSESHOE.

THEY laid out the Waite Place in this manner: —

Right into the pretty wooded pasture, starting from a point a little way down the road from the old house, they projected a roadway which swept round, horseshoe fashion, till it met itself again within a space of some twenty yards or so; and this sweep made a frontage — upon its inclosed bit of natural, moss-turfed green, sprinkled with birch and pine and oak trees, and with gray out-croppings of rock here and there — for the twenty houses, behind which opened the rest of the unspoiled, irregular, open slope and swell and dingle of the hill-foot tract that dipped down at one reach, we know, to the river.

The trees, and shrubs, and vines, and ferns, and stones, were left in their wild prettiness; only some roughness of nature's wear and tear of dead branches and broken brushwood, and the like, were taken away, and the little footpaths cleared for pleasant walking.

There were all the little shady, sweet-smelling nooks, just as they had been; all the little field-parlors, opening with their winding turns between bush and rock, one into another. The twenty households might find twenty separate places, if they all wanted to take a private out-door tea at once.

The cellars were dug; the frames were up; workmen were busy with brick and mortar, hammer and plane; two or three buildings were nearly finished, and two — the two standing at the head of the Horseshoe, looking out at the back into the deepest and pleasantest wood-aisle, where the leaves were reddening and mellowing in the early October frost, and the ferns were turning into tender transparent shades of palest straw-color — were completed, and had dwellers in them; the cheeriest, and happiest, and coziest of neighbors; and who do you think these were?

Miss Waite and Delia, of course, in one house; and with them, dividing the easy rent and the space that was ample for four women, were Lucilla Waters and her mother. In the other, were Kenneth and Rosamond Kincaid and Dorris.

Kenneth and Rosamond had been married just three weeks. Rosamond had told him she would begin the world with him, and they had begun. Begun in the simple, true old-fashioned way, in which, if people only would believe it, it is even yet not impossible for young men and women to inaugurate their homes.

They could not have had a place at Westover, and a horse and buggy for Kenneth to go back and forth with; nor even a house in one of the best streets of Z——; and down at East Square everything was very modern and pretentious, based upon the calculation of rising values and a rush of population.

But here was this new neighborhood of — well, yes, — "model houses;" a blessed Christian speculation for a class not easily or often reached by any speculations save those that grind and consume their little regular means, by forcing upon them the lawless and arbitrary prices of the day, touching them at every point in their *living*, but not governing correspondingly their income, as even the hod-carrier's and railroad navvy's daily pay is reached and ruled to meet the proportion of the time.

They would be plain, simple, little-cultured people that

would live there; the very "betwixt and betweens" that Rosamond had used to think so hardly fated. Would she go and live among them, in one of these little new, primitive homes, planted down in the pasture-land, on the outskirts? Would she — the pretty, graceful, elegant Rosamond — live semi-detached with old Miss Arabel Waite?

That was just exactly the very thing she would do; the thing she did not even let Kenneth think of first, and ask her, but that, when they had fully agreed that they would begin life somehow, in some right way together, according to their means, she herself had questioned him if they might not do.

And so the houses were hurried in the building; for old Miss Arabel must have hers before the winter; (it seems strange how often the change comes when one could not have waited any longer for it;) and Kenneth had mill building, and surveying, and planning, in East Square, and Mr. Roger Marchbanks' great gray-stone mansion going up on West Hill, to keep him busy; work enough for any talented young fellow, fresh from the School of Technology, who had got fair hold of a beginning, to settle down among and grasp the "next things" that were pretty sure to follow along after the first.

Dorris has all Ruth's music scholars, and more; for there has never been anybody to replace Miss Robbyns, and there are many young girls in Z——, and down here in East Square, who want good teaching and cannot go away to get it. She has also the organ-playing in the new church.

She keeps her morning hours and her Saturdays to help Rosamond; for they are "coöperating" here, in the new home; what was the use, else, of having coöperated in the old? Rosamond cannot bear to have any coarse, profane fingers laid upon her little household gods, — her wedding-tins and her feather dusters, — while the first gloss and freshness are on, at any rate; and with her dainty handling, the gloss is likely to last a long while.

Such neighbors, too, as the Waites and Waterses are! How they helped in the fitting up, running in in odd half hours from their own nailing and placing, which they said could wait awhile, since they weren't brides; and such real old times visiting as they have already between the houses; coming and taking right hold, with wiping up dinner plates as likely as not, if that is the thing in hand; picking up what is there, as easily as "the girls" used to help work out some last new pattern of crochet, or try over music, or sort worsteds for gorgeous affghans for the next great fair!

Miss Arabel is apt to come in after dinner, and have a dab at the plates; she knows she interrupts nothing then; and she "has never been used to sitting talking, with gloves on and a parasol in her lap." And now she has given up trying to make impossible biases, she has such a quantity of time!

It was the matter of receiving visits from her friends who *did* sit with their parasols in their laps, or who only expected to see the house, or look over wedding presents, that would be the greatest hindrance, Rosamond realized at once; that is, if she would let it; so she did just the funniest thing, perhaps, that ever a bride did do: she set her door wide open from her pretty parlor, with its books and flowers and pictures and window-draperies of hanging vines, into the plain, cozy little kitchen, with its tin pans and bright new buckets and its Shaker chairs; and when she was busy there, asked her girl-friends right in, as she had used to take them up into her bedroom, if she were doing anything pretty or had something to show.

And they liked it, for the moment, at any rate; they could not help it; they thought it was lovely; a kind of bewitching little play at keeping house; though some of them went away and wondered, and said that Rosamond Holabird had quite changed all her way of living and her position; it was very splendid and strong-minded, they supposed; but they never should have thought it of her, and of course she could not keep it up.

"And the neighborhood!" was the cry. "The rabble she has got, and is going to have, round her! All planks and sand, and tubs of mortar, now; you have to half break your neck in getting up there; and when it is settled it will be — such a frowze of common people! Why the foreman of our factory has engaged a house, and Mrs. Haslam, who actually used to do up laces for mamma, has got another!"

That is what is said — in some instances — over on West Hill, when the elegant visitors came home from calling at the Horseshoe. Meanwhile, what Rosamond does is something like this, which she happened to do one bright afternoon a very little while ago.

She and Dorris had just made and baked a charming little tea-cake, which was set on a fringed napkin in a round white china dish, and put away in the fresh, oak-grained kitchen pantry, where not a crumb or a slop had ever yet been allowed to rest long enough to defile or give a flavor of staleness; out of which everything is tidily used up while it is nice, and into which little delicate new-made bits like this, for next meals, are always going.

The tea-table itself, — with its three plates, and its new silver, and the pretty, thin, shallow cups and saucers, that an Irish girl would break a half-dozen of every week, — was laid with exquisite preciseness; the square white napkins at top and bottom over the crimson cloth, spread to the exactness of a line, and every knife and fork at fair right angles; the loaf was upon the white carved trencher, and nothing to be done when Kenneth should come in, but to draw the tea, and bring the brown cake forth.

Rosamond will not leave all these little doings to break up the pleasant time of his return; she will have her leisure then, let her be as busy as she may while he is away.

There was an hour or more after all was done; even after the Panjandrums had made their state call, leaving their barouche at the heel of the Horseshoe, and filling up all Rosamond's little vestibule with their flounces, as they came in and went out.

The Panjandrums were new people at West Hill; very new and very grand, as only new things and new people can be, turned out in the latest style pushed to the last agony. Mrs. Panjandrum's dress was all in two shades of brown, to the tips of her feathers, and the toes of her boots, and the frill of her parasol; and her carriage was all in two shades of brown, likewise; cushions, and tassels, and panels; the horses themselves were cream-color, with dark manes and tails. Next year, perhaps, everything will be in pansy-colors, — black and violet and gold; and then she will probably have black horses with gilded harness and royal purple tails.

It was very good of the Panjandrums, doubtless, to come down to the Horseshoe at all; I am willing to give them all the credit of really admiring Rosamond, and caring to see her in her little new home; but there are two other things to be considered also: the novel kind of home Rosamond had chosen to set up, and the human weakness of curiosity concerning all experiments, and friends in all new lights; also the fact of that other establishment shortly to branch out of the Holabird connection. The family could not quite go under water, even with people of the Panjandrum persuasion, while there was such a pair of prospective corks to float them as Mr. and Mrs. Dakie Thayne.

The Panjandrum carriage had scarcely bowled away, when a little buggy and a sorrel pony came up the road, and somebody alighted with a brisk spring, slipped the rein with a loose knot through the fence-rail at the corner, and came up one side of the two-plank foot-walk that ran around the Horseshoe; somebody who had come home unexpectedly, to take his little wife to ride. Kenneth Kincaid had business over at the new district of "Clarendon Park."

Drives, and livery-stable bills, were no part of the items allowed for, in the programme of these young people's living; therefore Rosamond put on her gray hat, with its soft little dove's breast, and took her bright-striped shawl upon her arm, and let Kenneth lift her into the buggy — for which there was no manner of need except that they both liked it, — with very much the feeling as if she were going off on a lovely bridal trip. They had had no bridal trip, you see; they did not really want one; and this little impromptu drive was such a treat!

Now the wonders of nature and the human mind show — if I must go so far to find an argument for the statement I am making — that into a single point of time or particle of matter may be gathered the relations of a solar system or the experiences of a life; that a universe may be compressed into an atom, or a molecule expanded into a macrocosm; therefore I expect nobody to sneer at my Rosamond as childishly happy in her simple honeymoon, or at me for making extravagant and unsupported assertions, when I say that this hour and a half, and these four miles out to Clarendon Park and back, — the lifting and the tucking in, and the setting off, the sitting side by side in the ripe October air and the golden twilight, the noting together every pretty turn, every flash of autumn color in the woods, every change in the cloud-groupings overhead, every glimpse of busy, bright-eyed squirrels up and down the walls, every cozy, homely group of barn-yard creatures at the farmsteads, the change, the pleasure, the thought of home and always-togetherness, — all this made the little treat of a country ride as much to them, holding all that any wandering up and down the whole world in their new companionship could hold, — as a going to Europe, or a journey to mountains and falls and sea-sides and cities, in a skimming of the States. You cannot have more than there is; and you do not care for more than just what stands for and emphasizes the essential beauty, the living gladness, that no *place* gives, but that hearts carry about into places and baptize them with, so that ever afterward a tender charm hangs round them, because "we saw it *then*."

And Kenneth and Rosamond Kincaid had all these bright associations, these beautiful glamours, these glad reminders, laid up for years to come, in a four miles space that they might ride or walk over, re-living it all, in the returning Octobers of many other years. I say they had a bridal tour that day, and that the four miles were as good as four thousand. Such little bits of signs may stand for such high, great, blessed things!

"How lovely stillness and separateness are!" said Rosamond as they sat in the buggy, stopping to enjoy a glimpse of the river on one side, and a flame of burning bushes on the other, against the dark face of a piece of woods that held the curve of road in which they stood, in sheltered quiet. "How pretty a house would be, up on that knoll. Do you know things puzzle me a little, Kenneth? I have almost come to a certain conclusion lately, that people are not meant to live apart, but that it is really everybody's duty to live in a town, or a village, or in some gathering of human beings together. Life tends to that, and all the needs and uses of it; and yet, — it is so sweet in a place like this, — and however kind and social you may be, it seems once in a while such an escape! Do you believe in beautiful country places, and in having a little piece of creation all to yourself, if you can get it, or if not, what do you suppose all creation is made for?"

"Perhaps just that which you have said, Rose." Rosamond has now, what her mother hinted once, somebody to call her "Rose," with a happy and beautiful privilege. "Perhaps to escape into. Not for one, here and there, selfishly, all the time; but for the whole, with fair share and opportunity. Creation is made very big, you see, and men and women are made without wings, and with very limited hands and feet. Also with limited lives; that makes the time-question, and the hurry. There is a suggestion,— at any rate, a necessity,— in that. It brings them within certain spaces, always. In spite of all the artificial lengthening of railroads and telegraphs, there must still be centres for daily living, intercourse, and need. People tend to towns; they cannot establish themselves in isolated independence. Yet packing and stifling are a cruelty and a sin. I do not believe there ought to be any human being so poor as to be forced to such crowding. The very way we are going to live at the Horseshoe, seems to me an individual solution of the problem. It ought to come to pass that our towns should be built — and if built already, wrongly, *thinned out*, — on this principle. People are coming to learn a little of this, and are opening parks and squares in the great cities, finding that there must be room for bodies and souls to reach out and breathe. If they could only take hold of some of their swarming-places, where disease and vice are festering, and pull down every second house and turn it into a garden space, I believe they would do more for reform and salvation than all their separate institutions for dealing with misery after it is let grow, can ever effect."

"O, why *can't* they?" cried Rose. "There is money enough, somewhere. Why can't they do it, instead of letting the cities grow horrid, and then running away from it themselves, and buying acres and acres around their country places, for fear somebody should come too near, and the country should begin to grow horrid too?"

"Because the growing and the crowding and the striving of the city *make* so much of the money, little wife! Because to keep everybody fairly comfortable as the world goes along, there could not be so many separate piles laid up; it would have to be used more as it comes, and it could not come so fast. If nobody cared to be very rich, and all were willing to live simply and help one another, in little 'horseshoe neighborhoods,' there wouldn't be so much that looks like grand achievement in the world perhaps; but I think maybe the very angels might show themselves out of the unseen, and bring the glory of heaven into it!"

Kenneth's color came, and his eyes glowed, as he spoke these words that burst into eloquence with the intensity of his meaning; and Rosamond's face was holy-pale, and her look large, as she listened; and they were silent for a minute or so, as the pony, of his own accord, trotted deliberately on.

"But then, the beauty, and the leisure, and all that grows out of them to separate minds, and what the world gets through the refinement of it! You see the puzzle comes back. Must we never, in this life, gather round us the utmost that the world is capable of furnishing? Must we never, out of this big creation, have the piece to ourselves, each one as he would choose?"

"I think the Lord would show us a way out of that," said Kenneth. "I think He would make His world turn out right, and all come to good and sufficient use, if we did not put it in a snarl. Perhaps we can hardly guess what we might grow to all together, — 'the whole body, fitly joined by that which every joint supplieth, increasing and building itself up in love.' And about the quietness, and the separateness, — we don't want to *live* in that, Rose; we only want it sometimes, to make us fitter to live. When the disciples began to talk about building tabernacles on the mountain of the vision, Christ led them straight down among the multitude, where there was a devil to be cast out. It is the same thing in the old story of the creation. God worked six days, and rested one."

"Well," said Rose, drawing a deep breath, "I am glad we have begun at the Horseshoe! It was a great escape for me, Kenneth. I am such a worldly girl in my heart. I should have liked so much to have everything elegant and artistic about me."

"I think you do. I think you always will. Not because of the worldliness in you, though; but the *other*-worldliness, the sense of real beauty and truth. And I am glad that we have begun at all! It was a greater escape for me. I was in danger of all sorts of hardness and unbelief. I had begun to despise and hate things, because they did not work rightly just around me. And then I fell in, just in time, with some real, true people; and then you came, with the "little piece of your world," and then I came here, and saw what your world was, and how you were making it, Rose! How a little community of sweet and generous fellowship was crystallizing here among all sorts — outward sorts — of people; a little community of the kingdom; and how you and yours had done it."

"O, Kenneth! I was the worst little atom in the whole crystal! I only got into my place because everybody else did, and there was nothing else left for me to do."

"You see I shall never believe that," said Kenneth, quietly. "There is no flaw in the crystal. You were all polarized alike. And besides, can't I see daily just how your nature draws and points?"

"Well, never mind," said Rose. "Only some particles are natural magnets, I believe, and some get magnetized by contact. Now that we have hit upon this metaphor, isn't it funny that our little social experiment should have taken the shape of a horseshoe?"

"The most sociable, because the most magnetic, shape it could take. You will see the power it will develop. There's a great deal in merely taking form according to fundamental principles. Witness the getting round a fireside. Isn't that a horseshoe? And could half as much sympathy be evolved from a straight line?"

"I believe in firesides," said Rose.

"And in women who can organize and inform them," said Kenneth. "First, firesides; then neighborhoods; that is the way the world's life works out; and women have their hands at the heart of it. They can do so much more there than by making the laws! When the life is right, the laws will make themselves, or be no longer needed. They are such mere outside patchwork, —make-shifts till a better time!"

"Wrong living must make wrong laws, whoever does the voting," said Rosamond, sagely.

"False social standards make false commercial ones; inflated pretensions demand inflated currency; selfish, untrue domestic living eventuates in greedy speculations and business shams; and all in the intriguing for corrupt legislation, to help out partial interests. It isn't by multiplying the voting power, but by purifying it, that the end is to be reached."

"That is so sententious, Kenneth, that I shall have to take it home and ravel it out gradually in my mind in little shreds. In the mean while, dear, suppose we stop in the village, and get some little brown-ware cups for top-overs. You never ate any of my top-overs? Well, when you do, you'll say that all the world ought to be brought up on top-overs."

Rosamond was very particular about her little brown-ware cups. They had to be real stone, — brown outside, and gray-blue in; and they must be of a special size and depth. When they were found, and done up in a long parcel, one within another, in stout paper, she carried it herself to the chaise, and would scarcely let Kenneth hold it while she got in; after which, she laid it carefully across her lap, instead of putting it behind upon the cushion.

"You see they were rather dear; but they are the only kind worth while. Those little yellow things would soak and crack, and never look comfortable in the kitchen-closet. I give you very fair warning, I shall always want the best of things; but then I shall take very fierce and jealous care of them, — like this."

And she laid her little nicely-gloved hand across her homely parcel, guardingly.

How nice it was to go buying little homely things together! Again, it was as good and pleasant, — and meant ever so much more, — than if it had been ordering china with a monogram in Dresden, or glass in Prague, with a coat-of-arms engraved.

When they drove up to the Horseshoe, Dakie Thayne and Ruth met them. They had been getting "spiritual ferns" and sumach leaves with Dorris; "the dearest little tips," Ruth said, "of scarlet and carbuncle, just like jets of fire."

And now they would go back to tea, and eat up the brown cake?

"Real Westover summum-bonum cake?" Dakie wanted to know. "Well, he couldn't stand against that. Come, Ruthie!" And Ruthie came.

"What do you think Rosamond says?" said Kenneth, at the tea-table, over the cake. "That everybody ought to live in a city or a village, or, at least, a Horseshoe. She thinks nobody has a right to stick his elbows out, in this world. She 's in a great hurry to be packed as closely as possible here."

"I wish the houses were all finished, and our neighbors in; that is what I said," said Rosamond. "I should like to begin to know about them, and feel settled; and to see flowers in their windows, and lights at night."

"And you always hated so a 'little crowd!'" said Ruth.

"It isn't a crowd when they *don't* crowd," said Rosamond. "I can't bear little miserable jostles."

"How good it will be to see Rosamond here, at the head of her court; at the top of the Horseshoe," said Dakie

Thayne. "She will be quite the 'Queen of the County.'"

"Don't!" said Rosamond. "I've a very weak spot in my head. You can't tell the mischief you might do. No; I won't be queen!"

"Any more than you can help," said Dakie.

"She'll be Rosa Mundi, wherever she is," said Ruth affectionately.

"I think that is just grand of Kenneth and Rosamond," said Dakie Thayne, as he and Ruth were walking home up West Hill in the moonlight, afterward. "What do you think you and I ought to do, one of these days, Ruthie? It sets me to considering. There are more Horseshoes to make, I suppose, if the world is to jog on."

"*You* have a great deal to consider about," said Ruth, thoughtfully. "It was quite easy for Kenneth and Rosamond to see what they ought to do. But you might make a great many Horseshoes, — or something!"

"What do you mean by that second person plural, eh? Are you shirking your responsibilities, or are you addressing your imaginary Boffinses? Come, Ruthie, I can't have that! Say 'we,' and I'll face the responsibilities and talk it all out; but I won't have anything to do with 'you!'"

"Won't you?" said Ruth, with piteous demureness. "How can I say 'we,' then?"

"You little cat! How you can scratch!"

"There are such great things to be done in the world, Dakie," Ruth said seriously, when they had got over that with a laugh that lifted her nicely by the "we" question. "I can't help thinking of it."

"O," said Dakie, with significant satisfaction. "We're getting on better. Well?"

"Do you know what Hazel Ripwinkley is doing? And what Luclarion Grapp has done? Do you know how they are going among poor people, in dreadful places,—really living among them, Luclarion is,—and finding out, and helping, and showing how? I thought of that to-night, when they talked about living in cities and villages. Luclarion has gone away down to the very bottom of it. And somehow, one can't feel satisfied with only reaching half way, when one knows—and might!"

"Do you mean, Ruthie, that you and I might go and *live* in such places? Do you think I could take you there?"

"I don't know, Dakie," Ruth answered, forgetting in her earnestness, to blush or hesitate for what he said;—"but I feel as if we ought to reach down, somehow,—*away* down! Because that, you see, is the *most*. And to do only a little, in an easy way, when we are made so strong to do; wouldn't it be a waste of power, and a missing of the meaning? Isn't it the 'much' that is required of us, Dakie?"

They were under the tall hedge of the Holabird "parcel of ground," on the Westover slope, and close to the home gates. Dakie Thayne put his arm round Ruth as she said that, and drew her to him.

"We will go and be neighbors somewhere, Ruthie. And we will make as big a Horseshoe as we can."

XXII.

MORNING GLORIES.

AND Desire?

Do you think I have passed her over lightly in her troubles? Or do you think I am making her out to have herself passed over them lightly?

Do you think it is hardly to be believed that she should have turned round from these shocks and pains that bore down so heavily and all at once upon her, and taken kindly to the living with old Uncle Titus and Rachel Froke in the Greenley Street house, and going down to Luclarion Grapp's to help wash little children's faces, and teach them how to have innocent good times? Do you think there is little making up in all that for her, while Rosamond Kincaid is happy in her new home, and Ruth and Dakie Thayne are looking out together over the world, — which can be nowhere wholly sad to them, since they are to go down into it together, — and planning how to make long arms with their wealth, to reach the largest neighborhood they can? In the first place, do you know how full the world is, all around you, of things that are missed by those who say nothing, but go on living somehow without them? Do you know how large a part of life, even young life, is made of the days that have never been lived? Do you guess how many girls, like Desire, come near something that they think they might have had, and then see it drift by, just beyond their reach, to fall easily into some other hand that seems hardly put out to grasp it?

And do you see, or feel, or guess how life goes on, incompleteness and all, and things settle themselves one way, if not another, simply because the world does not stop, but keeps turning, and tossing off days and nights like time-bubbles just the same?

Do you ever imagine how different this winter's parties are from last, or this summer's visit or journey from those of the summer gone, — to many a maiden who has her wardrobe made up all the same, and takes her German or her music lessons, and goes in and out, and has her ticket to the Symphony Concerts, and is no different to look at, unless perhaps with a little of the first color-freshness gone out of her face, — while secretly it seems to her as if the sweet early symphony of her life were all played out, and had ended in a discord?

We begin, most of us, much as we are to go on. Real or mistaken, the experiences of eighteen initiate the lesson that those of two and three score after years are needed to unfold and complete. What is left of us is continually turning round, perforce, to take up with what is left of the world, and make the best of it.

Thus much for what does happen, for what we have to put up with, for the mere philosophy of endurance, and the possibility of things being endured. We do live out our years, and get and bear it all. And the scars do not show much outside; nay, even we ourselves can lay a finger on the place, after a little time, without a cringe.

Desire Ledwith did what she had to do; there was a way made for her, and there was still life left.

But there is a better reading of the riddle. There is never a "Might-have-been" that touches with a sting, but reveals also to us an inner glimpse of the wide and beautiful "May Be." It is all there; somebody else has it now, while we wait; but the years of God are full of satisfying;

each soul shall have its turn; it is His good *pleasure* to give us the kingdom. There is so much room, there are such thronging possibilities, there is such endless hope!

To feel this, one must feel, however dimly, the inner realm, out of which the shadows of this life come and pass, to interpret to us the laid up reality.

"The real world is the inside world."

Desire Ledwith blessed Uncle Oldways in her heart for giving her that word.

It comforted her for her father. If his life here had been hard, toilsome, mistaken even; if it had never come to that it might have come to; if she, his own child, had somehow missed the reality of him here, and he of her, — was he not passed now into the within? Might she not find him there; might they not silently and spiritually, without sign, but needing no sign, begin to understand each other now? Was not the real family just beginning to be born into the real home?

Ah, that word *real!* How deep we have to go to find the root of it! It is fast by the throne of God; in the midst.

Hazel Ripwinkley talked about "real folks." She sifted, and she found out instinctively the true livers, the genuine *neahburs*, nigh-dwellers; they who abide alongside in spirit, who shall find each other in the everlasting neighborhood, when the veil falls.

But there, behind, — how little, in our petty outside vexations or gladnesses, we stop to think of or perceive it! — is the actual, even the present, inhabiting; there is the kingdom, the continuing city, the real heaven and earth in which we already live and labor, and build up our homes and lay up our treasure; and the loving Christ, and the living Father, and the innumerable company of angels, and the unseen compassing about of friends gone in there, and they on this earth who truly belong to us inwardly, however we and they may be bodily separated, — are the Real Folks!

What matters a little pain, outside? Go *in*, and rest from it!

There is where the joy is, that we read outwardly, spelling by parts imperfectly, in our own and others' mortal experience; there is the content of homes, the beauty of love, the delight of friendship, — not shut in to any one or two, but making the common air that all souls breathe. No one heart can be happy, that all hearts may not have a share of it. Rosamond and Kenneth, Dakie and Ruth, cannot live out obviously any sweetness of living, cannot sing any notes of the endless, beautiful score, that Desire Ledwith, and Luclarion Grapp, and Rachel Froke, and Hapsie Craydocke, and old Miss Arabel Waite, do not just as truly get the blessed grace and understanding of; do not catch and feel the perfect and abounding harmony of. Since why? No lip can sound more than its own few syllables of music; no life show more than its own few accidents and incidents and groupings; the vast melody, the rich, eternal satisfying, are behind; and the signs are for us all!

You may not think this, or see it so, in your first tussle and set-to with the disappointing and eluding things that seem the real and only, — missing which you miss all. This chapter may be less to you — less *for* you, perhaps — than for your elders; the story may have ended, as to that you care for, some pages back; but for all that, this is certain; and Desire Ledwith has begun to find it, for she is one of those true, grand spirits to whom personal loss or frustration are most painful as they seem to betoken something wrong or failed in the general scheme and justice. This terrible "why should it be?" once answered, — once able to say to themselves quietly, "It is all right; the beauty and the joy are there; the song is sung, though we are of the listeners; the miracle-play is played, though but a few take literal part, and many of us look on, with the play, like the song, moving through our souls only, or our souls moving in the vital sphere of it, where the stage is wide enough for all;" — once come to this, they have entered already into that which is behind, and nothing of all that goes forth thence into the earth to make its sunshine can be shut off from them forever.

Desire is learning to be glad, thinking of Kenneth and Rosamond, that this fair marriage should have been. It is so just and exactly best; Rosamond's sweet graciousness is so precisely what Kenneth's sterner way needed to have shine upon it; her finding and making of all manner of pleasantness will be so good against his sharp discernment of the wrong; they will so beautifully temper and sustain each other!

Desire is so generous, so glad of the truth, that she can stand aside, and let this better thing be, and say to herself that it *is* better.

Is not this that she is growing to inwardly, more blessed than any marriage or giving in marriage? Is it not a partaking of the heavenly Marriage Supper?

"We two might have grumbled at the world until we grumbled at each other."

She even said that, calmly and plainly, to herself.

And then that manna was fed to her afresh of which she had been given first to eat so long a while ago; that thought of "the Lamb in the midst of the Throne" came back to her. Of the Tenderness deep within the Almightiness that holds all earth and heaven and time and circumstance in its grasp. Her little, young, ignorant human heart begins to rest in that great warmth and gentleness; begins to be glad to wait there for what shall arise out of it, moving the Almightiness for her, — even on purpose for her, — in the by-and-by; she begins to be sure; of what, she knows not, — but of a great, blessed, beautiful something, that just because she is at all, shall be for her; that she shall have a part, somehow, even in the *showing* of His good; that into the beautiful miracle-play she shall be called, and a new song be given her, also, to sing in the grand, long, perfect oratorio; she begins to pray quietly, that, "loving the Lord, always above all things, she may obtain His promises, which exceed all that she can desire."

And waiting, resting, believing, she begins also to work. This beginning is even as an ending and forehaving, to any human soul.

I will tell you how she woke one morning; of a little poem that wrote itself along her chamber wall.

It was a square, pleasant old room, with a window in an angle toward the east. A great, old-fashioned mirror hung opposite, between the windows that looked out northwestwardly; the morning and the evening light came in upon her. Beside the solid, quaint old furnishings of a long past time, there were also around her the things she had been used to at home; her own little old rocking-chair, her desk and table, and her toilet and mantel ornaments and things of use. A pair of candle-branches with dropping lustres, — that she had marveled at and delighted in as a child, and had begged for herself when they fell into disuse in the drawing-room, — stood upon the chimney, along which the first sun-rays glanced. Just in those days of the year, they struck in so as to shine level through the clear prisms, and break into a hundred little rainbows.

She opened her eyes, this fair October morning, and lay and looked at the little scattered glories.

All around the room, on walls, curtains, ceiling, — falling like bright soft jewels upon table and floor, touching everything with a magic splendor, — were globes and shafts of colored light. Softly blended from glowing red to tenderly fervid blue, they lay in various forms and fragments, as the beam refracted or the objects caught them.

Just on the edge of the deep, opposite window-frame, clung one vivid, separate flash of perfect azure, all alone, and farthest off of all.

Desire wondered, at first glance, how it should happen; till she saw, against a closet-door ajar, a gibbous sphere of red and golden flame. Yards apart the points were, and a shadow lay between; but the one sure sunbeam knew no distance, and there was no radiant line of the spectrum lost.

Desire remembered her old comparison of complementary colors: "to see blue, and to live red," she had said, complaining.

But now she thought, — "Foreshortening! In so many things, that is all, — if we could only see as the Sun sees!"

One bit of our living, by itself, all one deep, burning, bleeding color, maybe; but the globe is white, — the blue is somewhere. And, lo! a soft, still motion; a little of the flame-tint has dropped off; it has leaped to join itself to the blue; it gives itself over; and they are beautiful together, — they fulfill each other; yet, in the changing never a thread falls quite away into the dark. Why, it is like love joining itself to love again!

CPSIA information can be obtained
at www.ICGtesting.com
Printed in the USA
LVHW031256060423
743358LV00019B/70

9 783382 133450